The Secrets We Keep

Gigi Lynn

Cover photography by Natalie Nelson at Cheznous Images
(Cheznousimages.com)

To my mom who shared her love of reading and who called me Gigi. I miss you.

Chapter One

Hateful to me as the gates of Hades is the man who hides one thing in this heart and speaks another

Homer, *The Iliad*

Let me say in my defense that I had an excellent reason for every lie I told or truth I withheld. But Sir Walter Scott is uncomfortably accurate. It was not long before I felt like a startled spider trying to catch and mend the sticky and tangled ends of a very twisted web.

It began so simply. I awoke one late summer morning with an aching head and an uncomfortable heaviness in my chest. Aunt Beatrice had spent the previous night's supper talking about Robert's return from his service in the Navy, remarking on his gracious afternoon visit, and making plans for us to call on him and his father the next afternoon. She then spent the rest of the meal speculating on the effect of his inclusion in upcoming neighborhood social events, which conversation had stolen my peace and ruined my appetite.

I didn't think I could break my fast with more of the same. It seemed providential when I rose and saw that a week of sleeting rains had been interrupted by the jewel like gift of a warm, thawing breeze and a clear blue sky. I decided right then that, for a day of freedom and a chance to avoid another discussion about Robert, I was willing to make my Aunt Beatrice's tenant visits. With only a twinge of guilt, I wrote a note making my offer and arranged for it to be delivered after she awoke.

I signed it Elizabeth so as not to provoke her. My aunt insists on calling me Elizabeth, unless she is particularly exasperated, and then she calls me Elizabeth Louisa. Everyone else calls me Liza, and sometimes Robert calls—used to call me Liza Lou.

I rushed through my own early breakfast, put on a light cloak, and breathed a sigh of relief as I made my escape.

My note was not all lies; I did, after all, drop off a basket at Mrs. Cornley's cottage, and I took my worn dresses to Mrs. Fenton so she could remake them for her numerous offspring. If I made a detour to look at Squire Davies' new litter of puppies, my aunt would never know. If it took most of the day, that was not such a bad thing.

There was no escape, however, from talk of Robert. Though housebound, Mrs. Cornley had heard the news of his return and reminded me that she had always had a special fondness for Robert Amesley since he helped re-thatch her roof when he was fourteen. She reminisced, and laughed at my discomfort, about the times she had seen Robert and I, streaked with dirt, running through the woods around Bexhill and climbing rocks like imps.

She was relentless in her pursuit of information. Had I seen Captain Amesley, and how had he changed? The answer to the first question, of course, was yes, but I didn't want to talk about the difference between the bold, imaginative, but kind youth I had known so well and the formal, self-contained man who called the day before. He was bigger than I remembered, broader in the shoulders, tanned and hard. Only for a moment as my aunt chattered, had I recognized my childhood friend when those disturbing, all-seeing gray eyes, warmed with a spark of laughter and invited me to join in his mirth.

Mrs. Fenton didn't need to ask how Robert looked. She had sighted him briefly as he rode past on his way to town. She detailed all the changes that I was trying to ignore. Her conjecture shared between interruptions from her children, though kinder, was perhaps more painful. Was the cutlass wound in his leg, received in a skirmish in the Dardanelles, healing well? Did he have someone capable to care for him? Would he stay in Bexhill or live in London?

It was with almost frantic relief that I alighted from my cart at Squire's. The Squire's daughter Maris was my best friend, but she was away this week visiting cousins, so I happily bypassed the manor and walked straight to the barn. I knew the squire wouldn't mind. He liked me and allowed me free access, partly as I was always willing to listen to him prose on about his breeding plans, but mostly because he could tell I loved the dogs.

Sitting with my back against the sun-warmed barn, my lap filled with two wriggling puppies, restored a measure of my composure. My head still ached, but when the squire found me, I was able to smile naturally.

"Miss Liza, I see you found Lottie's last two pups," he looked under his eyebrows at me and nodded once as if in satisfaction. "This one goes at the end of the week to Lord Branson. He will make a fine hunter," he picked up one puppy and walked over to put him in the pen. "This one," he turned back to me and motioned with his chin to the liver and white pup I still held, "he ran afoul of a wagon," he reached down and scratched the pup behind the ear and looked over his splinted leg. "I don't know as I'll be able to place him."

I felt a pang of sorrow to hear it. I looked down at the dog's sweet face. With his dark mask, he reminded me of the Harlequin in our Christmas pantomime. The little trickster knew we were talking about him. His head cocked to the side and seemed to grin and dare me to run and play. I laughed, and the squire joined me.

"Put him with the other," he said, "and come and see Sophie's new litter."

He walked away without looking back, so I carried the little lame pup to the pen. When I put him down, he whined piteously. "Don't try to gammon me," I tapped his nose, "you are well cared for and as smart and brave as your brother, even with that leg. Go play now; the squire will find a place for you. I'm sure of it." I gave him one more rub and went to meet the squire who was waiting, with that same satisfied expression, at the door to his breeding shed.

"I bred Lottie with the Brittany that John Fieldstone brought over from France before the war. But, Percy Branham brought his setter down for my Sophie," he said as he opened the door. "These pups are already showing promise." We stopped before a straw and wool lined box. Sophie looked up with immense patience as five puppies pushed and nuzzled to nurse. "You did a fine job, didn't you?" The squire murmured as Sophie turned her head into his hand.

I dropped to my knees, hands on the side of the whelping box to admire the little white speckled pups. "They are handsome," I began. Then a pull on my skirt distracted me. I looked down into the limpid eyes of my little lame friend.

"Oh, what are you doing here?" I looked up at the

squire apologetically, "I was sure I closed the gate, but it must not have latched properly."

"I'm sure it did, but this one always finds a way out, which is how he hurt himself in the first place. I worry about him." He paused expectantly.

Our eyes met and held. I shook my head, "You know I'd love—" I glanced down and tried to bite back my instinctive smile, "Aunt Beatrice wouldn't allow—" I started as the little runaway made an awkward leap, scrabbling up onto my lap and lifting his face. My hands went to his floppy ear without my volition as my mind began to race.

"Maybe, if I—" I remembered the servant's staircase, "I guess I could take him back and forth," I murmured to myself, "Frank might help," I nodded, thinking of our groom.

While I was scheming, the squire got up and moved behind a half wall and began to whistle tunelessly as he gathered supplies in a leather satchel.

I watched untroubled, confident now that I could find a way to care for him without troubling my aunt, "I think I'll call him Quin."

Though we only spent another quarter hour in the shed, the wind was sharp and dark clouds scudded across the sky when we came into the yard.

"We'll see if Mrs. Davies has a pot on before you leave. I think you will still be able to beat the coming storm," he squinted at the southern horizon.

I followed him around to the side entry of the manor, where the squire dropped the satchel on a conveniently placed table and hung his jacket. When we entered his comfortable sitting room, Mrs. Davies bustled forward, gave my shoulder a firm squeeze, and peered intently into my eyes. "You look a little peaked, Miss Liza. Come sit down, and I'll bring you some tea." She plumped a pillow on a shabby sofa. "I see Mr. Davies cozened you into that dog,"

"Oh no," I began in protest, "I really don't mind. I'm more than happy to have him." But I spoke to her back as she sailed out of the sitting room after leveling a chiding glance at her husband.

I looked the squire apologetically, but he just waved casually and settled into his favorite chair with a comfortable sigh.

I sat and rested my now aching body. I turned my head toward the window and closed my burning eyes for a few moments.

Mrs. Davies returned with her usual energy, followed by a maid who placed a tray on the table. Once Mrs. Davies had served, she settled back and focused her bright eyes on me.

"So, tell us about Captain Amesley," she said as she lifted her tea, "we hear so much talk, but very little information."

"Can no one speak of anything but Robert?" I cried heedlessly.

The squire tsked at me. "Now, Miss Elizabeth, people are curious and proud, what with he's acquitted himself so well, making Captain and fighting so bravely, and many will want some of that glory to rub off. Taking part in those battles in waters all around the continent, and his last battle in the Dardanelles, which many, who have more hair than wit, might see as romantic, well, and of course it will cause people to talk. But remember, Miss Liza, for all everyone might see the adventure and excitement, four years is a long time to be away from the people you know and the comforts of home. The seas around Spain, Portugal, and the Mediterranean are chancy right now. And he'll never forget that cutlass wound in his leg. He'll feel it for the rest of his life."

I nodded wordlessly and bowed my aching head. I truly felt miserable and small. But I braced myself and visited a short while, giving what information I could, before taking my leave.

The wind was brisk, and the clouds roiled when I finally climbed back onto our cart and began the trip home. Maybelle knew the way, so my attention wandered. I felt fractious and out of sorts. Remembering the squire's scolding made me feel hot and restless.

I soon tired of my thoughts. "I just won't think of him, I won't." I held Quin up and looked into his soft brown eyes. He cocked his head and sneezed twice, his hind legs waving in the air and tail wagging enthusiastically. "I see you feel the same," I laughed.

"The problem is," I began but I couldn't say it aloud, not even to my dog. I squirmed in embarrassment, even four years later, when I thought of that day. It was clear in my mind when my memory of almost everything else during that sad and confusing time was hazy.

I lifted my heated face to the wind coming off the sea. The clouds, thick and dark, began to drizzle and mirrored my mood, and I slapped the reins, hoping to outrace the worst of the coming storm, if not my memories. They wouldn't be ignored.

My mother had passed away in the first month of 1803. My father, my younger brother John, and I, exhausted and heart-sore, were also a little relieved that she had escaped the pain of her final long illness. We did what needed to be done as if in a daze. It was only later, in high summer that I began to truly understand the depth of my loss.

Aunt Beatrice, my father's sister, came to live with us. She was as different from my reserved and steady father as two siblings could be. She was even more unlike my mother. Where my mother had been calm and cheerful and had understood, even encouraged, my high spirits, my aunt was anxious and excitable—and determined to mold me into her idea of a lady befitting my station. If I found her tiresome and exacting, I'm sure she found me—a young, wild, bereaved, fifteen-year-old girl—a trial. We fought, often.

One day, after a particularly difficult and tearful dispute with Aunt Beatrice, I met Robert, walking along the stream that divided our lands. Though patently uncomfortable with my tears, he sat and planted his back against a tree trunk and held me as I cried violently. And then he held me while I slept.

When I woke, curled around him, and clinging even in sleep, my first emotion was embarrassment. But it wasn't long before I became vividly aware and curious at the feel of his soft shirt, still damp from my tears and scented from his soap, his hard chest and the strength of his arms around me.

My heart began to beat heavily. My breath stuttered. Finally, I pulled away to look up at him, not knowing what to expect. His eyes were hooded and intensely focused on me, high color on his cheeks. I mistook the warmth in his eyes and stretched up awkwardly and kissed him. The memory of the hitch of his breath, the feel of his lips, soft and heated on mine haunted me.

We kissed and kissed again.

Time slowed while insects hummed, and the brook

whispered deep secrets I almost understood.

But too quickly, Robert gently, but firmly pushed me away and rose abruptly to his feet and backed away. His fingers ran through his hair as he stood with head lowered, breathing hard for long enough for me to come back to myself. He looked up, and our eyes met for a moment's stillness that seemed to last forever.

"Liza, I—" He covered his mouth with his hand. "I shouldn't have—" he started again and stopped. He shook his head, "I must go," he backed up a step, and another before turning around and briskly walking away, leaving me stunned and painfully embarrassed. I sat for the longest time with my head on my drawn-up knees as the stream continued to babble blissfully by.

Four years later, and the memory of that kiss was still enough to make my heart beat harder, my breath hitch, while the memory of him walking away was still painful and embarrassing beyond words.

As if in concert with my ignominious memories, lightening flashed and the rain began to fall in earnest. I didn't see the rut in the road. After a hard bump, my cart stuttered and listed to the side; Maybelle reared, and we came to a faltering stop.

I sighed deeply, hunched over and shivering in my seat for a few moments, wishing for comfort. There was none to be found, so I climbed down to survey the damage.

Though I tried to get Quin to stay in the cart, he bounded down, barking and weaving around my legs in his three-legged shuffle and hop, nearly tripping me up as I inspected the wheel at its unlikely angle. He caused Maybelle to skitter as I untied her harness. I tried and tried again to mount while holding my wriggling puppy.

Though gentle, Maybelle would have none of it, and I was not so nimble as to be able to climb up without a mounting block, and one handed as well. Finally, accepting the inevitable, I slapped her rump, knowing she would find her way and began my wet trudge toward home.

As I plodded along the fields north of town, something the squire had said made me begin to wonder. Perhaps Robert's experiences of the last four years—the people he'd met, the battles, horrors, and pain had erased, or at least dulled, the memories of our youth. Maybe in comparison to the hardship of war on the seas, my forward, inappropriate kiss faded in import.

With that perspective, I wondered if I could look with mercy, even humor on that woman/child's first fluttering awareness and forgive myself. I could certainly bury my feelings for him. They were, after all, so far in the past, or so I told myself, and half-believed. As I trudged through the deepening dark, I decided I could meet him now as a friendly acquaintance, with grace and poise.

I straightened my shoulders and lifted my head. The rain, uncaring, ran down my face and beneath the neck of my cloak, and I shivered violently. Lightning streaked across the sky, followed quickly by a booming thunder. The downpour continued, and I scowled at the sky, hitched my dog higher in my arms, and continued my slog through the ever-deepening mud. In my arms, and continued my slog through the ever-deepening mud.

Chapter 2

*We are so used to dissembling with others that in time we
come to deceive and dissemble with others*

Francois de La Rochefoucauld,
Moral Maxims

Though my father was fond of his dogs, he hadn't
demurred when Aunt Beatrice banished all animals from
the house, which is why I sat on the stoop at the servants'
entrance and removed my ruined shoes, throwing them
under a nearby bush. My stockings were also wet and cold.
When I took them off, Quin showed an unwelcome interest.
By the time I was able to pry them from his teeth and slip
them into a pocket in my cloak, I felt weak and winded. I
had to make arrangements for him, but all I wanted to do
was sit there, out of the rain, and close my eyes.

Nevertheless, I pulled myself and my dog up and
turned to the door. "If there is a saint for little dogs, now is
the time to petition, Quin," I told him under my breath.

The staff were already beginning supper preparations
as I snuck by the busy kitchen and butler's pantry on my
way to the winding back staircase. As I turned out of sight
of any passing servants, I breathed a sigh of relief. I relaxed

too soon, though, as with another turn, I barreled into a
maid descending with a pile of linens. She shrieked and
backed up, falling inelegantly on her seat. In the dim light I
recognized my maid.

"Quiet, Susan," I grabbed her arm, "come with me," I
whispered urgently.

"What is that?" She squeaked, looking in horror at the
writhing bundle of wet fur.

"I need your help," I whispered as I pulled her along
with me up to my room.

"Oh, miss. You know your aunt will—" she protested
as we climbed.

"That's why I need your help," I whispered, "I know I
can't keep him with me in the house all the time," I poked
my head around the corner and looked up and down the
hall. It was blessedly empty, "I believe Charlie won't mind
an extra dog in the stables at night, no, nor for part of the
day either if I need. For his exercise I can take him with
me every time I go walking. If you will help, and don't you
think Frank would help too, bringing him to and from the
stable when I am unable to get away?" I pleaded.

She rolled her eyes, "Oh, miss. We will be caught, if
not today . . ."

"Well," I said recognizing capitulation, "today is
enough. We'll worry about tomorrow, later."

We had just walked into to my room, had yet to close
the door, when I heard my aunt puffing up the stairs, "Elizabeth Louisa, where are you, you difficult girl?"

Susan and I looked at each other in horror. She muffled her screech with a hand, while I pulled her further into
the room and closed the door. I looked around frantically
for a hiding place. But I knew Quin wouldn't stay where I

placed him. In desperation, I pulled my stockings out of my pocket and offered them; he pounced happily. I placed him on the floor between my feet and lifted my muddy hem over him, just in time, as Aunt Beatrice sailed into the room.

"Where have you—" she froze and frowned as she inspected me from my hair, clinging in wet flags down my back, to the mud encrusted hem of my cloak. "Oh, for pity's sake, Elizabeth, can't you—" She shook her head and fluttered her hands nervously. "Never mind that now. We have no time. Captain Amesley is here."

"But he called yesterday, and surely you returned his call today," I said nonplussed. Why had I spent all day away from home if Robert was going to arrive just as I returned?

"What does that matter? Why shouldn't he come again to visit his nearest neighbor?" Her shrill voice seemed to give her pause. She took a deep breath and shook her head, "it is of no consequence. He came to see your father," she looked around nervously.

"I see," though that was anything but the truth.

"Your father is not at home but will be soon. I've asked him to wait, and Captain Amesley asked after you. I need you in the drawing room now." She rung her hands and glanced over at Susan. In her distraction, she didn't see the obvious guilt on my little maid's face.

"Help her change," she fluttered, "and can you do something with her hair?"

Susan went to the door and stopped a passing servant, murmuring requests.

Aunt Beatrice put a hand to her brow, "Elizabeth, what am I to do with you? What are we to do? Captain Amesley is . . ." She shook her head and flapped her hands nervously.

"You go and sit with Robert," I suggested with as much patience as I could muster, "tell him I was out visiting, my cart wheel broke, and I got caught in the storm—which is the truth," I stressed, "but I'll be down directly." I couldn't move, or Quin would be revealed, but I made a shooing motion with my hands.

Aunt Beatrice nodded distractedly and sneezed, "Yes, yes. I'll go down." She sniffed delicately, "Elizabeth Louisa, what did you walk through? It smells like," she sniffed and sneezed again, "wet animal." She shuddered and wrinkled her nose, looking around suspiciously.

I silently willed her to leave, and after a moment, she shook herself and scowled at me. "Quickly, don't just stand there," she ordered as she turned and scurried out the door.

I was light-headed, but my body felt weighted, my stomach knotted. Why now, I asked myself. What would bring him here again today?

No answer presented itself, so I lifted my skirts and stepped over Quin who was contentedly shredding my stockings. I dropped my cloak to the floor. My dress was more difficult as my hands were numb. Susan pushed them away and unbuttoned and stripped the dress and my wet underclothes away.

"The water will be a moment." Susan said apologetically "While we wait, see you if you can untangle your hair." She put a comb in my hand.

I nodded, gave a weak smile, and shivered uncontrollably.

She scowled and pulled the blanket off the bed and led me to the chaise. She rekindled the fire, then gathered clothes for me as I sat listlessly. After another look at me, she laid the clothes on the bed. She shook her head and stirred the fire again, sighing in dissatisfaction before she removed the comb from my hand.

She tugged mercilessly at my head, but I didn't have the energy to remonstrate. I let her comb and twist and pin my hair. I felt unaccountably close to tears. The water came finally from the kitchen, and it helped a little to wash the mud away, but I was glad to sit again wrapped in my blanket.

"Alright, miss, you'll have to stand now," Susan said as she pulled me up by my elbows, stripped the blanket away, and dressed me like I was a baby. I no longer felt cold. Quite the contrary, I felt uncomfortably warm. Susan handed me a handkerchief, and I blotted my face and neck.

She shook her head as she handed me my stockings, but when I just stood there swaying, she took them from me and pushed me to sit again on the chaise. She dropped to her knees,

"Oh, your feet are frozen," she said in concern. She chafed them a little before putting on my stockings and shoes.

"Miss Liza," she searched my face, "are you sure . . ."

"Aunt Beatrice is waiting with Captain Amesley," I interrupted, "I must go down." I tried to smile reassuringly, but her concern didn't abate.

"Will you get Frank to take my dog, his name is Quin, down to Charlie. Tell him I will explain everything tomorrow."

Susan shook her head again, but I must have looked quite pitiful, for she patted my arm and gave me the assurance I needed, "I'll make sure the little dog gets settled for the night. You go down."

Robert's back was to me, as I came to the drawing

room. My eyes traced the slight curl of his dark hair, the
snug fit of his wool coat over broad shoulders that ta-
pered to his lean hips. My disloyal heart beat harder, and
I thought bitterly of my earlier assurance. I lifted my chin
and searched for the poise of new insight, took a deep
breath, and stepped forward.

"Oh, there she is," Aunt Beatrice moved quickly to my
side.

Robert turned, and the squire's scolding returned to
me as I noticed that he leaned on his cane and was pale
under his tan. His brooding eyes followed me as I walked to
greet him.

"Captain Amesley, how nice to see you again," I curtsied. Robert took my hand and bowed over it.

"Miss Henshaw," he was equally formal. When he
raised his questioning brow, my breath hitched. His serious,
searching eyes, his firm lips and square jaw started an ache
in my heart and brought a sting of tears. I looked away and
saw Aunt Beatrice watching avidly, "I was just telling Captain Amesley," she said to me, "that your father is called out
by the Lord Lieutenant on some business this evening but
will be home any moment."

Her countenance brought me back to myself, and I almost laughed. My aunt was torn on the subject of the Lord
Lieutenant and indeed all things to do with the militia. She
felt more than a mild distaste for the Duke of Norfolk. He
was slatternly, an unforgivable breach of etiquette to her
mind; it was rumored that the only time his servants could
get him to bathe was when he was in his cups. And, of
course, most people disliked the militia. They were as often
a source of mayhem as of stability and safety. Paradoxically,
Aunt Beatrice was proud of her brother's position as dep-

uty lieutenant, even though my father always said he was
only appointed for his ability to keep immaculate records. I
looked without thinking to Robert to share the joke and met
an unsettling, quizzical smile.

We sat, and Robert and Aunt Beatrice discoursed.
Aunt Beatrice shot me frantic glances periodically, but my
mind wandered, and I was so uncomfortable. I listened
dully as I alternated between deep, cold internal shivers and
burning heat.

The relief when I heard the rumble of my father's
voice from the hall surprised in me a sudden, overwhelming need. I jumped up and rushed out of the drawing room
before Robert could even come to his feet. I ignored Aunt
Beatrice's shocked reproach.

"Well, hello," my father said as he removed his gloves
and hat and handed them to Philips, the butler. He looked
tired, but he smiled gently, "there's my Liza." His eyes
wandered over my face, "You're looking a little flushed, my
dear."

"I was caught in the storm," I brushed some raindrops
off the shoulder of his jacket, "and then I had to rush to
change so as to come down to entertain Captain Amesley,
who is waiting to see you? I'm a little warm."

"Captain Amesley," his attention sharpened noticeably,
and though he patted my hand, his arm was stiff beneath
my fingers, "did we have an appointment?"

I looked at his face, already turned toward the drawing room, but I was too tired to try to make sense of his
tension, I just shook my head and moved to lean my head
against his shoulder.

His attention returned to me, "Liza, my dear, are you well?"

"I am only a little tired, Papa. Come and talk with

him, and then I will to up and rest."

I walked back into the drawing room, this time on my father's arm. He went straight to shake hands with Robert, "Captain Amesley, I'm sorry I wasn't here to receive you."

"No sir. I came with small hope I would find you home, but I thought it worth the attempt. It was presumptuous of me."

"Think nothing of it," my father clapped Robert on the shoulder, "neighbors have no need to stand on ceremony. What can I do for you?"

Robert's uncomfortable, quick glance at Aunt Beatrice and at me snagged my wandering attention. He cleared his throat, "I have a few small questions. Not pressing at all really, but I was riding by." He looked nonchalant, but I was watching his hands, and they told a different story.

Father raised his brows and nodded. "Well, come into my study. We'll talk. And a little brandy won't come amiss, what with this storm," he rubbed his hands together briskly.

Aunt Beatrice cleared her throat gently, "If I could speak to you a moment first," she pulled on father's sleeve.

"What, now?"

"It will only take a moment; I'm sure dear Captain Amesley won't mind." She looked coquettishly at Robert.

"Beatrice, Captain Amesley is . . ."

"It is no inconvenience," Robert assured, "I am content to wait," he bowed. What else could he do without being churlish? And I had never seen Robert churlish.

"I will be with you momentarily," my father returned his bow. Then he took my aunt's elbow.

"Very well, Beatrice," he said impatiently and walked with her across the hall to his study.

Paradoxically, after trying to avoid private speech, or

any thoughts, of Robert, I was glad of this few moments alone with him. It was clear he had something of import on his mind, and I wanted to know what it was. Whether it was the force of old habits or the pounding in my head, subtlety was impossible. "What is amiss?" I asked baldly, "what do you need to ask my father?"

He considered me thoughtfully for a few seconds, then he turned his back to me and walked to the window overlooking the front drive, "It is nothing, Liza."

"Nothing?" I said to his back and measured the distance between us thoughtfully.

"Nothing," he repeated, rocking forward and back again on his heels, "I've been out of the neighborhood for some time," he clasped his hands behind his back, then released them, "I would simply like to get his perspective on the state of the parish. It is nothing to cause you concern." He turned to me again, shrugged his shoulders and lifted one eyebrow.

With his third assurance that there was nothing awry, a thought came to me in a moment of dazzling clarity. Though in many ways I was looking at a stranger, at the same time, I still knew this man better than I knew anyone. His self-possessed but brittle aloofness may have been unfamiliar, but I recognized those nervous quirks. In my heart and with a cold assurance, I knew that he was lying.

I felt bereft and chilled to my bones. I moved stiffly to the fireplace and held out my hands.

He followed me, "Liza, what's wrong?"

"It is nothing, Captain Amesley," I repeated both his word and his tone.

"Liza, we have never been on such terms that you need call me Captain. Certainly, such long and sure friends as we have no need for such formality."

I looked up into his face, expecting to see the cold dishonesty, but saw instead a raw entreaty that shook me.

"We were friends," I mused aloud, "weren't we?"

"Yes, how can you doubt?"

My control broke and scattered under a sudden fury. I was surprised by its force. "You left. You left without word." I flapped my hand in agitation. "Everything changed, and I needed . . ." I stopped myself abruptly and tried to slow my breathing. "You left with no word to me," I said in more measured tones. He started to speak, but I held up my hand to stop him. "In over four years, I received less than a dozen letters," I accused.

"Liza," his hand, lifted as if to calm a wild animal made me unaccountably even more angry, "don't be unreasonable. Come, sit. We will talk. I'm sure once you understand . . ."

I stiffened, "Don't be so magisterial. I'm not a child anymore."

"I can see that," he answered gravely, taking two tentative steps toward me. "I tried to write." He shrugged uncomfortably, "at first I was—I didn't know whether you would want to receive letters from me after I," his cheeks flushed, and I could feel mine heating again as well. I looked away. He continued doggedly, "then later I tried to write, but it is not so easy to post letters from a ship of the line. But, you must know, I thought of—"

I know he continued to talk, but I was taken with a sudden violent coughing. I felt a rush of heat move from my head to my feet; a sudden nausea overtook me. I felt lightheaded, and my vision began to gray.

I heard no more.

Chapter 3

In order that all men may be taught to speak truth, it is necessary that all likewise should learn to hear it

Samuel Johnson, *The Rambler*

I opened my eyes to find Robert leaning over me, holding my hands. I looked around anxiously.

"What are you thinking coming down like this?" His low voice shook with anger, and maybe something else, "you might have just sent word you were ill. If I had not caught you when you fainted, you might have done yourself serious harm."

"Robert," I turned my hands to grasp his, "wait," his words resolved themselves into meaning, "I fainted? I never faint."

"Well, you did today," his grip on my hands squeezed painfully, "Don't do it again, I beg you," He pulled me up into his arms.

I thought I'd remembered what it felt like, but this was something new. It was a sweet languor seeping through the pain and confusion. How much was illness, how much memory? How much was Robert?

Overwhelmed by a rush of emotion, I brushed my fevered forehead against his shoulder, and said before I thought, "I have missed you."

Robert's hand tightened on the back of my head. "Liza," his breath escaped in a huff, "now you tell me this?"

I pulled back and saw his expression, as I'd only seen once before, hooded and hungry.

"Liza—"

Awareness returned and with it panic—too much change, too fast. There was so much I didn't know about this new and secretive Robert and, honestly, I was confused about how I felt. I had, unwittingly opened a door that I was not ready for him to storm through. I needed to re-trench—and quickly.

"Robert, let me up. I must—" my words were broken off by a violent shivering.

My aunt's startled, but suspiciously delighted shriek assaulted my ears. "Oh, my dear, what is happening here?"

Robert looked up but didn't let me go. He rubbed my back briskly, ignoring my aunt and speaking directly to my father. "She fainted. She is hot to the touch and wracked with chills. Will you send for the physician, sir?"

"Phillips," my father yelled to the butler in the hall. My aunt shrieked again, but Robert stood and lifted me.

"Ma'am, if you'll lead the way, I will carry Liza to her room."

"Robert, your leg. I can see it pains you. I can walk," I insisted.

"Liza hush, my leg is healed. It may ache in weather, but I can carry you up a flight of stairs with no further damage."

And he did, while I tried to focus on the frustration at being treated like a child, tried to ignore the beating of my heart and the overwhelming sensation of safety.

My aunt clucked and muttered and called my maid.
Together they put me to bed. The physician called in a
short time later and diagnosed influenza. My father wrung
his hands, patted my shoulder gently then left. Aunt Beatrice and Susan took turns sitting by while I spent the next
three days in laudanum-laced sleep.

Of that time, I only remember a blur of fevered
thoughts and worries, compresses, beef broth, and barley
water, which was only effective because the afflicted rose
from the sick bed just to avoid drinking it.

Sometimes in that space between waking and sleeping,
I imagined Robert's deep calm voice and the scent of the
sea, but when I woke, he was gone.

For three days I hardly left my bed. After the worst of
the symptoms eased, and for the rest of the week, my aunt
required that I remain abed except for an hour or two in
the afternoon, when I was allowed to sit quietly in the sun-
ny west salon.

Robert visited for a brief time each afternoon. I told
myself that it was only boredom that made me look forward to his arrival. Most men might bring flowers or a
delicacy, but Robert knew me better than that. He brought
reminders of our childhood together—a rock worn smooth
by the ebb and flow of the tide, an egret feather, a walnut
shell that he had cleverly carved into a small basket, the
abandoned nest of a ruddy turnstone, a branch of sea holly,
silver and blue. I could track his progress through the coun-
ty by his offerings. I tried not to be charmed by his gifts,
but they spoke to me in a way that a bunch of posies never
could.

After a brief visit with me, Robert would disappear
into my father's study. With too much time and nothing else

to think about, what was happening in that study, coupled with my earlier assurance that he was hiding something, weighed heavily on my mind. Possibilities chased each other in my thoughts like Quin chasing his tail. I wondered and worried about how to discover information. Inspiration came in the most unexpected way.

Toward the end of the long week of my semi-convalescence, I came downstairs to find my Aunt and her maid setting out a formal tea. I paused at the door for too long, and Aunt Beatrice saw me before I could retreat.

My aunt was on the board of the 'Female Friendly Society for the Relief of the Poor, Infirm, and Single Women of Good Character Who Are Impoverished.' It was a mouthful, but the poor-levy we paid to the parish did not serve all those who were in need. The Female Friendly Society did much good in those uncertain times. These worthy ladies were planning a dinner and a huge charity ball to be held on the night of the first full moon after the harvest.

I had never attended my aunt's meetings, mostly from a lack of interest and, also, probably due to my aunt's fear that I would embarrass her.

However, there I was, standing in the doorway as I heard the chatter of women being welcomed at the door.

"Oh dear," Aunt Beatrice paused as if struck, "Elizabeth, I should have reminded you of my committee meeting," she shook her head impatiently. "They are here; you'll have to attend," she scrutinized me carefully, probably looking for dirt or a tear in my dress, "you look well." She sounded surprised and I blushed but firmly reminded myself that I had taken special care before coming down so that it would lift my spirits, not in expectation of seeing Robert.

"Just sit quietly and," she pushed me gently toward the sofa, "well you won't have a chance to do anything else with Lady Charlotte Ramsgate and Althea Dinmore coming. Lady Ramsgate is bringing her daughter, Lady Helen. Martina Crossley and her daughter, Alice will be here too."

A brief look of distaste crossed her features, "well, Mrs. Crossley is no better than she should be, but we must have her," a short pause and a satisfied smile, "but I will show her today," She rubbed her hands in glee, smoothed her dress, and turned as her guests entered the salon.

Though uninterested in the workings of my aunt's committee, I couldn't help but be aware of the events that gave her such pleasure. She had talked of little else for weeks. Through a connection of my father's, she had met and curried favor with the current steward of the Court Lodge. As the wild fowling season had not yet started, the Duke of Dorset was not in residence, so the steward had written and received permission for her to use The Manor for the ball.

The Manor at Bexhill was an important neighborhood attraction. It was granted to the Sackville family by Queen Elizabeth herself, though the present Duke lived primarily in Kent. The manor included seven reception rooms, nineteen bedrooms, two cottages, and a detached ballroom.

It was quite an accomplishment for my aunt and would increase her consequence among her friends immensely. She was determined to make this ball the grandest in the parish.

Though Aunt Beatrice was in high spirits, I settled in grudgingly, expecting to be bored beyond bearing. And at first, I was.

They rustled skirts and chattered as they arranged

themselves, and my aunt began to pour. I had to attend and respond as they discussed my illness and recovery, but I lost interest somewhere between talk about the weather and their health and that of their families. They might have discussed fashion as well, though I can't be sure as I had taken to staring out the window and wondering if Robert would brave the overwhelming female atmosphere in the salon or cravenly escape, as I wished to do.

I was stirring my tea in a desultory manner, when something Mrs. Martina Crossley said caught my attention.

"Mr. Josiah Routledge says he is determined to find coal under Bexhill," she cleared her throat, but there was no need. We were already listening as Mr. Routledge, of Rosiers, was one of the most prominent figures in Bexhill, "Arabella, Duchess of Dorset and Lord Whitworth are providing substantial backing."

I didn't roll my eyes, but I wanted to. Mrs. Crossley wasn't intimate, any more than any of us, with either the Duchess or Lord Whitworth.

Lady Ramsgate sniffed, "they say they are looking for coal, but we all know what those tunnels will eventually be used for."

"Do you think he's consorting with free traders?" Mrs. Dinmore looked around the circle, eyes wide, "Millfield, is quite magnificent, isn't it? Will Mr. Routledge be coming to the ball, do you know?"

My jaw dropped at the abrupt move from smuggling, to Mr. Routledge's new mansion, to the ball. I was brought to myself as my aunt firmly pressed my foot with hers.

Aunt Beatrice picked up the teapot with poise and offered a refill to Mrs. Crossley's, which she accepted with a small nod.

"I believe he will attend," my aunt answered Mrs. Dinmore, entirely ignoring the reference to smugglers. "That reminds me, have you met the Hattons? They have taken possession of Edgecombe and are accepting callers. Shall we invite them to the dinner?"

Mrs. Crossley made a moue of distaste. "I think it's vulgar, the way they drive their coach and four through the village," but I could hear the envy in her voice, "when everyone knows he was in trade."

Lady Ramsgate hid her smile behind her cup, "One has met them, of course. I thought they were very mannerly. Not at all common. They do have some good blood in their line. The late Mrs. Hatton's grandmother was connected in some way to the Duke of Hampton, though there is some Irish on his father's side." She shrugged away her distaste, "I found Mr. Hatton quite elegant, and the son and daughter to be well behaved. I think we must have them. And of course, they will make up the numbers."

"It is good to have more young people in the neighborhood," Lady Helen Ramsgate inserted. She had been so quiet that I had forgotten she was there. "And Miss Hatton is quite nice, I think, and Mr. Hatton very agreeable. It must be difficult to move to a new place where you know no one. I think it would be the kindest thing to—"

"Yes, of course," her mother waved her hand and Lady Helen, once again, lowered her head.

I felt sorry for Lady Helen and was relieved when, just then, Phillips knocked quietly and opened the door to announce, "Captain. Amesley, ma'am." I should never have doubted his courage, I thought in relief.

"Oh, dear Robert," my aunt turned to him, "I suppose you're here to see Arthur. Will you take some tea first?"

"I thank you, no. I won't interrupt for long," he said, taking her outstretched hand, "Phillips thought it might be acceptable if I just slipped in to bring this book to the convalescent." He pressed a small leather-bound book into my hands, smiling warmly into my eyes.

"Thank you," I said, aware of my fascinated audience, but also disappointed. A book seemed so—so prosaic after his previous thoughtful offerings.

I looked down and opened the book at random and smiled against my will. There pressed between the pages was a delicate spiked rampion. His sweeping handwriting noted the plant's Latin name, location, and date. Another page held common thrift, a third, shepherd's purse. I looked up and met his eyes. Whatever he saw in my face made him nod and smile.

He turned, briefly made his excuses, bowed over the ladies' hands, each in turn, and took his leave, as quick and invigorating as a sea breeze. I wished I could join him.

"Well, Miss Elizabeth," Lady Ramsgate said archly, "Mr. Amesley bringing gifts. That's very promising."

"Oh, Lady Charlotte, it is nothing," my aunt came to my defense, "dear Robert was tutored by my brother when he was young. He is always a thoughtful neighbor."

"Well, maybe that is best," Mrs. Crossley said, though she looked disappointed, "his father was so wild, and," she paused dramatically, as she lifted her teacup, "blood will out."

"That was many years ago," my aunt said repressively, "young spirits in a difficult time."

"Oh, do tell," Mrs. Althea Dinmore leaned forward, placing her teacup precisely in the center of her saucer and choosing a lemon scone.

"Oh, this was before your family came here," Lady Ramsgate interjected, as she lifted her lorgnette. She watched Mrs. Dinmore's fidgeting with raised brows for a few moments before she condescended to continue, "when we were all quite young. Amesley, Captain Amesley's father, could hardly be kept home; he lived mostly on the continent. He took up many of those French ways. Although," she paused meaningfully and raised her eyebrows, "their family repaired their fortunes during that time."

"No," Mrs. Dinmore offered me the cream, "was he involved with the gentlemen?" She sat back and lifted her tea, "This is a lovely set, Beatrice, such a charming tea."

"Well, I'm not one to gossip," continued Lady Ramsgate, "but they always did have a generous cellar and his mama wore the finest French lace." She raised her handkerchief and coughed.

Mrs. Crossley nodded and leaned forward. "I heard there was a woman," she whispered. I watched riveted as she paused to spread jelly on her biscuit with a delicate hand. "My mama said Amesley came back after a year or two going back and forth to France with a broken heart and spent a wild year drinking excessively, boxing, cock-fighting, and taking every reckless dare."

"But," Aunt Beatrice inserted firmly, "Marianne saved him."

"Ah, yes," Mrs. Dinmore said, "Marianne was a good sort of girl, such a tragedy when she died."

I regretted even more that I hadn't joined Robert in his retreat. Robert's father was always gentle and kind to me. I knew that the next time I saw him this conversation would come to mind. I squirmed even then.

"She may have been the soul of refinement, but her

poor sister's husband gambled most of his family's fortune away," Lady Ramsgate's smile disappeared behind her cup.

My aunt, ungently this time, nudged my foot, and I realized I was staring at Lady Ramsgate, teacup suspended half-way between my saucer and mouth, with my mouth agape again. I lowered my eyes demurely and lifted the cup the rest of the way and sipped. And almost choked when she continued, "I've heard their son, that Mr. Perry Gerow, is quite wild when away from his own class. He consorts with," she looked at me and cleared her throat, "a certain class of women."

I spilled my tea and surreptitiously wiped with my napkin. I listened in fascinated horror as Mrs. Dinmore took up the story, "you know Amesley hired Mr. Gerow, out of care for his sister in law—very generous, I'm sure. And though Mr. Gerow has the best company manners," she brushed crumbs from her fingers, "and his family's good looks, it's unfortunate that he has never a feather to fly with. He'll be looking out for a rich wife, I'm sure."

She looked at me. And I felt the blood rise in my cheeks. I had met Perry Gerow socially, of course. He was steward for the Amesleys. I had always found him to be polite, if reserved. If these ladies were to be believed, while out of company, he wasn't so nice.

Finally, in defense, I put my teacup aside and kept my eyes on my folded hands. Over the next half hour, I learned more shocking things about Mr. Amesley, and his steward, Mr. Perry Gerow, and other local families whom I thought I had known all of my life. I was privy to uncomfortable speculation about the officers of the King's German legion, and of Colonel Abernathy and the other officers of the local militia. It was more than a little discouraging to be given a view into the hidden underbelly of fine society.

When tea was over, they continued to work, and my aunt did have her anticipated victory. I was happy for her, but I was also distracted and overcome with a new respect, may I say even fear of these well-bred ladies. And I had some pressing questions about how they got their information; Even the Duke of Wellington would have benefited from an intelligence gathering network as thorough as my aunt's friends. Their knowledge and supposition, though perhaps not always fitting, was certainly extensive.

"I think you acquitted yourself quite well," my aunt said after her friends left, "though Elizabeth," she said sternly, "in future strive not to gape like a codfish, no matter what is said at tea."

"How does she know these things?" I asked

"How does who know what things, Elizabeth?"

"Lady Ramsgate. All that she said about Robert and his father, about Perry Gerow and his family situation? How does she know so much about the Hattons? They only just moved into the neighborhood. And the commander of the local militia, Colonel Abernathy? Why, he's from Devon. How would she know so much about him?"

"Oh, that's Charlotte, she always did like to—well, Liza, it's best to never assume, even if she's left the room that she can't still hear you." After a pause, she continued, "her dresser is no better. And you know how servants will gossip," she said self-righteously, seemingly not aware of the irony.

Chapter 4

Sigh no more ladies, sigh no more, Men were deceivers ever,
One foot in sea and one on shore; To one thing constant
never

Shakespeare,
Much Ado About Nothing

Tea with my aunt's friends, though harrowing, gave me
ideas. I felt a little guilty about applying such underhanded
means. But though my memory of the night I fainted was
foggy in many ways, Robert's rigid back and subtle discomfort, the space he'd put between us, and his nervous gestures
made me positive that all was not fine, as he had thrice assured me. I told myself that since Robert lied to me, which
he never had before, and was closeting himself in secret
meetings with my father, he deserved to be spied out. Also, I
rationalized, I wouldn't be serving it up with tea. I, after all,
do know how to keep a secret.

I started by asking Aunt Beatrice what I hoped were
discreet questions and got a scolding for my trouble, "Men
will talk, and not everything is a fitting topic for tea. It's not
for you to go nipping your nose into things that that don't
concern you, missy."

Which was the veriest hypocrisy, as I was aware. Naturally, her stricture had a much different result than she intended. I was even more determined to discover Robert's secret.

I watched for an opportunity to eavesdrop, reprehensible I knew, but the only way to find the truth. The only relief from my fretting came when I was able to sneak out to the stables to play with Quin.

Finally, after a further two days of worry and watching, mixed with long periods of stultifying boredom, my opportunity came, and it was as easy as tripping down the stairs, and as unpleasant.

Aunt Beatrice finally declared that, if I was sensible in my choice of activity, I might be allowed to leave the house for short periods of time, and she might resume her usual visits around the neighborhood.

Since my idea of sensible differs from my aunt's, I watched her carriage roll down the drive before I came downstairs. I planned to celebrate by taking Quin for a walk in the back woods. I was feeling cheerful and had dressed accordingly in a morning walking dress of Scotch cambric, trimmed with green embroidered bands. My short scarf had a matching pale green border. I wore my half boots and a chip straw bonnet.

I was half-way down before I saw Robert at the bottom of the stairs. I stopped when he looked up and smiled. "You look charming, Liza."

What I felt was flushed and unstable, which made no sense. I should have become used to seeing him.

"I see you are going out. You must be relieved to escape the confines of the house."

I relaxed under his compassionate look, "Yes I am. I am going for a short walk."

"It is a fine day, but still quite wet out. If you can wait a moment, I will take you for a drive instead."

I shook my head, "I thank you, but I am anxious to move, and I know you want to speak with father. I will be fine. I have my boots." I looked down, "oh, I forgot my gloves." I backed up with an apologetic smile and turned to rush up the stairs.

I could feel his eyes following me as I ascended. I thought about that and the warmth I felt at his gaze as I walked to my room. I took my time and was relieved that the hall was empty when I descended again.

I heard the rumble of voices as I passed my father's study, but I was halfway down the hall before I realized his door was not completely closed and that no one, but I, was in the hall. I tiptoed back and leaned close to hear.

I almost jumped when Robert's voice came clearly from just the other side of the door, "Colonel Fitzpatrick from the Secretary at War office has an assistant who is willing for a price," Robert must have been roaming around the room as his voice changed in volume and direction.

"How?" My father asked.

"I meet the messenger at a series of prearranged spots."

"What if he is intercepted?"

"The communiques are encoded——" He must have moved to the other side of the room and turned away from the door as I couldn't hear the rest of his sentence.

"But the Wilkins gang," my father's breath whistle through his teeth, "are you sure?"

A deep rumble, "——likely," then he must have turned for the next was clear, "I am sure they are doing more than smuggling spirits. If I'm right, and they are already sending information to Napoleon's agents. Why not carry my information as well?"

I gasped, horrified then clapped my hand over my mouth.

I had missed my father's response, "—a way in?"

"There are some rumors spreading about my father, and my grandfather in his time, avoiding taxes on their brandy and tobacco."

"Have a care, Amesley. You will blacken your name. You still need to operate in the bounds of good society."

I missed the first of Robert's mumbled response, "—and I now know one of their number quite well," his satisfaction was disturbing, "I'll start small—some brandy. Then when that interchange has been successful, I have a personal matter that they can help me with."

"Oh?" My father sounded disapproving.

Robert didn't seem concerned, "yes, something I need to smuggle in from France."

"Robert!"

He chuckled, "it will serve a double purpose. I will get what I need into England, and it will pave my way with the Wilkins gang so I can begin to send out those communiques to Etienne LeFevre."

"He's in place?"

"Yes."

"Have a care—" my father must have joined Robert in pacing the room.

The sound of rustling papers muted part of Robert's response. "Used to hardened—"

"Yes," my father's voice clear now, "but these are not marines under your authority. You may not remember how ruthless free traders are. Over the past five years, they have burned three houses of suspected informants. They beat John Rawlins and Peter Collins. The locals either support them or stay out of their way. Perhaps there—"

"I know it's a risk, but I must." I could hear the heavy treads of Robert's feet, "and I am no present danger to them; they will continue to trade unmolested. The possible benefits outweigh the dangers."

There was long pause before my father answered, and my heart sank. "If you have determined that this is the best way, I am with you."

"Thank you," he paused, "the information you can get in your position will be invaluable."

"It won't be easy, but I'll find a way," my father said, "but if we don't both hang it will be a miracle."

I could hear both men moving toward the door and ran down the hall and slipped into the salon just in time.

From there I stumbled blindly out to the stable. I couldn't breathe, and my stomach clenched in a tight knot. It couldn't be, they wouldn't betray—but what other explanation could there be for what I had heard?

I don't know what I said to Charlie, but I was soon trudging aimlessly through the wooded area behind our home with Quin gamboling at my side. The wild terrain was an understandable temptation, but he seemed to sense my disquiet. So ,while he explored eagerly, he came back regularly to nuzzle my hand or bump my leg in sympathy.

Robert's request for information and my father's agreement chased each other through my brain. I didn't want to assume the worst; I knew my father as upright and honest. Certainly, he had changed since my mother's death, but I couldn't believe that he would participate in anything that required him to misuse his authority.

And Robert. I was sure the squire was right. The horrors of war must change a man, but I needed to believe that fundamentally he was the same. I fought against the idea that they were contemplating such disreputable activity. I would have to find out more before I could make a judgment. There must be another explanation. I could feel my heartbeat slow, my breathing calm at this thought. Yes, I needed to know more.

And if I found that they were involved in something dishonest, horrifying as was this possibility, because of some misguided thinking or in a moment's weakness, I would have to face it and find a way to convince them to stop. After all, these two men had been solid fixtures my entire life. I couldn't stand by wringing my hands while my father and my—neighbor did something so ruinous.

I felt better. I would have to be very cunning and vigilant. I would search my father's desk when he was away. I needed to find out when Robert was meeting with these uncouth men and follow him, if I could. I would find the truth, and I would help them, I resolved. And thus, 'My Society for the Rescue of Men Caught in the Immorality Attendant to War' was established.

I was so deep in thought that I didn't notice Robert's approach until he crested the hill. I may have felt confident in my decision, but I wasn't ready to face him. I called Quin to me and hastily pulled the hem of my walking dress up and secured it with my tie. I tucked him into the resulting pocket. "Shh," I mumbled to an unhappy Quin as I skittered my way awkwardly up into a chestnut tree. It's thick leaves provided a shield from any casual glance. I braced my back against the trunk and lifted my feet onto my branch. I pulled Quin out of my skirt, holding him firmly, and watched Robert's approach through the leaves.

His limp was barely perceptible, but his gait was slow. Deep in thought, he made his way toward my hiding spot. A short way from my tree, he paused to pick up some sweet chestnuts that lay on the ground. Quin didn't seem to understand the need for quiet and wiggled so vigorously that I had to grasp at the limb above me and drop my feet to keep from falling. Robert stepped closer to the tree and looked through the leaves.

"Hello, again." His eyes traveled from my face down to my feet hanging just above his head. His smile changed from puzzled to diverted. "It's been a while since we climbed trees, Liza. It is more entertaining than I remember."

He reached up and grasped my ankle, revealed by the disarray of my skirt. I should have wrenched my leg from his hold. I should have kicked him. His actions were too familiar by far. What I did instead was freeze and stare into his raised face. He smiled languidly as his thumb made gentle circles above my boot. And I sucked in a surprised breath.

Dappled sunlight through the shaded copse and the quiet gurgle of the nearby stream lent an intimacy to the scene. My awareness narrowed to the fast beat of my heart, his intent gray eyes, and the brush of his fingers on my newly sensitive ankle.

"Come, Liza, let me help you down." If his eyes mesmerized, his voice beguiled, and I slipped inelegantly into his raised arms.

"Tell me about your dog," he whispered as his hand cupped my shoulder, rocking me gently, his other hand found the spot behind Quin's ear that made him quiver with joy. I couldn't blame his little traitorous heart.

I cleared my throat. "His name is Quin. He ran in front of a cart at Squire Davies'. I'm hopeful that in a few weeks when this cast comes off, his leg will be healed enough for him to run and hunt."

While I was talking, his hand slid down my back and pulled me closer. Sneaky, sneaky man.

I looked down at my ecstatic dog. "Perhaps you could not mention Quin to my father and aunt?" I looked up through my lashes to measure his response.

He smiled softly, "Secrets, my dear?"

He took Quin from my unresisting hands and placed him on the ground with a pat. Rising, he again claimed my shoulder. "I'm good at keeping secrets."

His hand glided down my back once more to rest on my hip. I braced my hands on his chest and pulled back, a little. It was feeble resistance against the pull of his warm gaze and my wandering thoughts.

His smile deepened, and he whispered my name as he clasped one of my hands, intertwining our fingers. He brought our joined hands to his mouth and nibbled until I was dizzy. Then he gently placed my wrist on his shoulder. My heart raced as his hand traced down my arm, caressed my neck, threaded through my hair at the back of my head, and tilted my face up to his.

I felt his breath at the side of my face. His lips quested slowly over my temple, my closed eyes. He whispered my name again against my cheek as his fingers sifted through my hair. My emotions flashed and rolled like the tide. I followed his lips like a flower the sun.

Robert laughed breathlessly, and finally covered my lips with his, pulling me close to his hard chest. My head spun as lavish sensation flooded my body.

His kiss was an exploration in brushes and sips. Teasing and luxuriant in turns. And I trembled and—

Pulled back in surprise as Quin barked and jumped against my leg.

Robert kissed me one more time and gently stepped back, one hand back on my shoulder to steady me.

I looked up into those familiar gray eyes, and memory returned with a bitterness I thought I'd outgrown. "Are you going to leave without word again?" I asked with shaky breath.

He took my face between his palms, "No Liza," he kissed me briefly, but deeply, "As you told me before you fainted into my arms, you are no longer a child." His heated look seared a path to my center. "I am here to stay."

I spent that night tossing and brooding and met the windy morning puffy eyed and irritable. I wavered between anger with myself and anger with Robert, my thinking whirling like a spinning top in my head. Why did I just stand there, melting and compliant as he kissed me into aching awareness when there was any possibility that he was involved in traitorous activity? I shouldn't, no couldn't, respond to a man I could not trust.

And there was always the possibility—No, I would not accuse him of trifling with me. Even if he didn't care for me, he had too much respect for my father, who had tutored him from the time he was eight until he left for Eton. He wouldn't dally with the daughter of a gentleman, one whom he admired. I had to trust his intentions were honorable, but, I argued, when he was in the middle of such ignoble pursuit, he shouldn't be making up to me.

I sat in front of the banked fire, lost in thought and

recollection. I felt heat rising up my neck into my cheeks when I thought of his touch, but I shook my head and reprimanded myself firmly.

Until I had extricated him from his present pursuits, I had no business accepting his kisses. It was weakness, and I had never been weak. My family's most common description of me is headstrong. It was lowering to realize that Robert could unravel me in a few stolen moments.

Susan came in with a tray of chocolate, took one look at my face and remained silent as I drank, silent still as she helped me dress. I sat blindly in front of the mirror as she brushed my heavy hair into a tidy knot, pulled a few locks out and curled them to frame my face. Then she stood silently behind me until I lifted troubled eyes and realized she had finished.

I turned away without looking at my reflected image. It had never bothered me before, but today I couldn't face myself. Today my uncertain looks just underscored my jumbled thoughts. I'm not tall, but not short. My eyes are sometimes blue, sometimes green. My hair is not red, not blond, not brown, but an indeterminate mix of all three. My small nose with its smattering of freckles is at odds with lips too full and wide. Physically and mentally I was muddle.

I thought of my one determinate feature—my firm chin. I lifted said chin and made a vow to be stronger, to resist Robert's pull until I could rescue him from his folly.

Chapter 5

*An excuse is worse and more terrible than a lie; for an
excuse is a lie guarded*

Alexander Pope, "Thoughts on
Various Subjects"

Since I had recovered from my illness, and as I had
been present during their planning, I was naturally enlist-
ed to run errands and take care of less important details
for the upcoming ball. This would rob me of time to col-
lect more details about Robert's illicit movements, or so I
thought.

One afternoon two days later, I did manage to slip
away. I took Quin and walked through the fields behind
Robert's estate. I came to the stable just in time to see
Robert's groom, Magnus, bring a striking blood gray out,
saddled and ready to ride.

Though he had always a love for the sea and had
planned from childhood to join the navy, Robert was a keen
horseman. Saevio was his favorite mount. His name, which
is Latin for ferocious, is apt. I slid behind a hawthorn bush
and watched Robert walk up, dressed in buckskins and
riding boots.

"Are you armed, sir?" Magnus was obviously in Robert's confidence.

"Yes," Robert's smile was fierce, "but don't worry yet, Magnus; this is just the opening salvo,"

"I could go with you sir."

"No," Robert gripped Magnus' shoulder, "I may need you later. Let me see what I can bring about at the Five Bells tonight. Then we will see."

"Very good, sir," Magnus yielded.

Robert mounted and rode away, the beat of the horse's hooves filled the air, and then faded quickly into the normal sounds of the stable yard.

I watched in frustration until I could no longer see him and until Magnus returned to the stable. On foot, I couldn't follow Robert to find out what he was doing at the Five Bells. I sighed deeply. My initial attempts at subterfuge were not very successful. I would have to get better. Right then, though, I needed to get back before Aunt Beatrice missed me.

Suddenly, I realized that Quin had wandered. I was looking through the undergrowth behind the stables when a deep voice startled me, "Miss Elizabeth Henshaw, what are you doing here?"

I screeched and turned, my heart beating hard and fast. I stared for a few moments at Perry Gerow, Robert's cousin and estate agent and tried to gather my thoughts.

"Oh, Mr. Gerow, you startled me."

"My apologies," he smiled, but his probing gaze made me wonder if all the gossip I'd heard was written all over my face. I could feel a blush rise up my neck into my cheeks.

His smile flashed, and his voice deepened, "can I be of some service to you? Would you like to come up to the house for tea?"

"Oh, no," I said quickly. Why had I never noticed his knowing smile and the roguish glimmer in his eyes? "I was just walking in the back woods, and my dog ran from me. I thought he might have come this way," I stepped away and looked around quickly. His reputation may have been questionable, but my aunt's friends didn't say anything about him accosting women of good reputation. Surely I was safe.

"Let me help you find him," he offered.

I shook my head, and then noticed his gun and game bag. "Very kind of you, but I see you're hunting."

"Nothing scares game off like a dog," he put down his game bag but retained his gun, "what is your dog's name? Perhaps if we call out to him, he would come."

I grimaced but could see no way out of his company, "Quin," I said baldly.

Mr. Gerow began to call and whistle, slapping his leg as we walked through the woods. I called as well, but then I realized I had an opportunity here. I didn't want to reveal my doubts about Robert, so I wouldn't ask about him, but I was convinced that Mr. Gerow would know more about 'the gentlemen' than I did. I quickened my pace to come up to him.

A little breathlessly I began, "Mr. Gerow, at the Manor yesterday," that seemed a little abrupt for an innocent conversation, so I backtracked, "you know we are getting ready for the grand ball in October?"

He nodded, so I continued, "We were interrupted by the noise of a mill yesterday. There were dozens of men fighting in the square. The magistrate was called, but before he arrived, they seemed to disappear. Had you heard about this?

He nodded briskly.

"I heard they were rival smuggling gangs. Do you know——" I paused in invitation.

"It is nothing a gently bred young lady need concern herself with," he said in the most condescending way.

I wanted to scowl as this was almost to the word what Aunt Beatrice had said, but I laughed lightly, "come now, I am simply curious. I think everyone, even young women, should be vigilant in these dangerous times. How can we know what to watch for if no one will explain what is happening, don't you agree?

"You have lived here your entire life. You know well enough about how these things work. You know the dangers of talking about them, about those men——you know what happens to people who ask too many questions. This would be especially harmful if you were to talk in the hearing of, say, someone who was involved in the trade——and you can't always assume the people you know aren't involved."

"I just——"

"Just because you are usually surrounded by the bevy of worthies who parade through your home doesn't mean that word of your curiosity might not get around," he stepped close to me. It took all of my energy and thought not to step back.

"Miss Henshaw, I tell you these things for your own safety," his voice lowered, and he inclined his head even closer, "I could not bear to see your hurt because of an inappropriate curiosity."

I forced myself to lift my chin and look straight into his eyes. He watched me silently for a few moments, nodded his head briefly, and turned from me, once again whistling and calling Quin's name. I let the breath I had been holding slide through my lips.

We found Quin not far from the chestnut tree where Robert and I had—met previously. Perry and I parted with the utmost politeness. I felt frustrated by my failure to garner more information, embarrassed by my clumsiness, and determined to avoid such direct questions of anyone in the future.

I also felt slightly uneasy and chastised myself for allowing myself to be so influenced by the committee women's talk. Perry Gerow had never done or said anything that was out of the ordinary. There was no reason for me to be uncomfortable in his presence. He was young and handsome, in a continental way, and had a certain charm. I knew his grandparents were part of the Huguenot emigration when Louis XIV sat on the throne in France. If he had some high spirits, it wasn't my place to judge.

By the next day, which was to be spent at The Manor, I had settled my nerves. Mr. Gerow had been very kind to help me find my dog. There had been nothing in his words or actions that should make me question his intent. The free traders are ruthless men, and of course, he would be careful, for himself as much as for me. I took his warning to heart. Oh, I did not plan to stop my quest, but I would be more careful about how and with whom I talked.

I tried to put my thoughts and plans aside for the morning as I followed my aunt and Lady Ramsgate on a tour through the manor. My job was to take notes as their ideas and plans became ever more elaborate and sumptuous. Though the manor is a splendid and stately home, I was distracted. Yes, the new gas lights His Grace of Dorset had installed throughout were amazing and the size and layout of the ballroom perfect, but what was that compared to my worry about Robert and my father and frustration at my failure to gather more information?

Soon the view out the windows of the quiet and sun-drenched grounds called to me. When Lady Ramsgate and my aunt started a quiet, but impassioned argument about the advantages of white wine claret and sweet madeira over negus and orgeat to be served by servants during the dancing, I was relieved to slip away to think in peace.

My thoughts brought no comfort. I walked through the brisk, bright day and frowned at the formal garden, its fountains surrounded by shrubs and autumn flowers planted in lines as straight as the King's German Legion's formations. Morosely, I passed the shelterbelt to the pond and river. I spent a few sulky minutes circling a lofty viewing tower before I sighed and climb to the top.

Finally overlooking the shore, I took a deep breath and found some perspective and with it my usual optimistic outlook. What did I expect? I had just begun, but I would learn quickly. I would prevail, I told myself as I watched the waves sparkle and break.

On my way back through the Manor grounds, I peeked into a stone grotto and came face to face with the head gardener. This worthy gentleman, thin and stooped, welcomed my intrusion. His bright blue eyes shone through a face wrinkled like an old apple. His tanned scalp was ringed with wispy white hair. He was also a natural, patient teacher and was in want of a student.

In the beauty and quiet of that arbor, I was a willing volunteer. For the first quarter hour, I was worried he would fall over as he wheezed out information about each flower and stem, but he surprised me with his stamina. After following him for an hour through the rose garden and into the hothouse, I had developed a deep respect for the depth and breadth of his knowledge, and I learned more about the various plants than I was sure I would ever need in my life. The stables had always drawn me more than the garden or hothouse.

And after more than an hour the sweet scent of so many flowers became cloying, and I began to tire. I was almost relieved when Aunt Beatrice found me even if it meant that I would again be following her and Lady Ramsgate through the Manor. But one look at the gardener distracted my aunt, and soon they were involved in discussion of arrangements and a possible bower to be added to a room adjoining the ballroom. I again slipped away.

I walked idly around the front of The Manor to sit by the old walnut tree. I liked to imagine that this tree was planted at the time that Queen Elizabeth granted the Manor to the Sackvilles. I knew it had been here in my great-grandfather's time. I sat in the shade against the trunk and had a clear view of the bustle on Church Street, High Street, and Sea Lane.

I was beginning to get drowsy when the sight of Robert turning his horse down the carriage lane of the Belle Inn caught my attention. Leaning against the corner of the building was a tall, stocky man wearing a tattered blue wool coat, his face shadowed by a tarred felt hat. He lifted his head as Robert passed and I saw his weather roughened face for a moment as he looked up and down the street before he turned and followed Robert's horse down the lane. It seemed my luck was improving.

I was up and striding toward the inn before I thought. As I approached, a better wisdom prevailed, and I corrected my direction, walking around the other side of the inn.

Though I felt some trepidation, I saw this as a rare opportunity to spy out what Robert was doing. I walked to the back of the inn and poked my head around the corner just in time to see the blue coat disappear through the back door.

I slipped along the back wall of the inn. My problem was that, the afternoon sun filled the western facing back yard of the Belle Inn. I would be clearly visible to anyone looking out the darkened inn into the yard.

I approached the first window tentatively, knelt down, and took the quickest glance through the window and again lowered myself to rest breathlessly against the sun-heated wall. It was a kitchen, busy with comings and goings of the serving girls and coffee boys. I listened carefully, but there was no outcry. I hadn't been seen.

I breathed in and out, steadying myself, before I moved to the next window.

I spent a little more time there bobbing up repeatedly until I had checked each man at the bar. The grimy panes gave me no good impression of the housekeeper's abilities. I looked again at each table in my view but couldn't see Robert.

I was feeling more confident, and I passed another window into the same room and looked into the next. This one gave me a view of a number of tables surrounded by rough-hewn chairs arranged haphazardly through the space. A few tables were occupied, but not with anyone I recognized. Just as I was about to turn away, I spotted Robert and the blue coated man in a shadowed corner. Their heads were close together, and they were engaged in an intense discussion.

No one seemed to be looking out, so I risked putting

my ear to the window, but I could hear nothing but a low rumble. I was bitterly disappointed. All I had to show for my daring was the information that Robert was involved somehow with a man who looked like he could make a living as a pugilist, not that I was supposed to know much about boxing, but my brother John was an enthusiast and had talked all the previous summer about a bout between Tom Cribb and George Maddox until I had been tempted to lift my own fists and punch my brother.

I stepped away dejectedly. Then I paused. If I could find someplace to secrete myself, I could wait until Robert and his associate came out. Then I could follow and listen.

I moved carefully toward the stable. Around the side I found a small cart. By its smell, I guessed it was for mucking the stalls, but I couldn't be overly nice. This was too important, so I held my hand over my nose and knelt down and waited.

After what seemed like an interminable time, Robert and Mr. Blue Coat came out. They were walking away from me, but the breeze was blowing my way, and I could still hear Robert say, "tonight then, I'll meet you at the Forge on Sea Road before I make my way to Hastings Beach."

My eyes widened as the man answered in an educated and well-modulated voice, "I'll see you then. Now remember, I'm on sentry tonight, and still proving myself to Wilkins, so I won't be able to help if you get into trouble."

Robert stopped and put his hand on the man's shoulder, "James, from here on out, it is best we have as little public contact as possible, anyway. Continue as you are; I'll make my way."

I sat quietly as I heard Robert's horse leave. I sat for a little longer to give Mr. Blue coat time to walk away. Still my heart raced. Finally, I had something.

Just then rough hands pulled me to my feet and spun me around so fast that my back bounced against the wall of the barn.

"What do ya think yer doing 'ere, missy." He stepped closer, looming over me and I froze. He was a giant of a man. Deep furrows etched between his brows and marked the way from his large red nose down to the cruel line of his mouth. I was frightened into frozen silence.

Then, memory of my experience with Perry Gerow days earlier came as saving inspiration. I grimaced at what felt like a growing bruise on my shoulder but looked up at him, breathing as evenly as I could, "I lost my dog. I thought he came this way," I squeaked. "Have you seen him?"

"I 'aven't seen no dog," he leaned in further and I backed up until I was pressed hard against the barn.

"I meant no harm," I pleaded.

I had noticed that when Aunt Beatrice includes too many details in her conversation, my father and other men tend to find reason to be somewhere else. I thought it worth a try.

"He is a puppy and curious, but good natured and friendly," I began to ramble inanely, "I know I should have tied him up, but I was working over at the Manor, and it seemed safe enough to let him run." I was getting into the spirit of my story now.

"It seemed cruel to make him stay in the hothouse while I worked with the gardener. He, the gardener I mean, not my dog," I said vacantly, "can tell you anything about all the plants and flowers in the region. It was very edifying. Of course, not for my dog. He doesn't care much for flowers and such. Except to dig them up, which of course, he shouldn't do. He is mostly interested . . ."

"Foolishness," his scowl deepened, "ain't no dog 'ere. Now you get out," the man growled and stepped back. I lost my balance for a few moments, but wasted no time taking his advice.

I looked back once before moving onto the street and saw him watching me with angry suspicion.

There was one unexpected benefit from my afternoon snooping. Back at the Manor, my aunt pulled me aside with a hiss and a nose wrinkled in disgust.

"Liza, you smell like . . . a sty," she whispered while looking around, "How is it that you always manage to—" she looked me up and down, "and your dress is—" there was a clatter and the sound of approaching steps, and horror filled her face, "Go home. Now. Go home and change right this instant.

During the half hour walk from Church Street, I formulated a plan.

Chapter 6

It is double pleasure to deceive the deceiver

Jean de La Fontaine, *Fables*

At home, I washed quickly and changed, just not as my aunt expected. What I did instead was I walked down the hall to John's empty room. Though he was only fifteen, he was tall, and in the years since he had left for school, he had filled out.

I took a pair of buckskin breeches, a shirt, jacket and three wrinkled stocks, two to bind myself, one for my neck. I decided to wear my own riding boots. Lastly, I took an old dark cloak and his favorite round hat as it had a nice wide brim.

Other than having to adjust the gusset ties on the waist of the trousers for a little more room in the hips, I found everything fit well enough. I took the last stock to the mirror and surprised myself with a nervous laugh. Beau Brummell would have despaired. The rumor was that the arbiter of men's fashion spent five hours dressing each day and gave the cravat his special attention. I didn't have five hours. I didn't have one, and it showed. No one would ever mistake me for a dandy. I shrugged and looped the stock around my neck.

I was frowning at my third attempt to tie the cravat and growing ever more anxious when the door opened. My heart sunk, and I turned to see Susan standing stock still in the doorway holding a basket of freshly washed linens, staring in horror.

"Oh, Miss."

"Susan, come in and close the door. I need your help."

She continued to stand there in stunned silence.

I went to her and pulled her into the room, closing the door behind her, "I am having the devil of a time tying this cravat. Do you know how?"

"Why would you need to tie a cravat?" She asked plaintively. "Miss, why are you dressed in Master John's clothes?"

"Why, so I'll look like a boy, of course," I smiled at her.

Her stony face told me she wouldn't be put off.

I walked to my bed and sat in discouragement. I looked at the floor and thought about Susan. She had started service in our home when she was thirteen. She was bright and a hard worker, and she moved up the ranks of servants quickly. She had been my personal maid for nearly five years. Though only three years older than I, she had been more than a maid in the difficult years after my mother passed away. And she came from around Brighton, so I knew none of her brothers or cousins were part of the smuggling in Bexhill.

I sighed. I was going to need help, trusted help—no one could know what my father and Robert were involved in. She might not be willing, but she wasn't one to sit around of an evening sharing information with the other servants, and I knew Susan wouldn't betray me.

I looked up into her worried eyes and made a decision.

"I overheard my father and Captain Amesley planning something—planning to smuggle something, or perhaps some things, or some information," I whispered as if I could make it seem less horrible if I said it quietly, "into . . . or maybe out of the country with the Wilkins gang. I think, perhaps—I am sure they are into something dangerous and—"

"Oh no miss, I'm sure you are mistaken."

I shook my head sadly. "I wish I were, but they were talking about working with the Wilkins gang, and my father said, 'if we don't hang, it will be a miracle."

Susan blinked three times in silence. Then she spoke, but less assuredly, "I still can't believe it, but even if it is so, what can you do?"

I stood and walked to the fire. With my back to her, I said, "I saw Captain Amesley go into the Belle Inn this afternoon with a roughly dressed man. I waited, out of the way, for them to come out and heard this man tell Captain Amesley where the smuggling run would be tonight. I'm going to be there before they come. I'll find someplace to hide and watch."

"No," Susan gasped, "Miss, you can't."

"I must," I turned, clasping my hands in supplication, "I must, Susan. I have to know."

Susan shook her head, "and once you know, what will you do?" Her shoulders were hunched and she lifted her hands, "are you going to report Captain Amesley to the preventatives?"

"No!" I lifted my chin, "I could never betray him. And my father—no, I could never," I paced, my mind in a tangle. I hadn't thought that far.

"I'm sure it's not as bad as you think," Susan soothed, "and there is nothing you can do—"

"I can't just sit at home and let them ruin everything," I thought about what my life would be if my father and Robert were caught—if they were hanged. I sat again on my bed and, curled over my folded arms, I shivered.

Staring blindly at the patterns in my rug, I bounced my foot up and down, "I will have to find a way to stop them," I whispered. I stood and said louder, firmer, "I will find a way."

"And just how do you think you will do that?" Her voice was full of exasperation and she shook her head again, but she stepped forward and pulled the stock straight and began to knot and twist, tying it in a loose knot. How well she knew me. "It won't fool anyone who looks closely."

"This will just help me get through Bexhill before dark—no one will notice one more boy riding through town."

"What do you think to do with your hair?" She gave a long-suffering sigh.

I pointed to John's hat.

"Sit you down, and I'll pin your hair."

She pulled, perhaps a touch more ruthlessly than necessary, plaiting it tightly, wrapping it around my head. It worked. When I put on the hat, it covered my hair and came down low on my forehead.

"What will I tell your father and aunt about where you are when supper comes?" Susan asked.

"Well, I thought I could be ill again?"

"And you want your aunt up here upset that your influenza has returned, ready to call the physician just to find you gone?" Her skepticism stabbed at my confidence.

"Maybe not." I frowned out the window, "well, what then?"

Susan straightened the bedclothes and took my dress and draped it over her arm, "It will have to be a bit of the headache. I brought you an early supper, and you went to bed."

I grimaced. Headaches were the staple of my aunt's many health concerns. I never, never had headaches. I refused. But I could see no other way. I nodded hesitantly.

"Don't stir yourself up about it," Susan understood my reluctance, "it's the best excuse as she will certainly believe you would take to your bed with a headache. It's what she does."

I put my arms around her and hugged her briefly. When I pulled back, she looked surprised and was blinking back tears.

"Oh, miss be so careful. Even a young boy could be hurt or killed if he were caught by the Wilkins gang.

"I know it's dangerous, but I must know, Susan. I must," I looked down at myself to check that I was dressed as well could be.

Susan shuddered, "I never will be able to hold up my head again, you look so bad."

"No one will ever know you had a hand in dressing me. I will ride through town and keep my head down, and no one will think twice about me. After that, I hope not to be seen at all."

"Miss Liza, your horse," Susan's anxious eyes met mine, "he will surely be recognized."

"I thought I would take old Blueboy. It's been years since he's been far from home. He will love riding out for something other than light exercise, and he can carry me there and back if I ride him gently."

Susan nodded, satisfied.

"But Susan, do you think you can get Frank out of the stables for a few minutes? Then I can get a saddle and blanket," I wheedled.

She rolled her eyes but moved toward the door. "I'll gather some bread and cheese from the kitchen and bring it to you after I send Frank on a fool's errand."

"Thank you," I whispered as she slipped out the door.

A little over an hour before dusk I finally walked Blueboy down the road to Bexhill. I had not gone far when I heard a familiar bark. I twisted in my saddle, hoping against hope that I was wrong, but Quin was closing the distance between us with his funny three-legged lope.

I raised my eyes to the heavens in question. No answer was forthcoming. If I took him home, chances were more than good that I wouldn't get away again, and even if I did, I might arrive after the smugglers. I needed to be in place before they got to the cove. I had no recourse but to climb off Blueboy, gather Quin in my arms, and walk further down the road until I came to a rock large enough to act as mounting block. I talked sternly to Quin as I continued on my way. He didn't seem properly cowed. And, paradoxically, his presence made me feel more confident—not so all alone.

I buttoned my dog in John's jacket and kept my head low as we approached Bexhill. It was early enough that there were still people out on the road, but I could mark my slow progress by the growing scent of salt and fish, the feel of the air blowing over the marshes, the hollow boom of the bittern and the song of reed buntings.

A little further and I came to that no man's land between Bexhill and Hastings, the fields of Glyne Gap. For a few moments my heart beat faster as I rode through the sea mists that linger there even when everything else is clear.

I neared Hastings Bay just as the sun poised on the brown and green hills at my left. I stopped short of the bay and tied my horse to a tree off the road. I rubbed him down as he nuzzled around on the ground for a few moments, shook his head, cocked his leg and dropped into a doze. Then I walked down to the beach with Quin capering at my feet. For a few minutes I lost myself watching the flecks of light in the ever moving blue-green sea and listening to the rumble of the waves. For me there has always been something hypnotic about the sight and sound of the sea.

But this particular stretch of sea is rich with a frightening history. Julius Caesar landed galleys on these beaches. William of Normandy beached his boats here and became William, the Conqueror. This sweep of coast around Bexhill is the most vulnerable spot on the coast of England. On a clear day, you might look to the east and see France, and we all feared that one day soon Napoleon would cross those waters and invade England.

In spite of the weight of history and the present danger, I spent a little time playing throw the stick with Quin while I scouted the terrain looking for a place to hide. I briefly considered the cliffs above the beach, but they were too far to hear anything over the rumble of the waves. Likewise, I decided against a fall of rocks and some tangled scrub. There was really only one choice, so as the sun set and sky took on that silvery between-time hue, I took Quin back and tied him near Blueboy.

I returned to the bay and the line of skiffs, fisherman's cobbles, and cutters tied up on the beach. I didn't want

to accidentally choose the smugglers' vessel, so I chose an
ancient, small skiff at the end of the dock. I doubted it was
even seaworthy, all peeling paint and listing to the side as
it was. So, I climbed in, wrapped myself with John's cloak,
pulled a length of canvas for cover, and settled in to wait. If
I carefully turned my head, I could see the boats on either
side and a bit of the bay.

It seemed a long wait, and by the time men began to
gather next to one of the larger cutters, not far from where
I lay, I was stiff and cold. I thought about my precarious
position and prayed and watched.

Suddenly, from the direction of the road, I heard the
eerie sound of pipes. A gloomy tune swelled and waned and
I shivered, but the men seemed untroubled. I doubted my
hearing and my sanity, and as the men continued to move
around the cutter with an efficiency that suggested years of
working together, I tried to ignore the music.

In very little time, it looked like they were ready to set
sail, and I thought all my efforts were wasted.

Then there was a flurry and commotion. I almost
gasped when I saw two men with pistols trained on Robert,
pushing him towards one of the sailors, I assumed he was
Wilkins.

My hands fisted and an unconscious whimper escaped.
"Breathe," I murmured under my breath to calm myself. I
worried they might hear my heart; it was pounding so hard.

"What do you want?" Though short and wiry with
comically bowed legs, this man's deep voice resonated with
power.

"I need to secure your services," was Robert's calm
reply, "I need passage to France tonight."

"That's not how we do it. We work through an agent,

so to speak,"

"So, I understand," Robert's voice held a haughtiness that I had never heard before, "however, my need is great, and before I feel comfortable entrusting my . . . future packages to you I would like to see a successful run. If all goes well, I'll make arrangements for you to pick up my next . . . cargo. I understand you've brought people into England before?" When Wilkins nodded, Robert continued, "It will take me a week or two to make arrangements, but I believe we could develop a mutually beneficial arrangement."

"You want to sail with us tonight?" There was a trace of laughter in Wilkin's voice.

"Yes."

"Well, aren't you a cool one, and playing a deep game? What makes you think we'll let you come?"

"Why," Robert drawled pompously, "money, of course."

"We have regular customers, you might say, but we're not against taking on a little side job." Wilkins smirked, looking Robert up and down.

"What is your price?"

"It depends on what you're wanting brought in, or taken out," Wilkin's strutted closer to Robert.

"Tonight, it is just me. Although, I'm not above adding some fine brandy to my cellar?" The request was clear.

Wilkins laughed and nodded, "very well." He measured Robert as he calculated and explained, "Tonight we're rowing out to that ship; see that light?" He pointed out to sea. I couldn't turn and look, but Robert nodded. "They have our load of cargo. We'll unload and they will sail back to France. We might let you join them." Then Wilkins named a price that made me gulp.

"That seems expensive for a short boat ride and a cask of brandy."

"You're not just paying for a ride," he sneered, "you're also paying so your business stays private."

A frightening silence stretched before Robert inclined his head.

"In advance," Wilkins demanded.

Robert shrugged and pulled out his wallet.

As he counted, Robert asked, "What guarantee that my future package won't be seized by the preventatives?"

"Don't worry about that, young blood. There is no sure guarantee, but we get information about where to expect trouble," he bowed in mockery, "if we was mis-informed, we have other solutions," he patted the pistol tucked into the waist of his breeches. A few others laughed. "We've fought our way through the marshes up into flat lands of Sussex before. We can again if needs be."

Another man walked up just then. In the light of the lantern I recognized Mr. James.

"All clear?" Wilkins asked.

"I thought I heard something earlier," Mr. James' accent was a rough traditional Sussex, much different than that afternoon.

"Well?" Wilkens asked

"It was only a stray dog. I walked around twice to make sure."

I jerked nervously, but calmed when he said, "All is quiet."

"Check again and keep your patrol tight. When we signal, if you see anything, ride to the cooper's house and tell him to stuff his grate and fire a furze beacon. If we're on spot, use the spout lantern, and the lander will have the

men and the transport carts and horses here within the
hour." Mr. James nodded and disappeared into the night.

Wilkins turned back to Robert, who ignored Mr. James
entirely, "the tide won't wait. Let's go." He gestured broadly
and bowed. "After you, sir."

Robert climbed into the waiting craft. The men followed with guns still trained on him, and they shoved off.

I dithered about whether to stay and see their return,
but I felt that I had pushed my luck enough for one night,
and I didn't want to meet the landsmen or crew. I waited
for what felt like a long time before climbing out of my
fishing boat, and almost fell on my face. My left leg was
numb. I slowly straightened and stomped my foot, rubbed
my leg through the painful tingling, watching the shadow
of the cutter move out to sea. I stretched and leaned down
to touch my toes. I was most grateful for the freedom and
comfort of men's trousers. I decided that I would keep one
set of my brother's clothes for possible future outings.

As I walked back toward the place where I'd tied Quin
and Blueboy, I mulled over what I'd seen and heard. I was
discouraged to find proof that Robert truly was involving
himself in the trade, but I also felt quite proud of the success of my venture. As I passed a shadow of gorse bush, I
was grabbed from behind and held in a bruising grip. I had
forgotten the guard.

A rough, low voice growled in my ear, "boy, what are
you doing here? What did you see? What do you think to
do?" The voice belonged to Mr. James. How could I have
forgotten?

With his hand over my mouth; the only sound that
could escape was a squeak. But I struggled and kicked. I
reached back as far as I could and hit and scratched. He

grunted, but there was no change in his grip. He was very strong. I was beginning to tire when one of my elbows sunk into his stomach. He gasped, and his hold loosened for a moment. I twisted and scrambled and broke free.

Before I could run three steps, he reached out and grasped my arm. Into my frantic mind came a memory of John telling me once what I should do if I received unwanted attentions from a man. I pivoted and drove my knee between his legs. He leaned over, with a high-pitched moaning. I stopped a moment and stared in surprise. It worked!

Then awareness of my situation returned. I turned and ran. I ran until I fell. I whimpered as I pulled myself up, moving slowly, my breath coming in jagged gulps. Then I ran again, fear giving me strength and speed.

Finally, I came to Quin and Blueboy. I pulled the reins over my horse's neck, untied Quin and grabbed him by the scruff and tried to pull us both up. Quin whined and wiggled, and I landed back on my feet and stumbled. Faintly, I heard swearing, and I looked around frantically hoping for a rock to stand on. There was nothing. Terrified, but determined, I lifted Quin over Blueboy's withers. He scrabbled and barked and Blueboy shied.

I muttered, "come on, come on, come on," as I jumped and pulled and inched up until my stomach was over the saddle. I panted as I wiggled my way to sitting. Behind me I heard halting footsteps, but I leaned over my horse's neck and kicked Blueboy into a run and left the guard behind me on the dark road.

Chapter 7

Nothing weighs on us so heavily as a secret.

Jean de La Fontaine, *Fables*

I felt heavy with too much information but little understanding when my father, Aunt Beatrice, and I climbed into the carriage to go to the military parade and review the next morning.

This thrilling event happens every autumn when the militia regiments, and in Bexhill our King's German Legion, return from their tented camps and summer training exercises. Everyone in the community comes, and the soldiers march, drill, and compete in feats of arms. The day always culminates in a mock battle on an open hillside just outside of town. My aunt was in high fiddle because the Legion commander, the Duke of Cambridge was to be there to review his troops with Lieutenant Decken, his adjutant.

Though the townspeople initially grumbled when German soldiers "invaded" Bexhill, the Legion's beautiful singing in St. Peter's church began to soften hearts. The increased custom at the inns and markets was also welcome. Perhaps a more crucial element of the change of heart was our constant awareness that our unbroken shoreline was the ideal place for Napoleon to land his fleet of flat-bottomed boats gathered at Boulogne. All in all, it didn't take long for us to embrace our own King's German Legion.

My family arrived early enough to pull our open carriage into an advantageous spot in the flat area before the green. Not far from us was a dais with seating for the Duke, officers, and other dignitaries. Across the way chairs had been set up for those who walked or rode. Some spread blankets on the hill west of the field and behind them local businesses manned their colorful booths offering lemonade, ale, bread and cheese, currant cakes and other delicacies. In spite of my exhaustion and worry, my spirits unaccountably lifted as the crystalline morning air filled with color, movement, and laughter.

We had no sooner stopped moving than Aunt Beatrice leaned forward, "Arthur, I see Lady Ramsgate. I really must speak with her."

Frank, our groom scurried to hand her down before my father could move. She turned to me, "Elizabeth, will you come with me? I see Lady Helen is here, as well."

"Thank you, Aunt," I certainly could see poor Helen, standing in Lady Ramsgate's shadow, but didn't want to follow her example, "I think I will stay and keep father company. Perhaps I'll join you later," I tucked my hand through my father's arm and smiled up at him.

What else could she say but a terse, "Very well." And after a minatory glance, she swept away.

Father and I watched as she paused often to exchange pleasantries on her determined way to the raised dais, surrounded by the red uniforms of Legion officers. After a minute, father turned to me and patted my hand, "Now Liza, I noticed a new hound in the stables this morning," I jumped guiltily before I noted the humor in his eyes. "Why don't you tell me how that happened."

I laughed and squeezed his arm, "when I visited the squire, oh before I was ill," my father's brows raised, "he had this poor, sweet pup that had tangled with a carriage and . . . well you saw his leg. I couldn't bear to leave him."

"I see," father fought a smile, "inevitable, I suppose, but how do you plan to keep—"

"Henshaw," a hearty hail startled us both. I turned and my heart bumped against my ribcage. At first glance it might seem I was looking at two pair of identical silver-gray eyes. A moment's study revealed a vast difference. Mr. Amesley, Robert's father's eyes were filled with cheerful delight. They overflowed with light and warmth. I felt the difference in my bones as I met Robert's probing scrutiny. It moved from the top of my head to my toes, I don't see how he could have missed any detail in-between. Since I had learned something of his activities, his stillness, his strength, his confidence was even more marked. His lean form and supple grace reminded me of the watchful readiness of a predator. I shivered.

"Amesley, Captain," my father returned Mr. Amesley's greetings, shaking both men's hands, "let Frank take your horses and you can join us in the carriage. Beatrice won't be back before the grooms unpack our luncheon.

And so, perforce, I found myself, after a little rocking and shifting, facing Robert who lounged with deceptive ease and smiled at me with lazy intent. I lifted my chin and boldly returned his study. I looked for some sign of his all-night foray into France and back. It didn't show in his dress or demeanor, both of which were impeccable. If there was any sign at all of his disreputable journey, it only served to make him more attractive, honing his cheekbones and deepening the shadows and angles of his face. He returned my scrutiny, and I felt the severe injustice, knowing the effects of sleeplessness were written more clearly on my face. I lowered my eyes and kept them stubbornly focused on my clasped hands until the trumpets announced the advancing parade of the Legion.

The green uniformed men formed into lines and saluted their leaders on the dais neatly and spread over the field. I felt a stirring of pride and confidence. How could we not triumph with both right and strength on our side?

I was so intent on the assembled troops, I didn't see Lord Ramsgate approach, "Amesley, Henshaw, Captain Amesley, if I may have a moment of your time." The men all inclined their heads.

"Forgive me Miss Henshaw," he bowed before moving a little distance away. My three companions stepped down from the carriage and followed, far enough to guarantee their privacy, leaving me to scowl at the display that had so recently thrilled me.

I shifted closer, hoping to catch some semblance of their conversation. I heard only occasional words that blew my way on the breeze, more as Lord Ramsgate grew upset and louder with his emotion when the men asked inaudible questions.

"Missing since last night," he said.

My father's voice murmured calmly, but too low to distinguish words.

Out of the corner of my eye, I saw Lord Ramsgate wave his arms, "blockade," I heard, and "combined forces," and, "but he was determined."

Again, my father spoke quietly.

Then I heard, "they moved East," and a few moments later, "search instigated."

I was so intent on keeping the appearance of disinterest but bending all my attention on their conversation that I didn't see what must have been Robert's infernal interference, but it was his arm that was pulling Lord Ramsgate even further to the side.

I watched as they stopped to speak with Colonel Abernathy, who commanded the militia stationed in Bexhill. He joined them as they moved to speak with one of the Legion's officers. I took special note of the officer's face so I could find a way to be presented to him next time I saw him, perhaps that night at the Squire's rout. The officers of the Legion and the militia were always invited to local socials.

The soldiers began marching in organized drills. I sighed and asked Susan, who had stepped up when my father left, to spread a blanket in front of the carriage. I decided, if I couldn't follow the news, I might as well be comfortable. I climbed down, opened my parasol, and divided my time watching the contests and noting other hushed conversations taking place around the edges of the field.

A few men gathered in animated talk. Then they dispersed and reorganized into different clusters of men huddled along the perimeter of the field. Each group in their time separated again and formed new groups. I felt like I was watching a brushfire as word spread and emotions ran high, but the fire only took hold among the men. I followed the pattern of the news until my view was obstructed by a cloud of sarsnet skirts.

I looked up into familiar faces. My best friend Maris and her brother, Frederick Davies, children of the squire, were returned from a trip to visit a relative in London. Frederick was resplendent in surprisingly colorful and doubtless fashionable clothes. They looked ridiculous to my eyes, but that may have been my preference for Robert's more restrained style of dress.

I saw Lady Helen had escaped her mother but continued to watch silently from the back of the group of my friends. Mr. Philip Martin was there, but sporting mad as he is, his attention was on the field where the soldiers were now fighting with sabers. And leading the group was Miss Judith Bellerton with her faithful shadow, Miss Alice Crossley.

I had known this group most of my life. We were a tight little community, hosting the same families for dinners and musical evenings and sharing the same partners at routs and dances. Through the years, we discussed the same topics at subscription balls at the assembly rooms. And the hostesses of the nobility and other landed gentry competed to provide the best and most creative entertainments.

I stood and greeted my friends. Today, however, there were two new faces.

"Oh Miss Liza," Miss Judith Bellerton tittered, "let me present Miss Amelia Hatton, and her brother," she smiled up at him, "Mr. Hugh Hatton." Her hand rested briefly, but somewhat possessively, on Mr. Hatton's arm, "this is our dear friend, Miss Elizabeth Henshaw." Judith looked back at me with lifted brows, "The Hattons have recently moved into their new estate, Edgecombe." Miss Alice Crossley nodded and giggled.

Behind her Maris rolled her eyes.

I said all that was polite, and so did they. Newcomers are always interesting, providing, as they must, some variety in experience and conversation. Of course, I had already been regaled with all their particulars of their family, history, and fortune so I wasn't surprised. That infernal tea.

We all paused a moment to watch a particularly intricate form as the soldiers split and reformed and began to fight each other. Suddenly, I realized I had an opportunity. I moved closer to Miss Judith, linking my arm with hers. "There is quite a stir today—all these hushed conversations, have you noticed?"

She lifted her chin, laughed, and patted my hand.

Ever predictable, Miss Judith. I felt an unreasoning twinge of guilt, but I swallowed it and smiled at her, "Oh Miss Judith, do tell; what are people saying?" I leaned forward and lowered my voice, "you certainly have heard."

"Of course," she preened, "it's nothing of so serious note. I don't know why all the secrecy. It's only that two of the riding officers have not checked in. Lord Ramsgate is concerned, isn't he Lady Helen?"

Helen folded her arms tightly in front of her but didn't answer.

Mr. Hatton chuckled, "well, it's more of a puzzle than you've perceived. Apparently, His Majesty's customs service was alerted to a big smuggling run in Norman's Bay last night."

I jerked and stared at Mr. Hugh in consternation, since I knew that the run had occurred far to the east in Hastings. I quickly lowered my eyes so no one would guess at my knowledge about the smuggler's run. But, how could they have been so mistaken?

Mr. Hugh thankfully didn't notice my puzzlement and continued to tell his story, "Lord Ramsgate worked with the other branches of the custom service to combine the preventative force in Pevensey, Bexhill, and Hastings. They posted dragoons and set their riding officers for ambush. They even contacted the Admiralty, who sent out a cutter to apprehend the blackguards—I assume all was hushed and ready for the dark of the moon. It would have been quite the sight. I wish I had seen it," his amusement made me uncomfortable, and I noticed Helen's hands clenched.

"The smugglers must have got wind of the trap because they never materialized," he shrugged, "but the news today is that apparently there was one rider who distrusted the information. He cautioned Lord Ramsgate against pooling all their resources in one place.

"Finally, perhaps just to shut him up, this rider was given the commission to take another fellow and ride east. As Miss Bellerton says, they haven't returned or sent word. There is a search out for them all along the coast from Cooden, through Bexhill, and Glyne Gap, all the way to Hastings."

That was the way I had ridden, only in reverse, as I was coming home the night before. "When did they ride east, do you know, Mr. Hatton?"

"Oh, it must have been past midnight into the early hours, I assume," he squinted up at the sky, "I declare, who knew there would be so much excitement in the country?"

I shivered though the day was almost uncomfortably warm.

My friends continued to speculate as to the whereabouts of the missing riding officers, but I had a difficult time attending. I was remembering something Wilkins, leader of the smuggling gang, had said the night before. He had been arrogantly confident that they wouldn't be interrupted by preventatives.

Who was giving false information to the local customs

service? Or perhaps more disturbing was the question of whether the local riding officers were truly working to prevent the smuggler's run? Could it be that someone had embraced an alternative way to secure an easier life or to supplement their meagre pay?

It was a sad reality that, since riding officers lived in the hearts of the communities they were supposed to police, they could be persecuted if they were too diligent in their efforts to prevent smuggling. But the two who rode east, where I knew the smugglers had been active last night, what had they been doing? And where were they now?

The announcement of the mock battle interrupted our discourse, but running through my mind, as the air filled with clash of blades and muskets, was the overwhelming thought that I should have met those excisemen on my flight home. I was relieved of course. After all, how would I have explained my presence on the road so late? But my heart beat heavy with a foreboding dread.

"Oh, I say," Philip Martin said, "let's move closer. They have a sharpshooter company equipped with Baker rifles. I have heard about their unmatched accuracy. We don't want to miss this."

Though invited, I declined. I would wait for my father and aunt. We spent a few moments saying our good-byes and reminding each other of that night's rout at the squire's.

Mr. Hatton seemed suddenly to become aware of Helen's silent distress. He offered his arm and spoke more quietly as my friends prepared to move on, "Lady Helen, don't let it worry you. Doubtless those men just stopped for a little liquid warmth and were tempted to imbibe too long. I'm sure they will show up with pounding heads and have their pay docked and spend some well-deserved time in goal," he patted her hand as the group prepared to move on, "your father will see to it, I'm sure."

I would like to have believed him, but I worried over what I'd heard until finally my family returned.

Though my enjoyment had been marred by the story of these two unknown men, I was distracted by the sharpshooters. Philip was right. They were impressive. The noise and power and skill of the shooting gave me a twinge of envy.

After my night's adventures and the revelations of this day, the sound of the guns also gave me an idea. Though my aunt would have a fit of the vapors if she knew that I could shoot, I had fond memories of a series of summer days five years ago when I had snuck out and followed my brother and Mr. Conley, our game warden, while they hunted. Upon discovery, John had complained, and Mr. Conley had scolded, but they had, very likely on a lark, taught me to shoot.

I looked sideways at my father, thinking of his hunting guns and his prize dueling pistols, handed down from his father. I would find a way to borrow one, I decided as we ate our picnic lunch, and slip away to practice, just in case.

Though the story of the missing riders was supposed to be a great secret, by the end of the culminating mock battle, everyone knew and was talking about it—and about smugglers—their ruthless practices and the failure of the government to stop them. Everyone seemed to assume the worst, that the smugglers had waylaid the two riding officers on their journey and had removed, permanently, any chance of being found out.

The older men and women were comparing the

Wilkins gang to the notorious Hawkhurst Gang, who terrorized the whole of Kent and Sussex during the last century. That gang used the Mermaid Inn in Rye as one of their bases. They terrorized, tortured and murdered anyone who dared to interfere. I wondered where the local gang, the Wilkins gang had their base—could it be the Five Bells.

The more people talked the more nervous I became about Robert's, and by association, my father's involvement with the Wilkins gang. I imagined my fear and horror if I woke one morning to find my father and Robert had disappeared. I had a frightening vision of searching in vain for their bodies.

As I looked at my father's earnest bespectacled face, I began to feel angry. How wholly un-suited he was to mix with that heartless band. My determination to save them grew. I had to find a way to extricate them before they shared these two young men's probable fate. There was no sure way to measure what the smugglers would view as a threat to their operations. Without meaning to, Robert could bring down their wrath and retribution upon himself and my father.

Surely today's events should have made them reconsider their actions, although I saw no signs of regret or doubt in either man. I might have to confront Robert and tell him what I'd seen, but I had no confidence my entreaty would weigh with him if two missing riding officers did not.

I needed to know more about how the smugglers worked so I could fight their influence over my family. If I couldn't get information from my father or Robert, I would have to find another way. It might be a little dangerous, but I would take great care.

Chapter 8

Music was invented to deceive and delude mankind.

Ephorus of Cyme,
Universal History

I came home feeling fractious and dispirited. I blamed my late-night adventure and the morning sun for my irritation. I assured myself it was only that. My aunt, fearing another headache, encouraged me to take a nap, and I climbed the stairs, intending to comply. But the second I opened my door and looked at my bed, I knew I would not be able to stop the whirling in my mind. I retreated to the music room instead. After all, I would doubtless be expected to play that night. And music is as effective as sleep when you are troubled in spirit.

Of all the 'ladylike' accomplishments my aunt had tried to instill in me, music was the only one that took. I understood written and spoken French, but when I opened my mouth, it sounded stilted to my ears. My watercolors, though proficient enough to please my aunt and my governess, disappointed me. I never felt that I captured the essence and beauty of my subject, be it fruit, flower, or landscape. And Aunt Beatrice had long ago stopped trying to get me to ply a needle. But music—oh music was a different thing, maybe because it wasn't a weak imitation of something else. I could feel in my mind and heart and let it all pour into the notes. Music was a perfect joining of someone else's creation and the feelings of my soul.

That afternoon I chose Beethoven. I pounded out Sonata No 23 in F Minor Appassionata to give vent to my frustration. I moved pensively into Moonlight Sonata. Finally, Sonata No. 4 in E flat major helped give me courage to meet the challenges of the evening before me.

After the music worked its magic, I even had an hour left to sneak out and free Quin from the environs of the stable and take him for a romp through the apple orchard and down to the stream. The remainder of my bad mood seemed to float away with the rippling water, and I laughed as I felt my feet sink in the springy cushion of moss and as I watched my dog explore the reeds that swayed in the light breeze.

While I was gone, Susan did everything that was needful for the evening. After being with me through two London seasons, she was an old hat at getting me ready for any and all entertainments, so when I came upstairs again, she had my dress laid out and was waiting to arrange my hair.

Every girl dreams of her season in London. I had fashioned my own dreams as I joined the other young ladies of marriageable age and was paraded around in a whirlwind of social engagements, all in hopes that I would attract a suitable husband. Though my father was not titled, he was a gentleman, and my portion was not small. My aunt assured me that if I could comport myself respectably, I might meet with success.

And it was exciting. My days and nights were filled with dinner parties, balls, the theater and opera, musicals,

Venetian breakfasts, rides in the park, visits to museums, and, a favorite of mine, the zoo.

In spite of this, I often felt out of place in the crowds, smells, and noise. What I mostly remember is feeling a deep and pervading homesickness, interrupted with moments of blinding brilliance and beauty.

I did meet some fascinating people. And I had a gratifying number of young—and some older men come to call, none of which my father approved as suitors. I say my father, but all three of us knew that it was my aunt's approval a man would need to gain, and her tastes were too nice. At the time I was secretly relieved as I didn't really want to marry any of them, nice though they seemed. All in all, my "come out" was a moderate success, but if truth be told, I prefer fall and winter at home in Bexhill. I was as pleased to attend the Squire's rout as I ever was to attend the most exclusive crush in London.

Not everyone in our neighborhood has a ballroom in their home, although we do have an assembly room in Bexhill, where subscription balls are held every Wednesday and Saturday. But anyone can host a rout party. Mrs. Davies had provided a place for conversation and music in the drawing room. There were cards set up in the parlor for the men who preferred that pastime, and in the dining room was laid a supper consisting of quail, sliced beef and ham, vegetables, sweetmeats, seed cakes, custard and pudding. A long sideboard overflowed with lemonade, a rum punch—the squire's special recipe, and other liquors.

Living among each other for long and, oh long, one would think surprises would be few. It wasn't so. Perhaps the longer, and more deeply, one knew a person, the more they held power to astonish. The small, daily choices and actions brought the greatest alterations. And as we constantly saw each other, we more readily noticed every variation.

The recent addition of Mr. Hatton and his children, Hugh and Amelia sent fascinating ripples through our company, and we were pleased with the Legion officers that swelled our usual numbers. In fact, to my satisfaction, I found it ridiculously easy and natural, as the evening progressed, to meet the young officer I had spied that morning talking with my father, Robert, Mr. Amesley and Lord Ramsgate.

Maris hailed me shortly after we walked in. I joined her and the other girls close to my age who were self-consciously ogling a group of officers who were visiting with the squire and Lord Ramsgate nearby. The girls greeted me familiarly but continued their discussion.

"There is something about a man in a uniform," Judith Bellerton's high-pitched giggle grated. And of course, two seconds later Alice Crossley joined in with her shrill titter.

"I honor them for their courage and strength," Lady Helen inclined her head, but the red flags that stained her cheeks exposed her outrage.

Judith shrugged and turned away from her, "well, and so do I. I found this morning's display quite stirring."

We all murmured assent.

"Why, and just last week I saw Franny Collins, oh I mean Mrs. Webber in town," she smirked, "it certainly looks like Corporal Webber is keeping her . . . happy,"

"Miss Bellerton!" Maris chided.

I blushed at Judith's lifted eyebrows and noticed that the discomfort of the other ladies matched my own. There were, not surprisingly, quite a number of marriages between local girls and the legion soldiers. Maybe Miss Judith thought to join their ranks, but I thought it poor taste to talk about them in such a manner.

"Miss Judith," Maris interrupted. I couldn't help but admired her poise and determination, "will you be performing tonight?"

"Of course," She just shook her head and lifted her chin, but continued to look, and not subtly, at the officers.

Finally, the squire acknowledged the attention. It had to be hard to ignore. He led three of the officers over to us, "Ladies, allow me to make these brave gentlemen known to you. Captain Richter." Easily recognizable from this morning, tall and blond, with direct blue eyes and a winning smile, Captain Richter bowed.

"Lieutenants Walter and Lang," once again a flurry of bows and curtsies.

"Gentlemen, may I present Lady Helen Ramsgate, Miss Elizabeth Henshaw, Miss Alice Crossley, and her sister Miss Rose, Miss Maris Davies, daughter of our host tonight, and Miss Judith Bellerton."

The squire only stayed a few moments to ensure conversation moved apace before he excused himself.

There was much to talk about, and with these officers so courteous and willing to be pleased, we enjoyed ourselves and were soon joined by many of the young men of the neighborhood, and we made a merry party indeed.

"Captain Richter," I said when the ebb and flow of our group brought me near him, "are you pleased to be returned from your summer exercises?"

"Yes," he turned to me willingly, "you won't be surprised to know that the barracks are much more comfortable than tents," his slight accent was attractive, "though I admit I prefer to be busy and doing something worthwhile. It is difficult to keep discipline when my men are idle, which now that the review is passed is," he waved his hand in lieu of finishing his sentence, and his smile caused wrinkles at the corner of his eyes. "So, we are doubly grateful for the gracious invitation to such an evening such as this."

"No more sunken ships to retrieve?" I teased. The soldiers' aid in the attempts to excavate the remaining goods from the wreck of the Amsterdam at Bulverhythe were well known through the district.

He chuckled, "No, and that, as you know, wasn't very successful. However, the local preventatives have asked for our help to keep sentry along the coast and also to aid in their search for their missing numbers."

"That is unusual, isn't it?"

"They have been known to seek help from the local militia in the past. The Legion is here, well trained, and willing. After last night, I believe they will accept any help we can give."

"I have heard recently some talk that the effectiveness of Customs Service and is being called into question?" I wondered if the local preventatives were experiencing some pressure from London.

"I too, have heard this talk," Captain Richter's brow furrowed, "but in their defense, their numbers are insufficient for such a long coast with countless spots to land," he looked around before continuing, "the war effort has taken so many of the men who might otherwise serve. And since the pay for a riding officer is not generous, and they have to provide their own horse as well, it might be difficult to find enough men to fill their need."

A startled exclamation caused us both to turn back to

the general conversation, and I saw that Mr. Hugh Hatton, along with Colonel Abernathy, commander of the local militia, had joined the group and had a captive audience for the story he was telling.

". . . satisfying evening, good company, tolerable brandy," he smirked, "but as I was riding along Glyne Ascent, I saw an eerie green light and heard a high keening wail. My horse reared and I had a d—difficult time bringing him about."

"Probably the brandy," Philip said under his breath and I stifled a laugh, but Mr. Hatton heard and took exception.

"I wasn't bosky, perhaps a trifle disguised," he admitted, "but I truly hadn't imbibed too deeply," he looked around his audience waiting for their nods, "And in the green light, I saw what looked like a woman, her dark dress wafting in an unfelt breeze, and I heard the saddest haunting pipes. She reached out her arms, and a cold breeze moved through me and stole my breath. I don't mind telling you I slapped my horse into a gallop and didn't stop until I turned into the lane before Edgecombe."

"You saw the cursed gypsy girl? Oh, that's smashing," Frederick said, "did you hear the wheels of the caravan? Everyone says they hear the squeaking of the gypsy caravan," Frederick's gauche eagerness was in stark contrast to Mr. Hatton's sophisticated cynicism.

"Gypsies?" he asked, looking down his nose.

"Oh yes, the story is well known in these parts," and Frederick cleared his throat and took a deep breath.

"Oh Frederick, don't," Maris swatted his arm,

But Frederick ignored his sister as usual, and his voice lowered dramatically, "One late summer long ago, gypsies

came and camped on the fallow fields behind Bettle Abbey.
They were allowed to remain out of kindness by the old
Earl, though everyone said he should have sent them pack-
ing. And maybe they were right, for one moonless night, his
young son, just home from Cambridge walked up the hill
and saw a beautiful, dark haired, dark eyed girl, dancing
around a fire. Some say he was bewitched; he couldn't leave
her until," Frederick looked around at his mixed audience,
"well, he pursued her . . . assiduously, and they met often
through the autumn and winter."

Maris sighed heavily.

Frederick rolled his eyes and continued, "But, the earl
found out and whisked his son away to London, where he
eventually married a young woman of impeccable breeding—and generous dower."

"I can't help but remark on the weaknesses of this story," Maris said, "where were her family? Were the wagons
of the caravan empty?"

Frederick continued to ignore Maris, "the caravan left
that spring, but the girl, spurned and furious, stayed. She
cursed her young man and his line to the fourth generation
and railed against all men. And then on another moonless
night, she walked down to the shore, moaning and crying,
and disappeared into the cold high tide. On stormy nights
and on nights of the new moon, she haunts the dark places
of the coast from Rye to Pevensey."

"Fine story for all-hallows eve," Mr. Philip murmured.

I didn't, I couldn't of course, share my chilling experience of hearing pipes the night before, but something in
Mr. Hugh's smirking face led me to say, "I wonder if everyone didn't turn tail and run at the first odd light or sound
of pipes, if we might learn enough to prevent young officers

from being lost—or worse."

Frederick's mouth dropped open, and I had the uncomfortable awareness of an increased focus from Mr. Hugh. I realized suddenly that he might have felt I was suggesting he lacked courage, and I was quick to appease, "Although, I dare say. . ."

"Aha," he interrupted me, "we have an Amazon in our midst, or maybe like Atalanta, she will race after the enemy, this ghostly gypsy, and wrestle her to the ground."

His mockery stung, and he continued, "Perhaps the Admiralty and H.M. Customs Service should look to their womenfolk for strategy." His grin invited all to join in his mirth, "you ladies could take up your feminine weapons and start a new committee, "The Brave Ladies' Society for the Eradication of Highwaymen, Smugglers and Dishonest Persons, and the Capture of Ghosts, Specters, and Other Night Phantoms."

Everyone laughed, some uncomfortably, as I felt my cheeks burn. I guess you could say it was all in fun, and usually I am not too proud to laugh at myself, but Mr. Hugh's laughter had an edge that I was not accustomed to. In all honesty, I did not like him.

While my friends continued to talk, I looked around for somewhere else to be, some other group I could join. I noticed Perry Gerow bringing a glass of lemonade to Miss Amelia Hatton, who sat with her chaperone near the window. He leaned close to talk with her, and she flushed a little and looked up at him through her lashes. I got the impression that I would not be welcome there.

Robert was talking with my father and Lord and Lady Ramsgate—not there. I had been assiduously avoiding Robert all night. My eyes roamed to the right and then returned, puzzled. Lord Ramsgate looked down his nose and puffed out his chest, but his voice was unexpectedly muted. Lady Ramsgate's eyes darted from her husband to the others in their group and back.

Robert's hands were gripped tightly behind his back, and his shoulders were uncharacteristically stiff. My father was the only one of their group who seemed at ease, with head inclined and a look of polite interest on his face.

I looked around quickly and then made my way towards the pianoforte just beyond their group. I riffled blindly through some sheet music that was sitting there as cocked I my ears to listen.

"—Not my fault. It would not do to ignore intelligence that I receive."

"It might not hurt now to look at the source of your information," I wondered if Lord Ramsgate could hear the subtle sardonic twist in Robert's voice.

The dirty look he threw Robert's way answered my question. "I have the utmost confidence in my source. He is above reproach."

I could almost hear Robert's raised brows.

"And we needed a show of force this time. Last month we received information of a run. We caught the black-guards but were greatly outnumbered. When we came upon them, two rows of batsmen with stout oak clubs, flails, and handguns stood back to back a couple of yards apart, making a corridor that stretched from the beach all the way inland to protect their tubmen.

Each tubman carried two kegs, one on his chest, one on his back. Those things weigh about forty-five pounds each, but when we came upon them, they ran. They just ran. Their lander had mustered more than two hundred ponies, horses and wagons. Their hooves and wagon wheels were muffled with rags, and when we tried to capture them, the beasts were so slippery that we couldn't hold them. They had been soaped or oiled."

Fascinated, I turned slightly to bring Lord Ramsgate into view and saw that Robert was looking at me with narrowed eyes.

I was saved when Squire Davies called for everyone's attention and invited them to take their seats for the music.

I took Captain Richter's proffered arm but was frustrated when he seated me just two rows behind Robert, who I couldn't help but notice, had chosen to sit next to and was conversing warmly with Miss Amelia Hatton. I wiped the scowl off my face as Judith rose to play a creditable Scarlatti Sonata.

Following Judith, Mr. Jones, our curate, was pressed and, with a blush played the violin, in a surprisingly spritely manner.

Others followed, but for me by far the most interesting performance was by Phoebe Lancaster. Mrs. Lancaster, against all evidence to the contrary, remained convinced that her daughter was an incomparable sight when she played the harp. She must perform at every musical evening. I tried not to listen but couldn't look away as her head bobbed and her lips silently counted. Occasionally her face would affect a surprised squint as her fingers froze for three or four seconds when she lost her place in the music. Then she would smile hugely and begin to play and nod in time again.

It seemed cruel to have Miss Amelia Hatton perform directly after. Even the least skill would show to advantage, but Miss Amelia was supremely talented on the pianoforte and played a very difficult, intricate Mozart Sonata No. 11 in A Major. The applause was gratifying for her, I'm sure

She demurred when asked to play more until Robert came forward and offered to turn her pages. She sang as she played her second number, and of course her voice was a lovely, clear soprano.

I watched and tried to convince myself that his dark hair and tanned skin didn't provide a striking foil to her silver blond, delicate beauty. The applause was enthusiastic. I sunk down a little in my chair as her brother joined her in a third number in a pleasing baritone.

I was next, and though I had planned to play a Haydn Sonata, after the display of virtuosity and such obvious favor, all my sensitivities rebelled. I sat at the pianoforte, lifted my chin and looked Robert right in the eye. I smiled as I played, but not even I was bold enough to sing along with a simple medley of familiar, and maybe not quite respectable, sailor's chanties, most notably one whose lyrics began with *What shall we do with a drunken sailor?* Further verses suggested some salty suggestion, and it had a rousing chorus of repeated, *'Way-hay, up she rises; Early in the morning.'*

At the end of my piece, Mrs. Davies quickly signaled that it was time to move into supper, and my aunt sent a look that promised a scolding once I got home. Robert stood in his unhurried way, bowed to Miss Amelia, and moved inexorably toward me.

"Did you enjoy the music tonight?" I asked.

Much to my discomfort, he simply chuckled as he took my hand, placed it on his arm and walked with me into supper.

Chapter 9

Suspicion always haunts the guilty mind; the thief doth fear each bush an officer.

Shakespeare, *Henry VI*

I had never realized that the newspaper contained information pertinent to me until soon after Robert left for the war. That's when I began to search apprehensively for any mention of the HMS Panther and for his name among the fallen. Even after he returned, though it was not as emotionally harrowing, I still took up the paper as soon as my father finished reading.

"I think we should call on Lady Ramsgate and Lady Helen this afternoon, Elizabeth," Aunt Beatrice interrupted my reading on the first day of the week after the rout party.

"Ahh," I choked as I lowered the paper and thought quickly, "Maris and I talked about gathering shells for her latest picture. This was not precisely a lie. Maris and I have often talked about collecting shells. And between us it is understood that if one claims to be shell collecting, the other offers her support.

"Well," my aunt made a moue of distaste, "take a groom."

"Mmm," I quickly shoveled some ham into my mouth and lifted the newspaper again.

What I did instead was wait until she was ensconced in the morning room engaged in her correspondence before I once again snuck into John's room. I had rethought borrowing my father's gun when it occurred to me that John would never know I had his gun if I returned it before he came down for holiday. I took his Manton pocket pistol, though I spent quite a few minutes admiring his dueling pistols. They are not beautiful in an ornamental way, but they are so reliable and accurate, even sleek, that I was tempted. But they were too long for me to conceal and heavy as well. Even with the pistol, John might be upset if he knew, but I was determined not to be caught again with only my knee to defend myself as I spied on Robert.

It wasn't unheard of for young women in our time to learn to shoot, but my aunt didn't feel it was proper. We all made sure she didn't know when Mr. Conley, our game keeper started to allow me to tag along when he taught John to hunt. I think Mr. Conley only brought me along to provide motivation for John. What young man wants to be a poorer shot than his sister? His plan backfired, but by the time Mr. Conley and John realized that I took to shooting like a duck to water, it was too late. So, they continued to allow me, if not to hunt with them, to at least join them when shooting at targets.

Quin and I hiked North and West, past apple orchards and fields sown with turnips for winter feed. We came finally to an abandoned mill, where I attached my targets and practiced loading and shooting without fear of discovery by passing riders or field workers. The clear, crisp morning allowed me to polish my skills, but also gave me time to

formulate the details of the next steps of my plan, which
included a trip to Robert's house, preferably when he was
away from home.

Two days later, Quin and I moved East through
the home wood where I could hang my targets on a tree
branch, shooting as they swayed in the breeze. I brought
bread and cheese and enjoyed my woodland bower of
hornbeam, birch, hazel and ash. I took the long way home,
rambling down a path that meandered back and forth
between our property and the Amesley's. Quin gamboled
about my feet and then ran off.

When he didn't come back immediately, I took off my
cloak and spread it beneath an elder tree. I removed my
boots and bonnet and reclined, watching the dappled light
glitter and flash. I felt peace and assurance steal over me.
Everything would work out. I would find my way to make
my father and Robert safe. I couldn't believe it was so bad,
not when the sun was shining, the nuanced scent of leaves
and needles and the deeper, darker smell of sap filled the
air, and a light breeze was singing through the woods.

"Oof," I woke when Quin's paw landed on my stomach, "Quin, enough," I pushed him off. He ran a few steps
down the hill, then came back and barked. I lifted my hand
to rub behind his ear, but he backed up, barked and again
jumped on my stomach.

"Okay," I pushed him off of and sat up, "you want me
to play. One moment while I put on my boots."

With shoes, bonnet, and cloak once again in place, I
followed Quin, who didn't pause to play, but looked back
often to check that I was still there. He left the path, and
after ten minutes, crossed the stream and moved into a field
of ripened hay. I looked around and realized that by leav-

ing the path and moving across the fields, Quin had cut a
straighter path, and we were actually not far from where
Wild Turkey Road bordered Robert's land.

At the edge of a hollow filled with Gorse bushes, Quin
stopped and barked once, his nose quivering and his little
body quaking. I stopped and looked around with my hands
on my hips.

"Well, what are you—" I stopped when the breeze
changed directions and a noxious smell assaulted my nose.

My stomach rolled, and I lifted the edge of my cloak,
putting it over my mouth and nose, stepping forward, "No,
no, no," I chanted to myself, as the hum of flies sounded
louder in my ears "please don't . . ." I pushed one of the
branches aside and froze, horrified.

I turned away quickly, but the image was seared into
my mind, the stiff dark stains on the gray uniforms, insects
and maggots crawling over the blotchy and bloated bodies,
a bloody foam around their mouths and noses.

I backed up, tripped and fell. And then I rolled to
my hands and knees and cast up my lunch. I couldn't stop,
even when there was nothing left in my stomach to empty.
Finally, I stopped heaving, stood, and tried to back away.
I tripped, scrambled, clawed, and crawled away, back into
the hay, where I curled into a ball, pulled Quin to me, and
rocked. I don't know how long I sat there, shaking and crying, but eventually I wiped my face on my sleeve and stood.

Home or Robert's house? The distance was about
the same, but instinct had me moving to Robert's. I was
surprised someone hadn't stumbled across the . . . riding
officers sooner. It was a sure thing that in a few days when
the harvest began, they would have been discovered. Was
it wicked of me to wish they had been found by someone

else?

I don't remember the trek, but I came to myself as I stumbled up the stairs to Amesley Hall, breathing heavily as I pounded on the door.

"Miss Henshaw," with raised eyebrows at such a disordered mess on his doorstep, Robert's butler opened the door wider and gestured me into the hall.

"Finlay, I need to see Robert."

"I'll see if he is home to visitors," he turned and began to climb the stairs.

I couldn't wait; I followed him up to the dining room and before he could announce me, I pushed around Finlay and walked through the door. All three men at the table rose when I entered, but my eyes locked onto Robert's.

"Liza," he moved forward and took both my hands in his, "what's wrong, my dear?"

I sobbed once and he put his arm around me and led me to a chair. Mr. Amesley nodded to Finlay, who retreated and closed the door as Robert seated me and kneeled on one knee before me, taking my hands again and rubbing them briskly.

I glanced up briefly at Mr. Amesley and Mr. Gerow who stood poised and attentive. Robert ignored them and brought my hands to his lips, then stopped and looked up at me.

"Your hands smell of . . .powder," his eyes gleamed with humor and with relief, "then, you are not hurt, no one has—"

I met his gaze and came to myself. The horror retreated, "No," a choking gurgle escaped. I was horrified. This was the wrong time to laugh, and if I started, I feared I wouldn't be able to stop. I reclaimed a hand and covered my mouth with a fist.

After a few moments, I took a deep breath, "Not me, it's those men," I dropped my fist on my lap and pleated my skirt, "Robert, I found . . . down at the edge of your hay field by Wild Turkey Road—Robert, those two riding officers everyone was talking about, I found them." I felt ill again and closed my eyes and took another deep breath, trying to calm my stomach. I would not succumb again.

"Ahh Liza," I felt his finger brush my cheek before he untied my bonnet and threw it on the table. His hand winnowed into the hair at the nape of my neck and rubbed gently.

"Father, perhaps Mrs. Hinton could bring some tea for Liza?"

Mr. Amesley nodded and went to pull the rope.

"Perry, send someone to bring Mr. Henshaw right away. And have Magnus go and get the Squire."

Silence and a heavy stillness met his order.

"Perry,"

I looked up and saw a very pale Mr. Gerow, eyes staring straight through us at some unseen horror.

I sensed Robert's interest surge and focus on his cousin.

He rose from my side and stood before Mr. Gerow, "Perry, what is it?" He placed a hand on his cousin's shoulder, "Tell me."

Perry's eyes moved to Robert's and he winced, looking away again.

"These men. You know something about them?"

It didn't seem possible that Perry could lose any more color, but it was so, and he seemed to fold in on himself, though he did not move. I stayed as silent as I could and willed them to ignore me.

"Yes, I think so," Perry shot another quick look at Robert and stopped talking.

"Come Perry, now is not the time to keep secrets. Two men are dead. If you know anything about it, you must tell me," Robert's hand on Perry's shoulder tightened.

Perry swallowed and nodded. "It isn't an edifying story, but you are right. The time for secrecy is over."

He cleared his throat, rubbed the back of his neck, "It started a while ago—last spring. Colonel Abernathy hosted an evening of cards—just a few of his militia officers and a few friends. He introduced us to a man named Marcus Connors who had just moved here from Rye.

"It happens that Connors had just opened a gaming hell, just off of Hastings Road between here and Bulverhythe, it is. During the evening, I fell into conversation with Mr. Connors. We played Vingt-et-un and shared a bottle, and he invited me to his new place for an evening of cards. I know such places aren't always reputable, but I am able to spot a Captain Sharp, so I wasn't worried."

He stopped and his eyes wandered around the room. He looked everywhere but at the three of us, frozen and waiting.

Finally, he sighed and continued, "I played too deep, and my luck was," his laugh was a discouraged huff, "I should have remembered from whence I come. The Gerow's have no luck but bad." He shrugged off Robert's hand and moved to the window.

With his back to the room, he continued, "I tried to recoup at the races, I was sure my luck would turn. It must, I thought," he turned and shot a pleading look at Robert. Whatever response he saw didn't give him comfort, "I suppose all gamblers believe that." His shoulders bunched up under his ears. He turned back to the window, but he offered no more excuses.

"Go on," Robert's voice was cool but commanding.

"Then the Huttons moved in. I thought if I played it right, I could get myself out of dun territory . . . a rich wife would . . ." he chuckled without humor, "it's a common enough solution, but then I met Miss Amelia and talked with her," his head bowed, his voice lowered, "I think if it were just up to her, she might have still have me—" he swallowed audibly, "I know she deserves better, but I thought if she would marry me, my problems would be solved, and I would never—" he stopped and cleared his throat, "but her brother found out about my debts and warned me off."

The clock ticked in the silence as we all watched his motionless shadow, haloed by the afternoon sun.

"I determined to leave, maybe America I thought, but a man I didn't know approached me, holding my chits. He told me they could be forgiven, all my debts wiped out, if I would just watch here and among our friends, and report anything interesting back to him. Nothing serious, he assured me; he just wanted to keep abreast of what was going on in his new home. Of course, I knew he lied, that it was much more than that."

"And I said no," he lifted a fist to the pane, "I said no. Debtor's prison would be better," his laugh was bitter. "You can see I meant it for the best, but one night, I was drinking with Lieutenant Lentz, in his quarters at the Legion barracks. He passed out and I saw a company patrol schedule on his desk. It wasn't very important information, nothing that would do damage by the time it actually made its way to the smugglers. It was in my pocket before I even gave a thought."

"Perry," Mr. Amesley began in deep disappointment.

Robert shook his head abruptly, and his father paused, watching his son with head cocked in question.

But they both turned back as Perry continued, "it was just to be the once. But of course, once he had me, he wouldn't stop. I was stuck. I suppose I knew it would be a trap, but I didn't want to know, my financial embarrassments consumed me."

Mr. Amesley cleared his throat but was stopped again by a gesture from Robert.

"I suppose I could enlist or still make my way to America?" Perry turned and finally looked at Robert.

"I don't think that would answer," Robert was firm.

Perry looked down at his hands and nodded, "You probably think I deserve to be shot," he tucked his thumbs into his waistcoat pockets, and turned back to the window, "if my mother weren't already dead, the disappointment would kill her. What little honor we had left, I have destroyed."

Robert approached and placed his hand on Perry's shoulder, "I think I could . . ."

Perry shook his head, "you cannot get me out. Last week, I told that man no more. I was done with giving information. And look at what they did to—" he turned to face us. His face looked ravaged and a little green, "I think these bodies were brought here as a warning . . . to me."

"Perhaps, but," Robert paused and shot a look at me. I might have missed it if I hadn't been watching so closely. He must have finally remembered I was still present, "we don't know that for sure. You are not caught yet, and for the sake of our family, I will do what I can. For now, go on as if this has nothing to do with you. Maybe, in fact, it doesn't."

Perry just shook his head. "I should leave. I don't want to embroil you in my disgrace," he attempted a brash smile, "Of course, I may be the next to find myself dumped by the side of the road."

"No. You will not die! I have need of you, and you owe me that help. We will continue as we were, and you will make this up to me. It will demand nerves of steel, but no one else need know about it. You and I will talk later. I need to know more about what and whom you've seen."

Robert gave Perry a quick hard embrace, "but for now Perry, what you will do is keep your mouth shut, send Magnus to get the squire, and you will go and get Mr. Henshaw."

Perry studied Robert's face. I wish I could have seen what he saw, for after a few moments, Perry nodded, rubbed his face, stood straighter and walked out.

It was quite a few minutes after Perry left that I remembered that Father and Aunt Beatrice were away from home. I barely heard Mr. Amesley's apologies and Robert's request for discretion, which request, when I remembered it later, I found quite insulting.

What filled my mind was that, Perry knew more than he'd led me to believe about smuggling at the least. And it appeared, though Robert hadn't known, that Perry Gerow had also become involved in some extremely questionable activities. Though I was loth to take advantage of his difficulties, they were of his own making, and my intentions were good. He could be a fount of information for me, and he could no longer take that superior tone when I asked questions. I would have to carefully cultivate a friendship with Mr. Gerow, and if I handled it right, I could find an ear in the fringes of the Hawkins gang, giving me access to the information I needed to stop Robert and my father.

The Amesley men moved me to the drawing room and plied me with the tea that Mrs. Hinton brought. While they sat with me, I thought about what would happen when the squire came. I had little hope I could insinuate myself unnoticed into that meeting. And the drawing room was too removed from Mr. Amesley's study, where I guessed they would convene. But the library, where Robert regularly worked, adjoined the study.

I spoke before I finished the thought, "This has been a difficult afternoon, for all of us," I tried a sigh, watching both men from beneath my lashes, "and you have much more important things to do than entertain me," I spoke over their reassurances, "and I find myself quite tired."

"Very understandable, my dear," Mr. Amesley leaned forward, "Mrs. Hinton could take you up to a——"

"Would you," I interrupted quickly, "allow me to rest in your library, Robert? It won't have this afternoon sun and will be quiet. I could close my eyes for a few minutes," I smiled gently, "just until my father comes."

The speed with which I found myself with a blanket and pillow resting on the sofa in the library certainly pointed to their anxiety to be shed of my presence, but since it suited my needs, I just smiled when the door closed behind them.

I waited a few minutes before I rose, unlatched the door so I could hear the squire's arrival, and quietly began to explore while I waited.

Chapter 10

A truth that's told with bad intent beats all the lies you can invent.

William Blake,
"Auguries of Innocence"

Through my youth I had run tame through the Amesley's home, as Robert had ours. But not since Robert had returned from the war had I been in the library. I left Quin sleeping on the sofa and wandered slowly past shelves filled with books, letting my fingers run along the spines. I could tell it was a bachelor's home as my fingers came away with a light film of dust, and there was no apparent organization. I found a Latin grammar next to Fanny Burney's *Evelina*. Dr. Johnson's *A Dictionary of the English Language* shared a shelf with *Lyrical Ballads* by Wordworth. *A Treatise on the Development of Modern Agriculture* sat side by side with Clara Reeves' *The Old English Baron*.

During the winters when we were younger, John and I had whiled away our time reading adventure stories. In one story, an important clue was hidden in a hollowed-out book. We had both been intrigued with the possibilities and decided to make one, but we never could convince our father to contribute one of his books for our experiment. Wouldn't that be the perfect hiding place, I thought, for ill-gained documents or plans?

I pulled books at random, letting the pages riffle through my hands before replacing them. On the bottom shelf, pushed back from the other books, a slim volume with a green leather spine and a moiré pattern coverboard caught my attention. Obviously old, it's title was worn with rough handling, so I pulled it out and opened to a page at random, gasped in shock, shut it, and pushed it back into its place on the shelf. I took a few moments to let my blush recede before I continued my inspection of the shelves, though my eyes wandered back to mark its place.

I was ready to give up on the shelves when I heard knocking and Finlay's answering tread. I moved silently to rest against the wall next to the library door and cocked my ear to listen.

"My Lord. Squire Davies," Finlay intoned.

"Mr. Amesley and Mr. Robert are expecting us. I should say they are expecting me," anyone who knew the Squire well would recognize his exasperation.

"I was at the manor on another matter," Lord Ramsgate's unmistakable nasal voice echoed through the hall as he justified his presence, "but when your messenger came, I felt it incumbent upon me to bear the Squire company in this troubling situation. It definitely looks suspicious, and—"

"Yes, yes," the Squire said.

"When the dead bodies of men in service to the crown," he sounded aggrieved, "are found in circumstances that are, well I don't hesitate to say, questionable, at the very least . . . well, all measures must be taken to discover and punish those who have put themselves above the law, no matter the culprit's history or position," his words were drowned out by steps descending the stairs.

"And just whom do you think has circumvented the law?" I'd never heard Robert's father use just that severe, but measured tone.

"The bodies were found on your land. I know your son has served in the Navy, but that won't protect him from just punishment if he is found to be involved. These men served the King," Lord Ramsgate voice rose in volume as he warmed to his subject, "they were killed while in service——"

"Your passion overcomes your reason, My Lord. How could you think to look to my son in anything having to do with the killing of these two young men?" I had the strongest urge to open the door and step out and defend Robert. Of course, he didn't kill these men. I stopped myself when I realized Robert would not thank me, not when his cousin was somehow involved.

"I am not accusing anyone. I am simply saying that no matter who has done this evil deed will be found out and punished. I'll see to it, myself."

The sound of steps descending the stairs caused a heavy silence. I wished I could see what was happening.

Lord Ramsgate cleared his throat, "well, as I said, the bodies have been found on your land. Of course, we must look here first."

"I have never met them—never set eyes on them," next to Lord Ramsgate's full volume, Robert's icy control was awe inspiring even separated by a door, I could feel the intense animosity between the two men.

"Where were you on the evening of Friday, last?"

"I don't understand how it is that you are here in my home and asking me these questions."

Something in Robert's voice when he spoke to Lord Ramsgate chilled me, though I did not understand.

"It is not improper for me, as director of the customs service in this area to add my weight to the proceedings," I had been the recipient of that tone of voice by Lord Ramsgate. I'm guessing most people in the neighborhood had, and it always was accompanied by a haughty stare.

The squire coughed and recovered, "I think, my Lord, I can be depended upon to conduct a series of interviews unaided. It is my job as magistrate."

"I'm sure in other matters, but this involves my men, and—"

"With all due respect Lord Ramsgate, your job," the squire paused and sounded not quite as pugnacious when he continued, "I'm sure your very difficult, but much more important duty today is to inform the families of these two unfortunate men of their recent demise. We could never allow ourselves to delay you in the work that only you can do. Imagine the comfort their families will receive to have the dreadful news from the leader of their men. It will certainly speak to the value you place on every one of your customs and riding officers."

"Well, it is I suppose as you say," Lord Ramsgate harumphed.

"While you do that, I'll get on with my work."

He was given no chance to argue. I heard the front door open, and Finlay in his emotionless voice said, "My Lord."

Silence reigned until the door closed and the echo of Finlay's steps faded.

"He certainly jumped quickly from bodies found on our land to looking at me as the murderer. I wonder why that is."

"I suppose he has come to know," the Squire said quietly, "as many in the area have, that you have been spending time with less than desirable company, some of whom are known to be involved in the trade."

"You, and he I might add, could at least credit me with more intelligence. If I were so lost to myself that I killed two riding officers, I wouldn't be so foolish as to deposit their bodies at the edge of one of my fields that is ready to be harvested."

"Of course, Robert, but it doesn't look good. Especially as you are the one that found—"

"I didn't find them. Liza found the bodies," Robert's hesitation was palpable, "she was understandably upset and is resting in the library until her father comes."

"As difficult as it will be, she will need to show me where they are so I can gather evidence."

"I don't think we need to add to her distress by making her revisit the scene. She described the location clearly. I can take you there."

"Hmm."

"I'll look in on her when you leave," Mr. Amesley said in the silence, "and then I'll wait with Perry for your return."

I started. I hadn't considered that they would think to check on me in the turmoil of the moment. That was inconvenient. I turned the doorknob quietly and gently pushed the door to. In spite of the quick beat of my heart, and on an inexplicable whim, I made a quick detour to the bookshelf. I pulled that little green book out and slipped it

under the blanket before reclaiming my resting position on
the sofa. It may not have been proof of traitorous activities, but it was less than decent. I squirmed uncomfortably,
realizing that I sounded like Aunt Beatrice. I shook the guilt
away. This book was in Robert's library. He very likely had
read it. I told myself that it was my duty to fully understand
my quarry's foibles. Anyway, it would fit easily in the pocket
of my cloak after Mr. Amesley left me alone again.

I closed my eyes and waited, trying to regulate my
breathing. Quin chose that moment to wake and jump
down, meeting Mr. Amesley with a cheerful bark when he
came into the library.

"Shh, let's not wake your mistress," he whispered, "you
can keep me company on a walk outside. I'm sure she won't
mind."

I stayed as still as I could and was exceedingly touched
when Mr. Amesley gently pulled the blanket to cover my
feet and left again, taking my dog with him.

I worried over Lord Ramsgate's determined suspicion
as I continued my search of the library. Unlike the shelves,
the desk was clean--no dust there. I carefully riffled through
the papers and journals on Robert's desk. I left his tally of
monthly expenditures and the rent collection lists where
they were. I slid some papers with what looked like archi-
tectural drawings aside and found a chart of moon phases
and map of the coast. I thought back to my night ride and
remembered the heavy darkness, the lack of a moon. Naturally smugglers would choose to work in the darkest hours.
I checked for the next new moon—October first, in three
weeks. The map gave no clues as to where I should go to
watch.

I sat and opened the drawer. Once again Robert's

orderly mind was evident. His quills, knife, paper, and his crested seal lined up neatly, but nothing else was there to help me. Where would he hide plans or information? Did he have a safe? I walked around the room, lifting paintings away from the walls.

I stopped by his chess table and sighed deeply. For all I knew there was nothing to find at this particular time, or perhaps he kept his secrets in his bed chamber, and I could think of no way to secretly search his room.

I opened the box of deep hued wood, intricately carved with birds and trees, sitting on the table and began to put the chess pieces on the board. When the game was set up, I lifted the box to move it to the side. It was surprisingly heavy and made a solid clunk when I put it down. I sat and my hands shook as I pulled the box in front of me. The bottom of the box seemed solid, but deeper than necessary to hold the chess pieces. No matter how I tried, I could find no place to pry the bottom. I lifted the box and looked underneath. I could see no seams or drawers. I put it down again and closed the box and studied the carvings on the top and sides, running my fingers over every raised figure. Finally, on the side, a bird beak moved when I pushed, and a drawer slid out. I pulled and stared at the gold coins stacked neatly inside.

I didn't count them, but there must have been at least forty or fifty guineas there. I had never seen that much gold all at once.

My stomach knotted. What did Robert need with that much available gold? What did he plan to do? I wanted to believe there was good reason, but my fear was a heavy band around my heart.

I don't know how long I sat staring at those coins, but

a door closing in the next room, brought me to my senses. Reluctantly I closed the drawer, replaced the chess pieces, and walked out the French doors of the library and into the rose garden. I hugged the side of the house, stopping by the window to the study where I waited numbly.

When my heart stopped pounding enough so I could hear, the squire was talking, "You could see the bodies had been dragged. They weren't killed where they lie. But why were they left there?"

"I rather think they were put there as a warning."

"Too whom? You?"

"Well, that is the question, isn't it? And I will soon find the answer."

"You don't have much time, Robert. Lord Ramsgate seems determined to place you under suspicion. What were you doing Friday night? Are you sure there's no one who can testify about where you were?

"I told you before, there is no one. And Lord Ramsgate has no proof."

"If we can't find the true killer, and Lord Ramsgate whispers in the right ears, you may find yourself with a noose around your neck, proof or no."

I squeaked and clapped my hand over my mouth.

I realized that the Friday night they were talking about was the night I watched Robert get on that boat to France. I had proof he wasn't even in the country when those men were killed, but how could I tell the squire that?

How could I not? No matter what other despicable thing he was caught up in, of this much I was certain and could attest—he wasn't a murderer. I couldn't sit by and watch him hang for murders he didn't commit.

I found myself breathing as if I'd run all the way from

home, and then I had an idea. I had been out that night. If
I was very careful, I might be able to tell a very small, but
true, part of my experience. To the squire, it would sound
like proof that Robert was not on the road murdering two
riders, without giving details about what he, or for that matter I, was doing. I could suggest—maybe it was not quite
honest, but in intent and outcome, it would be the right
thing.

   I rushed back into the library, breezed through the hall
and burst into the study before I could talk myself out of it.

   "He didn't do it. He didn't kill those men," I gasped.

   "Liza," Robert scowled at me, "What are you doing?"

   The Squire came forward and took my hand, "of
course we all believe he didn't do it, but Miss Liza, we have
to deal in evidence and facts."

   "I can prove he couldn't have done it."

   Robert froze. I could feel his stillness, like a pointer
scenting prey.

   I ignored him and spoke to the squire, "that night, the
night before the Legion revue, my dog escaped," I squeezed
the hand that still held mine, "you better than anyone know
how he is."

   The squire's eyes smiled.

   "He's been staying in the stable, but he got out," I was
thinking fast, trying to be so careful. I had never known
how difficult it is to tell the truth and mislead at the same
time. "My father and aunt don't know that I left the house.
They don't know about Quin at all," a memory intruded,
"or at least my father knows now, but he didn't then, and I
couldn't let Quin run all night."

   Then came the tricky part, "Quin and I often walk
this way. He loves to cross the stream and he likes Robert's

hounds. And he likes Robert," I paused, knowing the squire would assume that Robert helped me search for my dog and praying that Robert would remain silent.

He didn't. He growled.

But I kept talking, "everything just took much longer than I thought it would. It was actually quite late, or rather early when Quin and I finally made it home," I tried to look as earnest as I could while I said the most honest thing of all, "Robert was out even later and nowhere near Wild Turkey Road or the west hay fields. That isn't where Quin ran. You see he couldn't possibly have killed those men."

The squire's shock made me blush. "Miss Elizabeth, what were you thinking, out all night, even with—,"

I interrupted his scolding before he could say Robert's name, "it sounds bad when you say it that way. I didn't do anything very wrong," I cringed inwardly as I realized I could not say that the same was true for Robert, but I wouldn't let the Squire believe he'd dishonored me.

"Of course not," the Squire patted my hand, "anyone who knows you would never consider. It's ridiculous even to think . . ."

Paradoxically, the more he denied the possibility of amorous activity, the more annoyed I was by his assurance.

"But traipsing around the countryside at night with a man, no matter how innocent," the squire shook his head sorrowfully, "you realize if this became generally known, your reputation would be ruined."

"I'm sure it wouldn't be that bad. Everyone knows me. They would not believe . . ."

"Oh ho, that is all you know about it," the squire shook his head, "if there's one thing I have seen time out of mind, it's that the aristocracy and gentry believe what will give them the most entertainment and make them feel superior. They would talk about nothing else until the next scandal lit. They would glory to believe and talk about 'poor Miss Henshaw' whose reputation is besmirched."

"Liza," Robert came forward, "This is ridiculous. It's all a pack of lies."

"It is not," I put my hands on my hips, "every word I've said is true."

"Liza, you don't have to do this. I will be questioned, but there can be no proof, since I did not kill them. I won't have you needlessly telling a story that—"

"I must. You didn't kill those men. How can I put fear of a little gossip before justice?"

Robert shook his head at me and then turned to the Squire.

"We can't have Liza tell this story,"

"Robert," I cried.

He held up his hand, "but she has given me an idea. I will admit that there is a witness, whom I can't or won't name, who could account for my time last Friday. You could, in all honesty, say there was someone who had knowledge of my absence from the area that night."

"They will ask me—"

"Yes, but you would also have to refuse to disclose this witness's name?"

I had to admire Robert's clearheadedness.

"I could, I suppose, but," the squire bowed his head and rubbed his neck.

"I realize it will be generally assumed that I was carousing, but that will do little harm to my reputation compared to the harm that might be done to Liza's if her name were to be bandied about."

"I suppose," the squire's scowl didn't abate. He slapped his gloves against his thighs, "I see no better way, though I'm not pleased to be letting the parish believe you——" he glanced at me quickly and stopped.

"Small price to pay," Robert murmured.

"They'll ask to hear her testimony, this unnamed lady——and, I assure you, it will be assumed that she's a lady, at the inquest."

"I will, of course, be honor bound to refuse to name her."

The squire chuckled, almost, it seemed, against his will, "husbands will be looking sideways at their wives and fathers at their daughters for months to come, and all will be looking daggers at you," he shook his head one more time before bowing to me and sketching a wave to Robert as he left the study.

The door closed. Robert folded his arms and leaned against the desk and watched me in silence.

Chapter 11

And all who told it added something new, And all who heard it made enlargements too

Alexander Pope, *The Temple of Fame*

I knew what the mouse must feel like when the cat gathered to pounce. My heart beat a rapid tattoo inside my chest. Though hot and a little dizzy, I refused to speak first. Childish I admit, but when confidence is lacking, bluster must suffice.

He stood and made his lazy way toward me. "Liza, why would you perjure yourself like that."

"I told no lie. Quin did escape," I sounded breathless, unsure even to my own ears, "it truly was quite late before I got him home." I bit my lip to stop from babbling.

"Perhaps you spoke no overt lie, but you were certainly less than honest."

I shrugged. It seemed the less I said, the better.

"Why Liza?" Eyes half lowered, he watched my hands which were grasped tightly in front of me.

I dropped them into my skirts and huffed, "You didn't kill those men."

"Far be it from me to shake your confidence, but you can't know that for sure."

"Well, I do know it. You couldn't have."

"All men are capable given the right circumstance."

"Perhaps," I looked away from his intense stare and then looked back and studied his face, "I don't know, maybe you're right. I'm sure in the heat of battle, you must have—" I stopped at his bleak expression, "but I do know you didn't kill these men." I folded my arms but took another step back. Though still a few steps away, he was way too close for my comfort, "I would know."

"Well, in this you are right. I didn't kill these men, but—"

"Robert, I would know. I would have been able to tell as you talked with the squire."

He took a step closer, but I refused to retreat again. As it was, my back was almost to the wall next to the door. He took one more step and lifted my chin. His finger made a lazy trek up my cheek, his thumb quested along one eyebrow and then brushed gently around my ear.

My thoughts scattered as surely as a flock of lapwing, and a tingling warmth spread from my ear to—other places. When he lowered his head, I lifted mine instinctively, and our lips met and clung. He withdrew and I whimpered, but he only slipped his hand down my back and pulled me to him. Then he angled his head and kissed me again. Softly, slowly, lushly he caressed my lips with his, brushing languorously until I sighed, and our kisses grew wilder, deeper. I wrapped my arms around his neck and tried to move closer. Finally, my back hit the wall, this time with Robert pressed against me.

His lips moved to my ear and down my neck, and I

moved my head to the side to give him access, "Liza," he breathed, "you make me crazy." As is lips skimmed, he murmured, "what am I going to do with you? I worry—"

And suddenly, like being drenched in cold water, I remembered why it was that I was so sure he was innocent of these murders. I remembered his overnight journey to France. I remembered his discussion with my father and why I couldn't be kissing with him. Though my traitorous body wanted to stay, I unwrapped my arms and pushed against his chest as I turned my head to the side. Robert stilled.

Neither of us moved. The only sound was our labored breathing and the ticking of a clock. I could feel his eyes on my face, but I refused to look at him.

"Well then, Liza," Robert's voice shimmered with tightly held anger. He moved his hands to the wall on either side of my shoulders and pushed himself away from my body, "tell me, what exactly you were doing out all night, and with whom?"

I gasped at his effrontery and whipped my head back to stare him straight in the eyes, "How dare you—"

Words escaped me. I looked down at his cravat and waited until I could control my breathing before lifting my chin and meeting his eyes again, "I told you, Quin escaped."

"Yes, I remember, and I'll not accuse you of lying," there was fire in his eyes, "but Liza, I've just witnessed what you can do with a very little truth."

I refused to be cowed. Of the two of us, his deceit was far greater.

But he wouldn't give up, "and you will answer my question. What were you doing?"

I opened my mouth to say—well, I don't know what I was going to say, but I knew it would be at full volume. But just then Quin barked outside the door, and I became aware of voices in the hall. Both Robert and I paused to listen. Even through the door I recognized the shrill, worried voice of Aunt Beatrice.

By the time Finlay opened the door and Quin ran in ecstatically, Robert was behind his desk and I, though I don't quite know how, I was seated, still breathless and hot, on the settee in front of the fire.

"Elizabeth," my aunt swept in, taking in Robert, who stood when she entered, the dog and me. Her eyes made a quick, but thorough inspection from my wind whipped hair to my dusty half boots, "you told me you were gathering shells with Miss Davies."

I could almost feel Robert's examination of my face and person.

"We finished early, and I took a walk."

"And I'm sure I asked you to take a groom or your maid." Aunt Beatrice's voice shook with anger.

I cleared my throat, "that was yesterday."

"Elizabeth Louisa," I blushed and prepared for the indignity of a public scolding, "with the events of this week, you know I expected you to be adequately protected. I should not need to remind you daily. Oh, and just look what happened," she shook her head, "I allow you a great deal of latitude when we're in the country, but I don't think it too much to ask for you to obey my wishes when I instruct you to take a maid or groom. And look what has happened; you have embroiled yourself in this unpleasantness."

Unpleasantness. As if two violently murdered bodies were of the same nature as a passing rudeness on the street, and as if my stumbling across them was somehow my fault. Or to add insult to absurdity, as if I would not have found those poor men if a groom or Susan had been by me. By force of will, I didn't roll my eyes. In fact, there was nothing for me to do, but bow my head, and quietly say, "yes, Aunt Beatrice."

She just turned her gimlet eye on me, "well, since you don't seem to be able to act with propriety on your own, I will simply have to be more watchful," she sniffed in that manner that meant the discussion was at an end.

My heart sunk.

She turned now to Robert, "thank you, dear Robert, for caring for our Elizabeth in her," a pause, "difficulties."

He bowed, "it was nothing, ma'am."

"Come Elizabeth."

I stood, and almost tripped over Quin.

"What is this?" Aunt Beatrice looked down at my dog and lifted her skirt as she stepped away.

I gasped, choked, and started to cough as my mind raced for an answer.

A dry voice behind me chimed in before I could create a thought, "he is a sadly undisciplined and lame hound, but one must admit, he is loyal and cheerful."

Aunt Beatrice's eyes went from Robert to Quin and back again before she nodded once and swept out of the room. I sent a silent thanks while Robert looked heavenward and came around his desk and picked up Quin by the scruff when he tried to follow me out the door.

My dreams were haunted by bodies, bloody and bloated. And I worried myself sick about the inquest, which was two days later. My father and Aunt Beatrice walked on either side of me into the Belle Inn where twelve jurors gathered to examine the body and hear witnesses. Lord Ramsgate was not called as a witness, but he had talked enough beforehand to raise eyebrows and pack the room.

But when the time came, things went as the squire had predicted. I was only required to tell my part in finding the bodies and their location. The finding of murder was no surprise to anyone, and though the families of the two men called for justice, Robert, with alibi in place, was acquitted of any wrongdoing. As there were no other suspects as yet, the squire was enjoined to continue his investigation.

It made me angry to watch the young men chortle and elbow each other, and the highest sticklers lift their noses a little higher around Robert. I would have received much worse. But he is a man, and the Amesleys were so popular in the district, that no one gave them the cut direct. They were still invited to every entertainment.

For a few more days, my aunt watched my every move. They were not pleasant days. I was anxious. My aunt was cross. My father was distant.

I suppose there were opportunities I might have taken, but I found it wisdom to absent myself when Robert came to call at our house.

Wednesday we were to attend the subscription ball. In the carriage on the way to town, Aunt Beatrice vented the last of her ire in a long lecture about propriety. By the time we walked up the steps and the master of ceremony announced our names, my faults were forgotten, and Aunt Beatrice was as lively as ever she was.

On nights when there was a moon, people came from as far as Herstmonceux and Battle to the subscription balls in Bexhill. There was room in the assembly rooms for thirty couples to dance comfortably, and mirrors reflected the glow of the candles. Those not dancing visited around the perimeter of the ballroom. Refreshments were bland and stakes in the card room were customarily low to discourage too much time away from the dancing. We took out a subscription every year.

Maris found me almost as soon as we entered. Of course, she had questions about my 'adventure,' as she called it. I warned her that we were collecting shells that day but finished early and I took a walk, which was how I stumbled upon the bodies. She waved her agreement and eagerly returned to her questions, "but Liza, this is the most amazing thing. Weren't you frightened?"

"Mostly I was ill." It made me ill even then to think of it.

"Well yes, but still," she said, "it must have been exciting to be in the middle of—"

I didn't want to think about it anymore, so I pulled Maris around the dance floor. "I need your help."

"Of course," luckily she was easily distracted, "where are we going Liza?"

"I need Mr. Gerow to ask me to dance, preferably right before tea so I can talk with him longer," I nodded to Frederick and Mr. Martin but didn't stop.

Maris pulled her elbow out of my hand, "why would you—" she said to my back. Then she huffed in frustration and caught up to me. "Liza,"

"Also, Captain Richter, and Mr. Hugh Hatton. I don't like him, but he does like to hear himself talk, and he does seem to know things," I peered around a group of turbaned matrons.

"Liza," Maris gasped and laughed.

"Perhaps Robert too, but only if I can't avoid it."

"But I thought you and Robert were—"

I stopped and turned to her.

"Hmmm," whatever she saw in my eyes made her clear her throat and turn away, "Liza, there is Mr. Gerow." I followed her eyes and saw Perry leaning close to the infuriatingly lovely Miss Amelia. The candles highlighted both of their blond good looks. Apparently he hadn't given up all hope.

It didn't look like he would willingly dance with anyone but her, but my need was pressing, and he could only dance with her twice anyway. Dancing twice with the same partner is the limit in polite society. Any more than that would, at worst, besmirch a lady's reputation beyond recall, or at best, be seen as announcement of an upcoming marriage.

And then I saw Mr. Hugh walking toward the attractive couple, looking like a thundercloud, and I picked up my pace to intercept him.

When he was ten paces away, Maris and I stepped in front of him. He sent one infuriated glance Perry's way which I would have missed if I hadn't been watching him. Then he turned his shrewd eyes on us, and with a bow, he graciously yielded to social custom.

"Miss Davies, is your first dance taken?" When Maris shook her head, he offered his arm.

Before they left to join the line forming on the floor, he turned back to me, "and perhaps I could have the dance before tea is served, Miss Henshaw?" His piercing look made me distinctly uncomfortable, but I nodded and smiled.

I watched Perry leading Miss Amelia away from me with disappointment. There was one dance wasted. I accepted Mr. Martin's invitation to dance. It was still early.

Between dances I moved around the ballroom with a strategy worthy of the Duke of Wellington. Many conversations, especially among the women were of fashion, people and the social round. These I hardly monitored. The men talked about war, the inquest, smugglers and the Squire's investigation, which interested me much more.

I moved near to one group of men then another, but I would only hear a little conversation, most of it highly inaccurate, before someone would come to claim their dance. I couldn't help but chafe at the restraints of a ball. But over the course of the evening, I pieced together enough gossip to get a picture.

It was universally understood that smugglers were to blame for the deaths of the two riding officers. There were many fearful references to the Hawkhurst gang of fifty years or more ago.

Some conjectured that the riding officers were in league with the smugglers. I supposed that could be true, but it didn't really match Lord Ramsgate's version of the evening.

There was some talk of Lord Ramsgate's lack of effectiveness as the leader of the local customs service. This didn't trouble me. In spite of his explanations about the difficulties of his work, no one could claim he held any resemblance to Captain Clark, who over the last year had captured the crew of a sailboat heading for Normans' Bay with 540 casks of fine brandy and later captured a luger only a mile off The Star Inn with 500 parcels of tea. Notwithstanding Captain Clark, the local smugglers seemed to do their work unimpeded for the most part.

I did dance with Mr. Hugh. Afterwards he fetched me a cup of tea and then leaned negligently against the wall with a glass of champagne dangling from his elegant fingers. From talk of my discovery of the bodies, it was easy to lead him into a discussion about smuggling. And he seemed very willing to hold forth on the subject—and surprisingly well-informed.

"Oh Miss Liza," his smile was sardonic, "the stories I've heard, you wouldn't believe," the rising inflection of his voice encouraged me to ask for more information.

Difficult as it was for me to feed his vanity, I needed to know more, "do tell, Mr. Hugh," I begged.

"Those two men you found aren't the first Riding Officers to lose their lives at the hands of the Wilkins gang. Most of the time the preventatives are greatly outnumbered. When a patrol chances upon a smuggling run, all they can do is signal for assistance and wait. But sometimes braver, or more fool-hardy riding officers try to stop the smugglers and face the same fate as your two men."

"They are horrible, unprincipled ruffians," I couldn't help my outburst.

"I wouldn't underestimate smugglers, Miss Liza. They aren't just a bunch of thugs. Someone has to keep the accounts. Do you think a local clerk is involved? Or perhaps our estimable curate, Mr. Jones?" He laughed at my scandalized look.

"Of course, I know nothing about it," he said, "but I hear they sometimes even keep a surgeon and a solicitor."

His seeming enjoyment was unsettling, "And where do you think they get their horses? How many local farmers, upon a wink or sign leave their stables unlocked? They may awake in the morning to find their horses too tired to work the fields, but maybe they find a keg of the best brandy on the back stoop."

"I can't imagine that all farmers are so willing," I challenged.

"Oh, I'm sure you're right. But those unwilling, might find their sheep falling unexpectedly ill or their hayricks burning. Or a farmer might ride home after dark and run into a strong black cord stretched between two trees. Smugglers are very creative," he chuckled at my dismay.

"And when they do have horses of their own, I've heard they train them to stop at 'gee-up,' and bolt at 'whoah.' A poor revenue officer who is quick enough to catch a horse would pull the reins and call Whoa and find himself trying to hold a horse running headlong into the night."

All the while Mr. Hugh gleefully shared stories of trickery and violence, he maintained an outward attitude of fashionable ennui. But I noticed that his eyes constantly scanned the company. What, or who, was he looking for?

I was actually relieved when Robert came to claim his dance. I readied myself for a continuation of the skirmish begun in his study. I waited in vain.

"Liza, you're looking well," he bowed and took my hand, placed it on his arm, and led me to our square.

"Thank you," I could be polite and proper too.

As the music began we moved into the familiar figure of the dance, but he hardly looked at me. His hands were cool, his face a sophisticated mask. Forgotten were the argument, his accusations and high-handed treatment. The kisses.

The room seemed to grow hotter. I simmered as I moved into the star figure. I smiled but looked daggers at Robert. He nodded remotely.

I didn't want him to take me in his arms and continue his assault on my senses with hands, and lips and body. I didn't—much. But this polite disinterest was an insult.

"What are you doing?" I hissed when we next met.

"What am I doing?" His frosty smile grated, "I believe I'm dancing."

I lifted my chin as we separated in the grand chain.

We met again in the chorus figure, "You know what I mean. Why are you acting like this?"

He bowed across, "You mean like polite acquaintances?" A spark in his eyes alerted me. He wasn't as unaffected as he seemed.

I inclined my head and smiled for those who watched.

"Liza," I leaned forward to hear his quiet voice, "The whole assembly tonight is watching me, trying to guess who I was with a week ago Friday. Now they will know I wasn't with you."

As I circled, I scanned the room. He was right; an inordinate number of eyes followed his every move. Now I saw that wherever Robert looked, men smirked or scowled. Ladies lifted their fans and averted their eyes.

I don't know why it upset me. If they knew what he'd really been doing that Friday night, there would be more than raised eyebrows and cold looks. I was still angry, but now I was angry with everyone else, not just with Robert.

At the end of the set, Robert escorted me to my friends, bowed and walked away without another word. I watched as he walked around the ballroom. He joined his father and turned his back to me.

My heart was pounding, and my breath uneven when Perry Gerow approached and asked me to dance the next set. I needed more time and privacy than the movements of the dance would allow, both to calm myself and to be able to ask my questions.

I looked around and made a decision, "Mr. Gerow, I am quite warm and breathless," I worked my fan, "couldn't we forgo this dance and take some air for a few minutes out on the balcony?"

He offered his arm, gave one last miserable glance toward Amelia and led me out the French doors. I stayed in sight of the room so my aunt wouldn't follow and stood against the balustrade, looking out into a small garden with the fresh breeze cooling my face. I was able to regain a little calm. And as the music swelled in the ballroom, Perry and I had enough privacy for a quiet conversation. And it netted a more useful bit of information, though not in the manner I thought.

Chapter 12

Enter RUMOUR, painted full of tongues

Shakespeare, *Henry VI*

"Mr. Gerow, I have wanted to apologize for sending you on a wild goose chase last week. I didn't remember before Robert sent you to bring father to me that both he and my aunt were away from home."

Perry shook his head and flapped a hand, "Please, it was no problem."

"I wasn't myself that afternoon," I looked out into the garden but saw again in my mind those two bodies.

"It is understandable," his voice interrupted my disturbing memories. I looked up at him in gratitude.

For all I needed more information from him, the pain in his face caused me to pause. I patted his arm briefly before turning away again to look up at the stars.

"It is I who am sorry for your distress." He surprised me.

"It was upsetting, I admit," I picked my way with care, "but it has made me realize that, well, we are all affected, aren't we?" I felt his eyes upon me but found it easier when

I didn't meet his gaze. "I have heard whisperings tonight, wondering if those two men were perhaps involved with the smugglers before they ran foul."

"How would we know?" I felt his shrug. "It happens, of course. I'm sure they are often tempted to turn a blind eye in return for a fee. It seems unlikely in this case. Though smugglers by nature are quick in retribution, they are protective of their own."

"It has made me wonder how many of our neighbors are complicit," I probed, "I have heard of many whose cellars and homes are filled with run goods," I paused, "the goods can't be hard to find."

"Brandy, spirits, tea, tobacco, spices, silks, and lace," he listed, "there is no shortage for those who want to forgo the tax."

"Lace?" I felt breathless. There was a haberdashery in town where my aunt refused to shop. "I wonder," I said without thinking, "what I would find at Madame Fortunna's."

"No!" Perry surprised me with his vehemence, "I should not have said anything, especially to you," he paced away from me and back again, mumbling and gathering a few scandalized looks.

"Mr. Gerow," I said gently.

He shook his head. His voice was low, but still heated, "I have no patience for this; it is madness," he breathed deeply for a few minutes until he was calm but still pale, "I apologize for my rash words Miss Liza, but you are not purse-pinched. Learn from my mistakes."

I jumped a little.

"You heard everything, though I wish I'd remembered you were there before I started talking," he grimaced, "but you know what I have done, and what was done to keep me working with them," his eyes looked fevered, "pay full price for your lace in Hooe or Ninfield, Miss Liza. The savings you might gain here will not be worth associating with these blackguards."

I heard nothing else he said, but I must have responded reasonably, for he made no more objection before leading me back into the ballroom where I was soon dancing with Colonel Abernathy after which Captain Richter and Lieutenant Lang solicited dances.

I very purposefully did not watch Robert the rest of the night, but I still noticed that he danced twice with Amelia. Both of them smiled and laughed vividly while they circled the room. Nor did I miss that shortly after his last dance with her, he slipped out one of the doors with Perry.

I chatted with Lieutenant Walters for a few moments before excusing myself and heading in the direction of the ladies' retiring room. I quickly looked around, and then I passed right by that room and the hum of female voices within.

The hall beyond was quiet and dimly lit. I moved quickly, working my way to the door that Robert and Perry had taken. I looked both ways and saw no sign. A few men were making their way to the card room. I followed quietly in their wake. I waited until the hall was empty and listened at the doorway, even peeking around the corner making a quick survey of the room. Robert and Perry weren't there.

I continued down the hall, pausing to put my ear to the doors along the way. At one I heard a deep voice, a rustle and giggle. I blushed and moved on quickly to the next door where two men were involved in an argument if the tone and volume of their voices were anything to go by. I

couldn't tell what they were saying, but neither voice was
Robert's, so I moved on with an imagined clock ticking in
my head adding anxiety to my search.

I explored the halls on the ground floor and paused
before the stairs. Surely, he wouldn't have gone up to the
upper rooms among the storage and servants' quarters. I
sighed despondently. I could spend the whole night looking
for Robert and still miss him. I decided to return to the ballroom before I was missed. But as I turned, Robert appeared
right before me.

I stood mouth agape but after a moment, I had the
presence of mind to wonder where he'd left Perry.

But that thought flew when he spoke, "you've been
avoiding me."

"I thought that's what you wanted to prove to all the
gossips that I—"

"I don't mean tonight. That is something else; it will
pass in time," he waved a hand as if to brush it aside, then
he folded his arms and leaned forward, "I mean all of this
week I haven't seen you."

"I've been busy."

"Liza," he shook his head.

"Robert," I mimicked his tone.

"You're still angry with me?"

I would never have brought up our interchange in the
study at Amesley Manor, but I wouldn't back down, so I
lifted my chin, "I believe it was you that was angry."

"Yes, hmm, I apologize." He looked discomfited, "my
behavior was—" he lifted one hand and raked his fingers
through his hair, "not entirely honorable."

I lifted my eyebrows, hiding the hurt his words, and his
regret, gave me.

And then unknowingly he salved the wound, "I didn't handle—I was—" he sighed and looked me straight in the eyes, "I didn't like it when you pushed me away. You shouldn't take personally what a man says when he is frustrated is in his attentions for a woman, though that is no excuse for my behavior. I did not act well. I apologize," his voice and face were stiff.

I swallowed. And stared. And thought. Finally, I nodded.

His voice lowered as he moved closer, "I cannot, in truth, tell you that I'm sorry that I kissed you. I like kissing you. I'd like to do it again."

"Robert," I squawked this time.

"Not now, not here." With one hand he lifted my chin. He waited in awkward silence until, finally, I raised my eyes to his.

"I am sorry if our kisses have made you uncomfortable," he paused, "or afraid?" His eyes searched my face looking for answer to his question. He must have seen something because he released a breath and his shoulders dropped.

"Uncomfortable then. For that I am sorry."

I didn't know what to say. How could I tell him that I liked kissing with him, that I would like to step forward into his arms right then. But I stiffened my resolve and remained silent.

"Liza, listen carefully, my dear. I wasn't," he paused, "this is not a game to me." His fingers slipped up from my chin and brushed my cheek.

"I would not for the world do anything to harm you."

A promise—so sincerely stated. I could not remain unmoved. My heart picked up its pace.

"Nor would I have you hurt."

I felt the stiffness in my shoulders loosening.

He ruined that in his next sentence, "I understand you have been talking to Perry, asking questions.

I felt a rush of anger toward Perry Gerow, but Robert continued, "I must ask, please, that you don't ask questions about town. Especially with Perry, I know he can be charming, but he doesn't always act appropriately—with ladies."

I stiffened, "of all the gall! Perry Gerow," I ground out, "unlike some I could name, acted with complete propriety."

"Touché, little one." There was no smile on his face, but I heard it in his voice, "I still would like you to promise me you'll stop trying solve the mystery of those deaths."

"I don't know what you're talking about."

"You might try trusting me. I will take care of things."

I felt a quick flash of anger. Trust him? Did he think that he could so easily continue to hide his double life, that he was immune to the law?

"Oh, dear, I know that mulish look. Liza . . ."

He looked away from me, held his finger to his lips, and backed into the shadow of the stairs. His silence and speed made me blink.

Now that he was quiet, I heard voices moving toward me. The tittering laugh let me know before they turned the corner that one of the young ladies coming was Judith Bellerton. And where Judith walked, Alice Crossley would not be far behind. I had a fleeting thought that I'd like, in spite of all his superior, hypocritical advice, to join Robert in the shadows rather than be subjected to another of Judith's vacuous, malicious, or embarrassing chats.

There was no answer though. I must meet them.

The giggle came closer and I lifted my head and

smiled brightly as Judith, Alice and Miss Amelia Hatton came into view.

"Oh, Miss Liza," Judith said, "what a lucky chance, meeting you here."

"I was just," I motioned behind me, but could think of no excuse, "taking some air."

"Well, I declare I have been wanting to talk with you all evening, but of course, you must be swamped with questions," she waved expansively.

I froze, had she heard me asking questions tonight?

And then I sighed in relief when she continued, "your little adventure is the only topic of conversation."

Oh, right, the riding officers. How could I have forgotten?

"And you especially must be so relieved that Captain Amesley was exonerated," she simpered. And Alice Crossley snorted before she laughed.

I felt deeply embarrassed, knowing Robert was not ten steps away listening to this drivel. And did the whole parish believe Robert and I had an understanding? I wanted to stamp my foot and scream. But manners triumphed, and through gritted teeth I said, "I'm sure we all are relieved that the truth came out and hopeful that the culprit will be found."

"Oh, certainly." Her knowing tone annoyed me, "Were you expecting to meet someone here?"

"No, no," I asserted, in answer to her arch tone, "I was a little over-warm, and have a little bit of the headache," speaking the word seemed to make it truth; I realized my head truly was pounding. I never should have begun to use headaches as excuse. Even their mention seemed to make them reality.

"Oh, Miss Liza," Judith gushed, "let me take you upstairs. My maid, Martha, has the most effective remedy. It's a mixture of brandy and some nasty tasting herbal. But it will make you feel ever so much better."

She took my arm, but before she could move towards the stairs and Robert's shelter, I interrupted her, "I thank you for your concern, but I am much recovered. This few moments away from the heat and noise has done me such good. Let's do return," I smiled as I reclaimed my arm and made shooing motions toward the ballroom before turning to the one silent girl, "Miss Hatton, how are you finding your first Bexhill ball? I declare the dancing tonight is divine, don't you agree."

I linked arms with her and waited for Judith to lead the way back to the ballroom. I was surprised when Miss Hatton slowed our pace. We fell behind the other two girls.

"Miss Liza, may I call you that?" She continued at my nod, "and of course, I am Amelia." Her smile was perfunctory, "I haven't had much conversation with you," she put her finger to her lips and leaned forward to whisper, "may I call upon you?" I noticed her eyes were a little overbright.

"I will look forward to that Miss Amelia."

"Thank you," she made a small moue of distaste, barely noticeable, "but I will have to find a time when Judith is not near my home, which she often is. It's not her opinion I'd like to solicit."

I laughed in surprise.

She stopped, as if just hearing her own words, and blushed, "I had some champagne tonight. It's my first time. I didn't like the taste, but I didn't like to be disagreeable."

"I understand. I hope you can come to call without Miss Judith."

"Yes," she nodded, stopped then nodded again, "We wouldn't be able to talk if she came, and I'd like to talk with you. Some things Mr. Amesley and Mr. Gerow have both, but separately of course, said about you have led me to feel I'd like to know you better."

"That surprises me. They are presently both out of sorts with me."

"And yet you don't seem cowed by their disapprobation," there was almost a question in her comment.

"No, I don't suppose so."

"I wish . . .I'd like to be less affected by," she paused, "oh, you know, the tempers and humors of the men around me."

I couldn't formulate a response to that. But it didn't matter as we stepped into the greater light and noise of the ballroom.

"Courage, that's what they say of you, that you are courageous."

My jaw dropped, "I am astounded to hear that, Miss Amelia. Are you sure you heard correctly?"

A giggle seemed to surprise her, "well, that isn't exactly how they described you. I think they might have used the words headstrong and willful."

I glowered. "Well. I find them overbearing and stuffy," I fumed, "and it doesn't matter anyway, I am more than angry with both of them."

"Oh, but you are brave and so honest."

I cringed at that last.

She didn't notice, "my brother in particular is angry all the time, and now especially as he's started asking me to make the acquaintance of certain men, he is never happy with me," her scowl looked out of place on her delicate

face, "I don't like them. And I'm uncomfortable with
Hugh," she sighed, "it didn't used to be so, but it is now,
and I find it particularly distressing."

"I can't imagine that anything you do makes anyone
angry. You're very accomplished," I realized that my com-
pliment sounded like a complaint.

She shrugged, "I suppose so." She didn't sound happy
about it, "do you ever just tire of doing everything the right
way? I haven't noticed that it makes my life any easier or
happier. I would like to play a sailor's ditty," she clapped her
hand to her mouth, then took it away, "Oh, I'm just being
silly. Forget it, please."

"I don't think you're silly," and I didn't really, especially
after talking with Mr. Hugh earlier.

"Not silly," she paused and ruminated , "No. I'm not
silly. I am angry," a gurgle of laughter turned into a sob.
Her eyes widened in horror as they filled with tears.

"Oh dear." She looked around stricken.

"Let's take a turn about the room, Miss Amelia," I
pulled her into a stroll.

"You will think I'm the veriest goose,"

"I don't think it's gooseish to be angry. I find it quite
likely that you have every reason to be angry, men being
what they are.

A waterlogged giggle escaped, "but I am. I'm angry.
I'm angry," she said again with a sense of wonder. "That's
what this knot in my stomach is and my difficulty breathing.
It isn't nerves. I'm not overset. I'm angry," she said it with
more force and not a little satisfaction.

"What has your brother done to make you angry, if I
may ask," I was very curious. I nodded to Mrs. Davies who
was chatting with Aunt Beatrice. She smiled in approbation.

"Mr. Hugh certainly didn't look happy earlier to see you standing with Mr. Gerow."

"Oh, Mr. Gerow," she smiled tremulously, then her face fell into a glower, "No, Hugh doesn't like Mr. Gerow. He says he is just on the lookout for a rich wife."

Even though I knew, at least to begin with, that was true, I kept my mouth shut.

"What do they expect? They settle large amounts on us to make us more attractive to men and then complain when the money attracts men. Do men ever see women?" She continued without waiting for a response, "and how can I blame him? I have a large portion. I don't suppose there is a man alive who won't like me better for it. Hugh is not really my brother."

I felt dizzy trying to follow her conversation.

"Sometimes I wish I were poor, well not poor, poor, just not so very rich. It would be nice to just to know when men are nice and when they are thinking about money. Don't you think?"

I nodded, though I don't suppose I'd ever given it much thought, "What about your father?" I brought her back to the topic.

"My mother passed away three years ago."

I was taken back again by the non-sequitur, but felt her sorrow, "I'm sorry."

"Yes. It is difficult. Though my mother was married to him since I was five years old, now that she is gone, he is changed. Everything is changed, and my place with Papa and Hugh seems somehow more precarious, though I don't mean to say that they treat me badly. I just, oh I don't know, I don't fit as comfortably into our life as when she was there." She took a deep breath, then announced rather loudly, "Miss Henshaw, my tongue is tingling, and I'm talking too much."

"No, not at all," I assured her quietly, "you can trust me, you know." And somehow her artless, tipsy meanderings had tempered my feelings. She was still enviously beautiful and talented, but I felt some pity, maybe a little fellow feeling, even admiration, and certainly a great deal of curiosity.

"I have felt that—that I can trust you."

Our way was suddenly blocked. Robert bowed to Amelia, "Miss Hatton, you remember Captain Richter?"

"Captain," her gentle smile returned.

"Ma'am, are you available to dance this last dance?"

She nodded and placed her hand on his proffered arm.

After they walked a few steps, Robert reached out and took my hand and pulled it through his arm, "Dance with me, Liza," he murmured and pulled me onto the floor.

I had to pay attention to the forms of the country dance, and my mind raced with all I'd heard and seen tonight. It should have been enough to occupy my thoughts, but my heart raced, no matter how I tried to deny it. The heat in Robert's gray eyes, though hidden from those who watched, his challenging smile, the breadth of his shoulders, and his powerful grace overset me. What was I to do?

Chapter 13

Every inch that is not fool is rogue

John Dryden, *Poetical Works*

I had learned that smugglers murdered riding officers and were willing to drag them to a field, miles away to serve as warning to a beleaguered man who wanted to escape their influence. Smugglers burned a farrier's cottage because he decided he preferred his cellar to remain empty or perhaps informed to the authorities. Would they shy away from making a brave curate their next target?

That was my question the next Sunday when Mr. Jones, without a quiver, announced, "I take Psalms 37:1 as my text today, 'Fret not thyself because of evildoers, neither be thou envious against the workers of iniquity.'"

He very carefully, but boldly, expounded against sinners of all kinds who, to quote the curate, "do all manner of violence against honest souls in pursuit of their own ill-gotten gains," and enjoined us to follow the example of Ruth, as "The Lord recompense thy work, and a full reward be given thee of the Lord God of Israel, under whose wings thou art come to trust."

He continued with a plea that we do what is right, without weighing the consequences, even when our choices might be difficult or unpopular, but trusting to our God to bring all of the rewards He sees fit in His wisdom to bestow on his children.

I had always liked our Mr. Jones. Frankly, all of us were relieved when Vicar Tolison's advanced age caused him to turn over more of the work of the parish to his curate. Mr. Jones, though young and new to the church was gentle and learned, a good conversationalist, a worthy dinner guest. But I had never realized the depth of his conviction and courage.

His sermon was especially hazardous because, and he had to realize, many of his parishioners might very well have been involved, in one way or another, in the trade—either in the receipt of run goods, their silence, the use of their homes to hide contraband, or more active participation. If he preached too volubly against the smugglers, I worried he would end face down in the shingles at the outgoing tide. And then how could he help those of his flock who were damaged by the effects of the so-called 'gentlemen?'

I hoped that any who might be angered by his homily would assume that no one was listening, which is true enough in the general course of things.

In fact, a goodly way through his sermon, I found my own mind wandering. How was I to look into the haberdasher and millinery without bringing notice to myself or worse having word get back to Aunt Beatrice? I was not so full of myself to assume every soul in Bexhill would immediately recognize me, but neither did I trust that I could walk through town and enter a shop I'd never patronized and remain unnoticed. I would have to go incognito, but I didn't think John's trousers and braces would serve in this instance.

I was still mulling over my problem when at the church door Mr. Jones took my hand and asked, "Miss Liza, how are you doing?"

I was surprised by the tears that filled my eyes. Every time someone asked, the sight of those two men came back vividly to memory. And I had heard that question more times than I could count, but many people asked with titillating, horrible curiosity and some with a self-serving calculation. When my family and Robert inquired, I felt their sorrow and guilt, though what they felt guilty about I couldn't guess.

But our curate's sincere and unselfish concern overset me. I blinked and blinked again, smiled tremulously, and responded, "I am improving," and felt for the first time that I was.

A few minutes later I was standing, feeling unaccountably exhausted, next to my father and aunt who were talking with Lord and Lady Ramsgate and Lady Helen.

Lord Ramsgate looked bilious, "I don't like the cut of that man's jib." He was speaking of the curate.

"Oh, I don't think we can doubt his honor and loyalty to the crown." My father tended to take things literally.

It didn't matter, as Lord Ramsgate ignored his calm rejoinder, "I don't come to church to have some upstart man of the cloth call my actions into question and preach to me about sin and repentance."

I wondered what he thought church was for—probably an uninterrupted nap?

"And I expect," Lord Ramsgate continued, "for my

wife and daughter to receive the balm of comfort to prepare them for the week ahead."

I would need more than a calming sermon, I thought,
to live everyday with Lord Ramsgate's pinched voice and
voluble pomposity.

Helen's hat blew off in the breeze, and one of her
maids stepped after it. No one paid her any mind as she
caught the recalcitrant hat and returned it. With a dip of
a curtsy and, I was intrigued to see, totally unnoticed the
maid slipped away. I looked around me with new eyes at the
grooms holding horses and the maids with downcast eyes—
all those servants present and busy, but unnoticed.

The curate might call it blasphemy, but the idea felt as
if it came straight from heaven to my mind as I stood in the
churchyard. I received, like a benediction, a revelation of
my next ruse.

With the inspiration came a new energy and hope
and a number of ideas to bring my plan to fruition. When
Maris and Miss Sylvia approached, I wasted no time ar-
ranging an opportunity to reconnoiter .

"Oh, hello, isn't it just the most, lovely day?" I hardly
waited for their smiling response, "shall we walk down to
the beach?"

Aunt Beatrice turned her head and opened her mouth,
but I spoke first, "we'll take my maid with us," she closed
her mouth and nodded, "and perhaps when you get home
Aunt, you could send the coach to meet us and bring us all
home?"

Miss Amelia clapped in delight, and she and Maris
both went directly to arrange with their families.

"I think it is good for young women to take some light
exercise," Lady Ramsgate nodded, "Lady Helen would

be pleased to join you, I believe." Without a word, Helen stepped forward to join our group.

A very few moments later, we found ourselves walking down Church Street chatting easily.

Miss Liza," Amelia's hands were grasped in front of her, her knuckles white, "I feel I must apologize."

I reached out and took her arm, pulling a little so she would release her painful grip, "I can't think why. I was delighted to talk with you last night," I smiled my encouragement, "upon reflection, I have decided you are very brave, or will be once you've got in the way of it."

Her laugh was an embarrassed gurgle, "Oh Miss Liza, I hope so. I have determined to try."

"And what shall be your first act of courage?"

"Oh dear, I hadn't thought. Do you mean I should decide upon something brave?" Her brow creased in concentration.

"Sometimes, I think, an idea presents itself in the moment, and if you don't think too deeply and talk yourself out of it, you can speak or act."

"Such as changing your music choice at a rout?"

Now it was my turn to gurgle in embarrassment, "well yes. And I will admit that it was your incomparable performance that put me in mind to leave off my Haydn Sonata and try something more lively," I smiled and gently bumped her shoulder with mine, "but often, I find it best to have a plan, especially at first."

"I can see how that might be a benefit, especially as I'm not in the habit of doing more than thinking rebellious thoughts. I will give this some consideration."

"Well, I hope to watch your thoughts and feelings find expression."

She smiled, but already I could see her mind exploring possibilities."

Once we crossed High Street, we joined Upper Sea Road from where we had a clear view down to the broad expanse of sandy beach, revealed now by low tide. A few puffy clouds floated above our heads. Past the white foam where the sea met land, the water turned from a jewel-like green close to shore to a shadowed deep blue as it neared the horizon. Barely a ripple broke the vast expanse.

I looked behind me when I heard Maris ask, "Lady Helen, what did you think of Mr. Jones' homily this morning?"

I slowed down; I wanted to know if she agreed with her father.

Her voice when she began to speak was quiet and well-modulated, "I am so pleased to see that Mr. Jones understands that a "true Christian" needs to discharge his debt to God. I would much rather be challenged to do good than hear a sermon that places few demands upon my conscience or the endeavors of my life." As she continued, her voice took on more volume and force, "last spring when we were in London, I came upon a tract by William Wilberforce called 'A Practical View of the Prevailing Religious System of Professed Christians, in the Higher and Middle Classes in This Country Contrasted with Real Christianity.' I have since been reading the works of others of the Clapham group. I would like to find a way that I too could make a difference. Perhaps Mr. Jones has some ideas. I have been thinking I should look for opportunity to speak with him privately."

I couldn't have been more surprised if our quiet and contained Lady Helen had walked to the middle of the

street and begun singing and dancing. Were all of the
young ladies in our parish nurturing secrets and living lies?

I shook off that thought before we reached the end
of the street where the buildings gave way to fisherman's
huts, wooden net shops, and rope houses and ultimately to
the shingled beach. Miss Fortunna's was the last shop on
the road, but one. I slowed and took a long look. The shop
fronted the road with only three steps to the entrance. In
the windows an attractive chip bonnet caught my attention.
Ribbons and gloves lay on an artfully arranged gold silk. I
saw that this building was detached from the neighboring
shops and had a narrow, but well beaten path down to the
back garden and then to the shore. Even from the front
of the shop, the sound of the crashing waves muffled the
voices around us, and its location certainly would lend itself
to smuggler's work. I would have liked to look at the back
of the shop but could think of no reason to give my friends
and my maid. In spite of that I smiled as my plan began to
take shape.

The tide was out and not many were on the beach, so
we brazenly, even Lady Helen, removed our slippers, tucked
our hems up, and walked barefoot where the rocks gave
way to a stretch of hard sand. A flock of ruddy turnstone,
with their orange legs, dug and probed, seeking crabs, sand-
hoppers, or seaweed flies.

We walked East toward a group of rock pools that
I loved and were rewarded with a view of a great egret,
standing motionless in the water, waiting for unsuspecting
fish to glide by. After a few moments, my friends backed
away, leaving me standing still and silent, waiting with the
large, elegant white bird. I could hear girls' laughter carried
across the breeze. I watched them for a minute and smiled.

When I looked down again, a shore crab, brown-ish-green with a serrated edged shell, eight legs and two claws scuttled out from under some weeds and onto the rocks across the pool. The egret struck with a quick thrust of its blade-like bill, picking up the crab, and in quick scissoring motions, cracked the shell and swallowed the crab whole.

I stepped back, shocked and sickened. Tucking in its long neck, the bird took flight, and I took another step back. Tripping on a rock, I fell with a jarring thud onto my seat. The air cooled as a cloud covered the sun and the breeze picked up. A frisson of fear slithered up my spine. I looked around, but from where I sat I could no longer see my friends. I could see no one.

Then the cloud passed, and the sun came out again. I stood looking up and out at the horizon and shook off the shiver of premonition.

It was a beautiful day. I had a plan. My friends beckoned to me from further down the shore. As I walked towards them, I allowed my heart to once more swell and mirror the expansive sea and sky. All would be well.

For the next few days it seemed that everywhere I went I saw maids following their mistresses. I noticed how many servants moved through the streets of the town daily, sometimes alone, and sometimes in groups of two or three to deliver a package or do a quick errand if their mistress was otherwise engaged. Few of the aristocracy or gentry ever saw those servants. It was as if they didn't exist. And as for the proprietress of a shop? Surely the faces of maids ran together in their minds unless the maid were sent regularly.

I decided the best time to enter the haberdasher and millinery was in the evening just as the shop was about to close. One problem I didn't foresee was that of convincing Susan.

"Oh no, Miss," she looked horrified, "I will be turned off,"

"Of course, you won't, Susan. I couldn't do without you," at first I laughed off her concern.

"Oh yes I will, and without reference."

I shook my head and smiled gently, "I will take all responsibility. Well, and it is my responsibility."

"As if that would help," she scowled and lifted her clasped hands in entreaty, "Please—"

I felt a little guilt to pressure my maid so. With my new awareness of servants, I had seen more than I liked about how difficult their lives were. I didn't like to take advantage. I knew Susan could do nothing to stop me, but I wanted her help. It was an uncomfortable fix. Only the severest need spurred me on.

"All I need is to borrow one of your dresses, a black one."

"It's more than clothes, Miss, it's—"

"And maybe an apron. A pocket might be a good thing."

"The way you walk and talk. They would be sure giveaway. Also, you—"

"Definitely a cap to cover my hair."

"—would forget to keep your head lowered and voice low and respectful. No one would mistake you for a servant."

"A shawl too, don't you think?"

Susan looked up as if looking for divine intervention, but since my idea came from heaven, so to speak, I wasn't worried.

"Maybe I should borrow a pair of your shoes too. Mine might be too noticeable."

"I only have one pair," Susan sat on the bed and let her head fall on her fist.

"Truly?" I was stunned, "that doesn't seem like enough. I'll wear my old boots. They are a little tight but needs must. And I will get you another pair next week."

"I'd much rather you stay home tomorrow night."

I went to her and took her hands in mine, "Susan, I am sorry to pull you into this mess, but how else am I to find out when the next smuggling run is?"

She clung to my hands. "They will kill the both of us without question," she shook her head sorrowfully.

"Susan, we won't be caught." She opened her mouth, but I talked right over her, "I need to do this, and I think it will be much safer if you are with me." This was cruel of me, but I was determined to visit that shop. I needed her help. I absolutely had to find out where the next run would be.

"What more do you need to learn? You already know that Mr. Robert is doing business with the smugglers. You could talk with him. I think he would listen to you."

I wasn't as sure as she. "He has a package coming in, remember. I need to know what is in it so I can steal it, if I must, or talk to him about it or . . . or, I don't know, Susan, but I can't help if I don't know what I'm looking for. And he definitely won't listen to me if I don't know what I'm talking about."

I sat next to her silently, still holding her hands.

She looked up at me in misery and shook her head again.

I fell to my knees and put my head on our linked

hands. "Oh Susan, I know. I know the risks, truly I do," I looked up at her. I was pleading now, "please, please will you help me?"

She sighed deeply, "Miss Liza, you have to—you must follow me and do as I do. You must."

"I will. I promise," I leapt to my feet and gave her a hug, "we will be so careful, and it will be okay, you will see."

Chapter 14

A plague upon it when thieves cannot be true to one another!

Shakespeare, *Henry IV*

It was not difficult to come up with an excuse not to attend the committee ladies' tea, hosted by Mrs. Althea Dinmore this time. Aunt Beatrice may even have believed my excuse. Even if I'd wanted to go, I would have excused myself as this was the day that Squire Davies offered to come and remove Quin's cast.

Once he was free, Quin still gamboled about with his three-legged gait, but the squire said he might, in time, begin to use that leg a little more, though it might never be as strong as the others. I didn't care all that much. His bad leg hadn't kept us from traipsing through the woods and fields, and Quin was happy and smart and loyal. I couldn't have been more pleased with him even if he had full use of all four legs.

The time in our stable calmed me—the smell of the hay, the sounds of animals at rest, or maybe Frank's tuneless whistle as he cared for the horses settled my racing heart and galloping thoughts. And Quin always made me feel cheerful. Much better for me to spend the afternoon in the stable, rather than pace in my room and worry.

Finally, it was time. I met Susan in my bedroom. Sighing in hopeless dismay, she helped me out of my dress. She cringed as she pulled her oldest, black dress over my head and muttered as she added one of her aprons and tied it snugly to pull in the excess fabric. She handed me heavy woolen socks and my old boots.

If I hadn't known before how she felt, I could have guessed when she started brushing my hair. She always addressed herself to my hair with a little too much vigor when she was displeased, but I didn't complain as she pulled and twisted it up on the top of my head. I thought she deserved what little retaliation was available to her.

Then, with cap and bonnet covering my hair, I sat at my desk to write a note to my aunt. I described a circuitous, if not honest, route among our tenants that would last quite past supper. It also did include some truth. Or, at least I told her I was taking Susan with me. I read it over and decided that it was a masterpiece, my finest work so far. I felt quite proud. I paused a moment as guilt rushed over me. Since when did I take pride in my growing ability to deceive?

I fingered the stationary nervously. But what else could I do? I took a deep breath and handed the note to Susan. While waiting for her return, I promised myself that from then on I would only lie in pursuit of the truth.

When Susan returned, we slipped down the back stairs and out into late afternoon sunshine. The descent into town turned and opened into a broad overlook to the sea, white-capped deep gray, rippling in an unseen breeze onto a shore of bronze and pewter. As we walked closer, the air filled with scent of salt and fish.

Once in town, we left our cart at the stable of the Belle

Inn and resumed our adventure on foot. For the most part,
I kept my head down and followed in Susan's footsteps as
she swept through Bexhill. It wasn't long before I was loaded down with wrapped packages. I think this was another
form of punishment, but Susan said that if my hands were
full, I would be more likely to comport myself like a servant.

I was so grateful that she had agreed to come that I
didn't complain. But the packages were awkward and grew
heavier as the afternoon passed. What with juggling to
steady the ever-growing pile, my arms began to hurt. And
my feet hurt, and I had to keep constant watch so as to be
where Susan needed me to be, so I couldn't really watch or
even think. I would have liked to tell Susan that we'd done
enough, but servants can't, can they? So, Susan just kept
adding to the load.

We were coming out of the green grocers and I
stopped to look up, unconsciously dazzled as the setting sun
flecked the ever-moving sea with dazzling light and cloud
shadows. When I looked down and cast around for Susan, I
caught my breath. Across the street, Perry Gerow was walking out of the Five Bells followed closely by the same man
who Robert had met before the last smuggling run—James,
Robert had called him. If I hadn't been watching so closely, I would have missed it when Perry swung back a hand,
holding an oilskin package and Mr. James reached forward,
grasped the package and slipped it beneath his coat. They
both continued to walk, though not together, in the same
direction Susan was headed. I hurried forward and stayed
in Susan's shadow, but my mind was teeming.

Now what had Robert done? His cousin wanted to
escape the power of the smugglers, but Robert seemed to

be involving him even more deeply. I couldn't believe he would be so cruel. From across the street, I tried to keep my eyes on them, but I had to stop when I tripped and ran into Susan and dropped a few packages. By the time Susan had reloaded them into my arms, I looked up and the two men had moved on. I didn't allow myself to be distracted again.

My nerves were stretched thin when finally, as dusk began to leech the light out of the sky, we made our way down Upper Sea Road.

"Are you sure, Miss?" Susan whispered out the side of her mouth.

I nodded. She swallowed. And we entered Madam Fortunna's haberdasher and millinery.

I paused at the doorway, feeling a little guilty, but I determined to ignore that as I looked around me with wide eyes. A tall woman, dark of hair and eye was standing, with folded hands and lowered eyes, beside an older, buxom woman who was trying on hats. I felt some sympathy for the attendant maid who was also loaded down with packages. The dark woman, Madame Fortunna I apprehended, turned briefly, gave Susan's attire a brief, but thorough scrutiny, inclined her head minutely, and turned back to her customer. Me, she ignored.

I took advantage of her preoccupation and looked about with more attention to detail. Numerous small tables topped with very attractive hats adorned the middle of the room. One in particular would have tempted me had I not remembered that I was in guise of a servant, and no servant would buy that hat.

The perimeter of the shop was lined with counters stacked with laces, ribbons, and other trims. Toward the back were the threads, yarns, and sewing supplies.

I walked past the trims and fabrics and bent over the sewing supplies, carefully sneaking a glance through a broad gap in the curtains into a back room. Nothing to be seen but a storage and workroom with stacks of boxes, a table with piles of lace, feathers, animal furs, and silk flowers. Hat stands with bonnets in various stages of adornment testified of Madame's millinery skill.

I saw one wall lined with shelves and on the opposite wall a large floor to ceiling cabinet. Next to the cabinet was a stairway to an upper level, where I assume Madame lived. While we waited to be served, Susan looked over the selection of laces, holding samples up to the light, pretending to compare them. The sky continued to darken. Madame Fortunna took a moment away from her customer to light a few lamps. She paused near me and looked through the back room and gave both Susan and me a minatory look.

As she rejoined her higher-class customer, her manner became a little more brisk. I looked into the back room again and noticed through the window, the shimmer of a lantern coming up the path from the beach. Now Madame Fortunna's haste became understandable. It looked like she was expecting back door company.

I chose a spool of thread at random and took it over to the lace counter.

"I'm going to step outside," I said in an undertone, "I'll be back in a moment. Buy this and enough lace to keep her busy."

I didn't wait for her to argue, but looking back as I slipped out the door, I caught Susan's appalled look before the older lady stepped between us on the way to complete her sale.

No one was on the street as I walked around the side

of the shop. A line of bushes barred the way, but I pushed through them, dropping all my packages under the last. I crouched and made my way in the shadow of the building toward the back of the millinery.

In the slight glow of their lantern, I could distinguish two hulking shadows making their steady way up the path, the white of their shirts bobbing eerily in the near dark. I looked down and noticed my own white. I tore the cap off my head and replaced the dark bonnet. I untied the apron and ran back to tuck them under the shopping. The black dress was a blessing as it faded into the shadow. Back to the corner of the shop I made my way to watch as the lantern bobbed ever closer. To my surprise, when they came to a small hill topped with a tamarisk bush, they disappeared from view.

Obviously, Madame Fortunna was more than a humble milliner. Deciding quickly, I pulled myself onto the wooden porch attached to the back of the building and scrambled up to my knees. I tried the back door. To my surprise, it was unlocked.

Before I could talk myself out of it, I slipped inside, looked around quickly in the near dark and chose a spot on the far side of the cabinet. The last vestiges of light through the dirty window caught dust motes and highlighted patterns of dust on the floor. Her hats were beautiful, but I was not impressed with her housekeeping.

Quite suddenly, I realized that when Madame Fortunna came to lock the back door, she couldn't miss me. I looked through the curtain and saw her locking the front door, and I quickly slipped across the storage room and slid between a waist high tower of boxes and the shelves. I knelt on the floor between.

My heart pounded; my breath sounded as if I'd just run up two flights of stairs. I took one deep gulp of breath, held it while I counted to four, and let it escape slowly through my mouth. I wrapped my arms around my waist, made myself as small as I could, and waited.

Madame came in and pulled the curtain between the front shop and the storage room closed. Wasting no time, she unlocked the cabinet and removed a metal box. This she also unlocked. She counted her money before putting it in the box, again locking it and the cabinet.

Once her money was secure, she locked the back door and pulled curtains across the window so not a bit of light could escape. Even then she shuttered her lamp until it only let out a thin beam of light before hanging it on a hook by the door. I began to breathe a little easier as the shelves where I hid were now in deep darkness. I thought she might ascend the stairs, but then I heard the scrape of the table being pulled across the floor and the creak of rusted hinges. I heard her light steps going down, then only the muted sound of the surf.

I counted to one hundred, twice, then slowly crawled out of my hiding place. In the small glimmer of the hanging lamp, I could see where the table had been, the rug rolled back and a trap door propped open, six stairs descending, then a small landing where the stairs turned, leading into a gaping maw like Aladdin's cave. I felt cooler, fresher air and heard the low rumble and crashing of the waves, but that was all.

I took a deep breath. If I went down there, how would I get out? Of course, the smugglers were getting in from some entrance unseen from the road. Surely I could get out the same way after they left. I closed my eyes for a moment hoping I was not mistaken and started down. As I descended the stairs, the dark swallowed me. I opened my eyes as wide as I could, hoping to catch sight of deeper shadows in the dimness. I put my hand on the rock wall to my right, so I wouldn't fall, and when I got to the landing, I saw by a small glimmer of light, the bottom of the stairs and the sand floor, stone walls, the crates, barrels, and casks strewn all over the room below.

I heard a grunt, and someone swore. I realized if I stayed on the stairs, I would inevitably be seen, so I forced myself down and, more by feel than sight, found a very small space and squeezed myself between a stack of crates and some casks near the stairs. From the other end of the room two deep voices and one female voice moved toward me. My heart trembled to think what would have happened if I had stayed poised on the stairs.

"You were supposed to come tonight and take the brandy, not bring more."

"It will have to wait," deep and surly, his voice boomed in the dark.

"Put them here."

Heavy grunts spoke to the weight of the casks.

"Why didn't these come with the last shipment?" No more was Madame's voice subservient, "I can't have you just showing up at my back door of a night, especially with the moon waxing gibbous."

"These are the casks we had to sink partway to shore when the patrol came too near. We lifted them into our boats this morning and hid them under our nets and catch," deep voice explained,

"The patrols have been even more bothersome than usual this last week," this speaker's voice was high but more chilling, "and you'll do your job and keep your mouth shut."

"I don't need you to tell me my job," I heard the hate and the fear in Madame Fortunna's voice, "and it isn't my mouth you need to worry about?"

"I know a way you could use her mouth," the deep-voiced man sounded amused.

"I'll ignore that vulgarity," her voice took on an imperious tone, which I thought was brave considering the company. "What more can one expect from the unwashed and untutored?"

When no answer was forthcoming, she continued, "What is the holdup with the delivery? I was told he had buyers for this shipment."

"It's His High and Mighty's job to decide the when and where of delivery. Our job to bring the load in, yours to store it," I swallowed nervously, fearing the violence inherent in his voice.

"I do my job," the venom in her voice intensified.

"And get paid plenty for it." Even directed at someone else, that chilling high voice raised the hair at my nape.

Only the sound of heavy breathing met his reminder.

I heard retreating footsteps on the rocky path, but Madame Fortunna paced and muttered, so I remained silent and hidden.

In what seemed a very long time, but was probably only minutes, I heard the men returning.

"The preventatives have been even more vigilant after those ill-conceived murders," her voice was calmer, but her words were more frightening in spite of it, "What was he thinking, allowing those bodies to be dragged up and dropped at the door of one of the gentry? Why didn't they do what they always do and row them out and dump them overboard.

"She's right, I think," deep voice said, "these weren't townspeople or farmers to be used to scare the rest into keeping their mouths shut. It's death to any man caught killing a riding officer."

"It's not for the likes of us to question," the leader's tone brooked no arguments, "maybe Wilkins knows, but in the end, he will do what Himself says, and if Himself is playing a deep game, it makes no difference to us." He paused, and with menace continued, "so you'll keep watch for us and make hats while we move what we need, and when we need."

I suppose even Madam Fortunna recognized the finality of his words. The men made another trip away and back before she spoke again, this time quietly, "Will this be gone before the next shipment?"

"I don't know." The deep voiced man answered also quietly, and I guessed the other man, the one who scared all of us, must not be in the cellar.

"I assume we're still planning for the next new moon, no change in location?"

"No change," deep voice answered. "Although, you'd think we'd move further east with a watch set every few leagues and only a pistol shot needed to be bring riders raining down on us, but we're still at Little Galley Hill on the second. Word is a big package coming in this time."

The sound of heavy steps stopped their talk.

A big package. Is that what Robert had arranged? How could I find out? I needed to know before the run if I was to have any chance of stopping Robert. There were only ten days until the next new moon. What could I do before then?

The men made one more trip.

Pins and needles pained my feet and anxiety plagued my thoughts, but terror kept me still until the men left once more and I heard a door close and the clang of a lock. My heart sank. The cellar entrance had a lock. No matter the greater risk, I would have to go back through the shop.

Madame, guided by the small stream of the light of the final lantern, climbed the stairs to the shop. I waited until all sound of footsteps faded. Then I waited longer to make sure she had time to climb her stairs, ready herself, and go to sleep. When I was sure no one would be about, I climbed the stairs by feel, stubbing my toe on one of them. My head hit the door, and I stopped and rubbed it until the ache subsided. When I pushed up against the trap door, it didn't budge. I pushed again with every bit of my strength. The door moved minutely but was too heavy to open. I realized that Madame Fortunna had moved the table back over the door.

I was trapped.

Chapter 15

Liars are the cause of all the sins and crimes in the world

Epictetus

I turned around and sat on the stair in the dark. A terrible painful pressure began to build in my chest. I couldn't breathe, and my heart pounded harder and faster with every moment. A mind-numbing cold settled into my bones. I trembled and my head spun until I thought I would faint. I knew, without any doubt, in that instant that I was going to die.

The dark was so complete that I struggled to feel where I began and where I ended. Panic overwhelmed me when my hand, invisible to my eyes, searched for something solid to hold onto and met only air. A whimper broke the dark. It took a few moments for me to realize that the sound came from me.

Finally, my flailing hand hit the wall. I sobbed and reached out again, pushing firmly against the rock and scooted a little closer to it. It was cool, rough, and a little damp. That awareness helped a little. My heart began to slow, so I put my other hand on the wooden step where I

sat and felt the rough texture, warmer and smoother than
the wall, but nearly as hard. I breathed in and smelled the
damp sea air and heard again the muted sound of the surf.
Reason tried to reassert itself. I would get out. I shuddered
again. I had to get out or I would go crazy before morning,
I thought in panic.

I tried to slow my breathing, but my mind wouldn't
settle. What if Madame. Fortunna came down again? Even
worse what if those men came back? They would think
nothing of, how did they say it, rowing out in their boat and
dropping me over the side. I sat in the darkness listening to
the restless surf, and all that I'd heard about smugglers and
spies came back to me in clear and vivid detail.

Finally, I understood, in a way I hadn't before, that
this wasn't a game. These people were merciless. They
wouldn't spare me. A distinct picture of bloated bodies and
blood-crusted uniforms came to my mind's eyes. That could
be me, I thought in horror. Maybe Susan was right, and
more than right. Maybe I was not in any way prepared for
this work.

Oh dear, Susan. Susan would be beside herself. For a
moment, deep regret for her fear and anxiety swamped me.
Then a bright question rose from the confusion. Would she
think to keep my father and aunt from finding out what I
had done? They couldn't find out! I took another breath at
that thought. It seemed almost familiar to me, as if I were
coming back to myself. I breathed in and out, in and out,
but the dark still pressed down upon me.

Maybe good memories would help. I thought of my
comfortable room, my pianoforte, my books, some soothing
tea and biscuits. Thoughts of my family and my friends
filled my mind. Quin.

Oh no, I choked a little, what would happen to my poor little dog if I never came home? Once more tremors overtook me.

Why had I taken the steps that had brought me here? I spent the next few minutes imagining my life as it had been before I overheard that conversation in my father's study. If I somehow got out of this cellar, I would stop what I was doing. I did not want to die. I had no training in espionage. I was not smart enough or brave enough to do anything to stop these men. What had I been thinking?

I could go back to those simpler days, I could forget—

I saw, in my mind, a picture of my father, spectacles slipping down his nose, reading Plato. His delight in my childhood antics, his steadfast, reassuring presence through our sorrow and loss, and his understanding and encouragement of my youthful interests and pursuits were the foundation upon which I had built my life.

And Robert—a flood of memories of Robert flashed through my mind—Robert laughing in the breeze as he raced on Saevio, standing firm and squinting into the wind and spray while piloting his sailing skiff, smiling down in triumph from the crown of an oak and then reaching down to help me climb up to join him—a lifetime of memories. And the ache and force of my love took me by surprise.

A humorless laugh escaped. I could lie to myself no longer. Of course, I loved him. Unwise as it was, it was also undeniable. I was, and had been for some time, in love with Robert Amesley.

What could I do but continue? I couldn't be so selfish as to ignore what I knew and leave them to their fate. I thought of our brave curate Mr. Jones' and his courageous homily. I must do right and trust that all would come right in the end. My father and Robert needed me.

But as I stared sightlessly and felt the dark press down upon me, the thought came again, I really didn't want to die. I folded my arms on my knees and rested my head on them, and for the first time in years, I cried.

My crying was so violent, I almost missed the sound of banging. I lifted my head and—yes, again a bang. They had come back! I scrambled down the stairs by feel and moved awkwardly and painfully back into my hiding place and listened to the repeated banging, until with a clanging crash and a scraping sound, a sliver of light pierced the dark. With another scrape, the door opened wider.

"Miss?" A terrified whisper.

"Susan!" I squeaked.

"Shh. Where are you? Come out of there, Miss Liza."

I'm sure I have never been so glad to see a familiar face. I limped out and hugged Susan who dropped an old horseshoe to hug me back.

"There's no time," she whispered as she put her arm around my shoulder and led me out, "let's get out of this viper's nest."

We retrieved the shopping and, after hurrying through town to the cart, we made our sorry way home. Along the way, my story came out. I told Susan everything, all the choices I'd made, all the things I'd heard and my plans for what I would do next.

She remonstrated passionately my foolish determination to continue, but even the dim light of the moon was enough for me to find my courage again. I would not be moved. Finally, she fell silent in surrender. I realized how lucky I was in Susan. Even though she didn't approve, she had saved my life. I knew she would not expose me, and I knew she would continue to help.

The most difficult consequence of my evening in the cellar was the swinging of my emotions. As September passed and harvest season continued, my courage and determination wavered and then strengthened, just to waver again. I felt, at unpredictable times, irritable and anxious. I tired easily and felt listless, and then surprisingly I would be filled with a frantic energy.

While my emotions pitched and rolled, I helped to gather the last of the garden vegetables, clean the greenhouse, and prepare the ground for winter. The long hours, hard labor, and cheerful company settled my mind and heart. I knew what was coming. I was determined to follow through, but until that time, I resolved to fully enjoy these autumn days.

When the night of the new moon finally came, despite my trepidation, I set my face to do what I must. This time I had Susan's help as I bound my breasts and donned John's clothes. Even under Susan's anxious eyes, I felt the liberating effect the second I pulled on his trousers. I was set free, free to move certainly, but also freed from the heavy weight of anxiety and self-doubt and from society's unyielding strictures about what women could and should do. I didn't want to be a boy, but I certainly liked how I felt when I wore my brother's clothes—stronger, smarter, more daring. Maybe Susan saw it in my face. If so, it just added to her concern.

I tried to plan for everything this time. I would not be trapped again because I was heedless.

Dark clouds were beginning to gather, so I wore John's old greatcoat. I locked Quin securely in the stable. A quick mount, as I'd learned, is almost impossible with a dog, and silence even more difficult. I brought extra food, as I was determined to stay the whole night if Robert again made the trip to France. I needed to know about that package.

Right before I left the house, I had what I thought was a brilliant idea. Hiding in a boat, while it had its benefits, would limit what I could see. There are not many other places to hide on the shingles of the beach at Little Galley Hill. But as I was considering my options, I remembered my aunt's opera glass. It folded into itself, but when pulled to its full length made everything look three times larger.

I would have to be very careful, of course, as her opera glass was very ornate and valuable, covered in ivory and jewels, and she was justifiably proud of it. But with that amazing invention, I could hide safely among the rocks set back from the surf and watch the action on the beach. While Aunt Beatrice was downstairs writing letters, I had Susan distract my aunt's dresser, and it was the work of a few moments to slip into her room and take the glass.

I left early enough to scout the area before dusk, but even with all my planning, I almost came to ruin.

A little distance before coming to the beach the road turned, and off to the left was a hill with a copse of trees. The perfect place to leave Old Blue, I thought. But as we ambled around that turn I saw someone else who had that same thought. A mounted man was just leaving the road. I'd recognize that striking blood gray anywhere. And seeing Saevio made Magnus, Robert's groom and confidante, immediately recognizable, even from the back and wrapped in a dark cloak. In the split second before he turned, I frantically lowered my head and hunched so my chin, mouth, and nose were buried in the folds of my coat. I lifted my hand casually, coughed a greeting, and continued along the road hoping my disguise was sufficient. I felt his eyes on my back until I made the next turn.

What was this package that required Robert to bring his groom? And where was Robert? Why wasn't he riding Saevio?

I continued on the road, but I didn't dare stop on the closer side of the bay. I didn't want to cross Robert either coming or going. After some thought I rode right by the beach and found a place to tie my horse some ways East of Little Galley Hill. It would be a walk there and back, but I wouldn't be discovered.

A light drizzle made my careful search for a safe, but advantageous spot unpleasant. I was grateful for my brother's greatcoat, but no matter how I tried, some water trickled down the back of my neck, and if it continued raining, I would probably end up with wet feet. But I couldn't let such trifling concerns discourage me. I found a depression between some rocks, a little distance from the dock. I tested my opera glass, and the details of the boats came into sharp focus.

I positioned my coat and settled in for a long uncomfortable wait. I did worry about the lack of light—not only was there no moon, but clouds and rain obscured the view; how was I to see anything? But surely smugglers had to see as well. In all their experience, they must have found a way.

I waited. The rain stopped then started again. I took out the opera glass and studied the coastline west toward Bexhill then east toward Hastings. I watched the road, both ways. I counted the boats then split them into fishing skiffs, tub boats, cutters, sailing vessels and counted again. I noted how many were built clinker, with their planks overlapping, and how many carvel, with smooth hulls because their planks butted up against one another.

The depression where I sat slowly filled with water. I was just thinking about moving, even though the dark was now absolute, when a fishing boat slid into dock and disgorged three men. Soon another group of men made their way along the strand. I settled in to watch as the smugglers came by ones and twos and began to ready five small fishing skiffs. They did indeed have lanterns, shaded with blue glass, and shuttered to allow only slivers of unnatural eerie glow escape.

Before long, more than thirty men with carts and horses were assembled on the beach. I was so absorbed with the systematic industry of the smugglers, that I didn't see Robert arriving until he dismounted from a good-looking bay and strode boldly to the largest group of men.

Last time I listened but couldn't see well. This time I watched but couldn't hear. Both were unsatisfactory. Robert spoke for a time with the man whom I had decided was Wilkins. As he motioned seaward, I noticed a flash of light, a pause, and another momentary light.

Robert pulled a bag from his greatcoat pocket and gave it to the smuggler. I thought about the guineas in Robert's library. Is this what he had all that money for? The money seemed to satisfy the man, and Robert boarded one of the tub boats that were rowing out toward the shadowed ship. Each boat held two or three men.

My seat became progressively soggy. I shivered every once in a while, but what could I do but wait with increasing misery?

Finally, I saw the shadows of the returning boats, loaded down with casks and tubs. I searched each one as they approached. The fourth boat was not as heavily loaded, and I recognized Robert's form aboard. I pulled the opera glass from under my coat and wiped the lens on my shirt. Again, I lifted the glass and watched that boat as it pulled onto the beach. Robert leapt agilely to shore. Another man followed, then Robert turned back.

And he did something so unexpected it took me a few moments to understand what I was seeing. He leaned back into the boat and lifted the third passenger and cradled him—no, I blinked and shook my head.

When I looked through the glass again, I realized the third passenger was not a man—it was a woman that he cradled so tenderly against his chest. She was covered in a dark cloak and the light was so dim, but there was no mistaking. She was small and slim against his height and broad shoulders. Robert was carrying a woman up the beach beyond the reach of the waves.

Gently he let her down but held her shoulders until she was steady. In a light breeze, her hood fell back, and I saw her dark hair, darker even than Robert's, and her pale face gazing up at him. Even from this distance and in the dark, I recognized adoration. I watched numbly as he reached out and carefully pulled her hood back over her head. Then he put his arm around her and walked, leaning over her protectively, until he came to his horse. He lifted her into the saddle, took the reins and started to walk away from me.

I sat frozen watching the road even after Robert and his—his package disappeared from view.

Slowly, meticulously, as if I would break if I moved too quickly, I folded the opera glass and carefully put it in my coat pocket. I pulled my knees and my arms close to my body and shrunk into myself, heedless of the rain that beat down upon me. And something inside of me shriveled and withered. I was a dried, empty husk, silent and unseeing and mercifully unfeeling.

I don't know how long I sat there, unmoving, unthinking. When I came to myself, I wished I could return to that numb, dark, thoughtless place. Misery flowed, swelled, and broke over me, and my tears mixed with the rain.

I suppose the smugglers continued their work, rowing back and forth to the ship out in the channel, bringing back their contraband, and carting it away to Madame Fortunna's or another of their hiding places. I didn't watch. I laid my cheek on my knee, closed my eyes, and rocked back and forth, back and forth in agony.

I had to lift my head eventually. I couldn't breathe. My head pounded, and my eyes felt swollen and tender. I looked around and realized the tide had turned, and I was alone.

I stood and almost fell back into my depression in the rocks. I was stiff and my body throbbed. But slowly, painstakingly I crawled out of the rocks and up the incline to the road. And then I stopped, my footing unsteady, as if I wasn't on land at all, but on a storm-tossed sea with all the moorings set loose, pitching on vast and treacherous waves, and with no familiar landscape in sight.

In time I decided that since I was still breathing, I would move forward. Steering-way, I told myself. Rather than just getting pushed around by waves and wind, I had to keep the bow pointing into the waves to plow through them safely. My laugh sounded wild, irrational— frightening. I had already been struck sideways by the submerging wave. My ship had already rolled and sunk.

Old Blue was where I left him. I staggered to him and draped my arm around his neck, sobbing once against his warm bulk. He nodded as if he knew what I was feeling. I rested for a while, but eventually I pulled myself into the saddle and gently kicked my horse forward. It was just by luck that I didn't meet anyone. I didn't think to take precautions or even to watch as we made our slow way home. I just let Old Blue take the lead.

Eventually, he ambled straight to his pasture gate and stopped. I slid down out of the saddle, let him into his pasture, blindly rubbed him down, and set the gate.

I climbed the back stairs as first light began to leach into the sky. I turned my back on the dawn of a new, terrible, incomprehensible world where everything I thought I had known, I knew no longer.

Chapter 16

Truth emerges more readily from error than from confusion

Frances Bacon, *Novum Organum*

Susan was beside herself as she harried and scolded me out of my wet, sandy clothes and into bed. She asked and asked again, but I couldn't talk, not yet. So, she built up the fire, pulled an extra blanket over me, blew out the candles, and left me staring at the ceiling as the light of the new day spread.

Still sleepless a few hours later I rose, washed, and went downstairs to join my family for breakfast.

My father, as usual, was hidden behind his newspaper. Aunt Beatrice was chattering about her plans for the day. I looked out the window at the newly washed landscape, the raindrops sparkling in the blinding sunshine like scattered crystals, and the sky, a cloudless expanse of pallid blue.

Everything had changed, but the world continued on in its heartless course. My family was arrayed before me like a scene from a play, their customary dialogue moved forward without a discernible ripple. So familiar, but unrecognizable and unreal.

Father folded the newspaper and handed it to me, "Robert came this morning." My heart jumped. Everything in front of me—sights, sounds, smells, took on sudden, painful, bright transformation. "He tells me that quite early this morning the preventatives knocked on his door wanting to conduct a search of his home for contraband."

"How upsetting," my aunt handed me the platter of eggs, "I say, they are getting very impertinent, going out of their way to trouble good, honorable people. I hope he sent them on their way."

"He let them search." Father waited for me to pass the eggs. I hastily slid some onto my plate and passed the platter, "they were very thorough, apparently."

"Well," Aunt Beatrice paused, a slice of bacon halfway between her plate and her mouth, "I'm not sure I approve. Poor Robert is being hounded without purpose. He was found innocent of the murders at the inquest. To pursue him further is just harassment. It sets an alarming precedent. They will begin to assume they can come into anyone's home uninvited." The bacon disappear into her mouth. She chewed meditatively. "I certainly wouldn't allow them into my home to search," she said after she swallowed.

"If they come, you will certainly let them in," father's voice was unusually firm, "we have nothing to hide."

"Of course not!" She put down her fork, "but it's unseemly for them to cast aspersions on our good name and invade our home. It is vastly inappropriate—vulgar even."

"Nevertheless, we will cooperate with the local preventatives."

A disapproving silence settled over the room.

I wondered if the preventatives searched more than

the cellars and larders. I doubted that's where Robert hid his—contraband, I thought bitterly. And if they searched his library and his study, what would they have found? For that matter, I thought faintly, what would they find if they searched my father's study?

Panic threatened, and guilt settled in my heart and mind. If only I had been smarter, understood sooner, maybe talked with my father, talked with Robert. After I'd found those riding officers, I knew how serious it was, how dangerous. I should have—

"You don't look well, Elizabeth,"

I looked up to find my aunt's eyes fixed on my face.

"I didn't sleep well last night," I murmured.

"Why don't you go rest a little longer?" She placed a dollop of jam on her plate between concerned glances at me.

I looked at my plate and felt sick, "perhaps I will." I placed my napkin on the table and excused myself.

"I'll come up presently, shall I," she asked, "I'll bring a posset or tea?"

"Thank you, Aunt," I smiled, "but I think I'll just sleep a few hours. I'll be fine then, I'm sure."

Surprisingly, I did sleep. When I woke mid-afternoon, my hollow abstraction and my guilt had been replaced with a bright turbulent, and nearly unrestrained anger.

I pulled the pillow from behind my head and hit it again and again and threw it across the room. I threw my head back and screeched then climbed out of bed and, with hands fisted, looked around for something upon which to vent my fury. Feeling heat rise up my neck and into my face, I growled and stomped around the furniture, gesticulating wildly.

I picked up the carving of a curlew—a gift from Robert. Remembering his words and his smile, I threw it at the wall across the room. It fell unmarred to the floor, and I screamed in frustration. I started toward it meaning to try again, but angry tears blurred my sight, and I hit my thigh on the foot of the bed. I felt a sob rise as I rubbed my leg, panting from the hurt and from my determination to stop crying. He didn't deserve even one of my tears. I turned away and stomped to the window and left the bird where it had fallen.

How dare he? I had worried and had endangered myself, putting myself in the way of ruthless men and women hoping to learn more, trying to save him. And he spent his time and money and abandoned his honor to bring that woman here.

I stared sightlessly out the window and cringed as I thought about the way he had played with my affections while he secretly schemed, how he put money in the pockets of men who were breaking the law and terrorizing the neighborhood, all for a woman. Maybe this was his whole purpose, to bring her to England from the continent. Maybe he wasn't involved in traitorous activity, and maybe he had a reason to bring her here.

I tried for a few minutes but could find no worthy reason for smuggling a girl into England in the middle of a moonless night. Ruthlessly I berated myself for even now, having seen his perfidy, trying to defend his actions. No. He was a blackguard, a villain. I hated him. And I was furious at myself for being such a fool.

I shook with the force of my outraged tears. My breathing became labored and jagged. I knuckled my face and shook my head. Would he laugh if he knew how consumed with worry I had been, how anxious for someone who obviously didn't deserve even a thought or minute of my time?

And the height of his arrogance—blithely inviting customs officials into his home. Of course, they weren't looking for a woman. Who would even think of that? I certainly hadn't. How he must be laughing at how easy I was to distract, to deceive—the liar, the cheat. I pounded the wall next to the window. The dissolute, debauched, depraved, degraded degenerate.

My laugh held more than an edge of hysteria, and it scared me into silence. I put my head against the cool window and closed my eyes. I breathed as deeply as my stuttering lungs would allow. I breathed and breathed again, looking for sanity.

I couldn't do this anymore. I couldn't. And then over everything settled a fragile calm. I wouldn't do it anymore.

I would no longer worry about Robert's fate. He deserved whatever consequences his actions caused. I would lock him out of my mind and my heart. When I saw him, I would treat him with aloof hauteur. Yes! Cold-hearted contempt.

I washed my face and changed my dress. An afternoon walk with Quin sounded just right. And I would take my gun.

After checking the cloud covered sky, I pulled on my cloak and my boots, put my gun in my pocket and went to get my dog.

The fields were still full of harvest workers, so I made my way to the priory ruins, picking up fallen apples on the way. I set them in a row on the crumbling west wall of the ancient building, walked back twenty-five paces, turned and shot. One apple exploded. I felt a small flicker of satisfaction.

I wished I could say that I was disciplined enough that I wouldn't spare one thought for his touches, his kisses, that I didn't remember every word, every action. The ache was unrelenting. Why would he do this to me?

I rubbed the tears out of my eyes angrily as I primed and reloaded. Another shot, another apple.

It would be one thing for him to have gone to war and met someone and formed a connection. My heart sunk to think of it, but I tried to reason past the sorrow. We'd had no understanding when he left for the Navy. There were women on the continent, daughters of officers and diplomats. He surely didn't spend all his time aboard his ship. He might have brought someone home with him.

Trying to be rational, I supposed the possibility had existed that I would meet someone and find my feelings engaged while I was in London. Or I could have developed a tendre for someone locally, say with—here my thoughts stopped. I could think of no one. But I assured myself stubbornly, I could have fallen in love.

Either or both of us could have married someone else. He could have come home with his wife or met my husband, and we would have been nothing but childhood friends who had a former tender, youthful relationship. But that wasn't the case. Anger flared again briefly.

He hadn't cleanly broken those bonds between us. He'd come home and sought me out. He'd brought gifts and shared glances and laughed with me. He'd kissed me. He'd kissed with me and told me he wouldn't hurt me. Then he brought her here.

Another apple exploded, and the blast echoed back to

me on the breeze.

Maybe it was this woman on the boat that started Robert down this path. Perhaps his passion had overcome his honor. Did that change things?

No, at least not for me it didn't.

Two more apples blown to small fragments.

Would this girl be just a passing interest? I thought about this for a while, then realized that didn't matter either. More than preferring another to me, as painful as that was, there was the deception and the betrayal I could not tolerate. And a memory of his tenderness toward her that night on the beach was forever seared into my mind.

One last apple blown into the air in pieces. I lowered the gun, took a deep breath and nodded. No more. I was finished.

We were almost home when my fragile peace was broken. That conversation I'd overheard in my father's study so many weeks ago came to my mind in horrible detail.

Anxiety again settled in. What would Robert do now? Obviously, someone had some serious suspicions about his activities. Would that suspicion spread to my father? Would we also have preventatives at our door?

My father, I feared, did not have the same proficiency with secrets and subterfuge as Robert did. I couldn't imagine him calmly watching as authorities combed through his home and possessions, his personal effects.

Hopefully after Robert came this morning, my father destroyed any incriminating documents that might have been lying about in his study. If I talked with Robert and told him everything I'd seen and heard, would he mend his ways or at least allow my father to extricate himself? Would my father stop, even if Robert continued?

Another restless night and still I was staggering from the revelations and overwhelming emotions. I made no significant plans. I wasn't sure what, if anything, I wanted to do. So, I decided to do nothing, at least for another day.

Fate had other plans.

By mid-morning I could mope around the house no longer, and I noticed my aunt's concerned looks, so I spent the rest of the morning in the stable and stable yard. There is nothing like animals to calm a troubled heart.

Mid-day came and I still felt lazy and indifferent. But though Charlie and the grooms would say nothing, I could tell they were constrained by my protracted presence, so I petted and hugged Quin one more time and wandered out into the bright sunlight.

Where to go now? I couldn't face my bedroom. My emotions were so raw that music would deepen, not soothe my grief. I'd found the day before that I couldn't walk far enough to escape.

As I stood in the yard rolling a small stone back and forth under my foot and staring at the back of the house, an idea presented itself. We kept up a subscription to the circulating library in Bexhill, and I had a novel that I had been too busy to read as yet. It would be a relief if I could live in someone else's life for the rest of the afternoon. Eagerly, I retrieved Camilla, A Picture of Youth from my bedroom, and I headed to the morning room, which was blessedly empty.

The three North facing windows provided a pearly light that usually pleased me, but that day it just lit the dust motes floating in the slanting sun. The Persian carpet and the quercitron upholstery were faded, perhaps even shabby. At least the smell of the lemon oil that the maids used to polish the wood table and chairs in the center of the room assured me that they had already finished their work here, and I would be undisturbed. It was a little cool, so I moved towards chairs that flanked the fireplace.

And looked down in disillusionment. Listless flames told the story of servants who assumed no one would enter there that late in the day. I shrugged and chose one of the deep mahogany wingback chairs. Pulling it closer to the fire, I angled it so I could turn my back on the depressing room and make the most of the available heat. I pulled my feet up, wrapped my skirt around them and became acquainted with Camilla Tyrold and her sisters, sweet Lavinia and deformed, but kind, Eugenia, and their beautiful cousin, Indiana Lynmere.

I might have titled the novel Eugenia instead of Camilla, but maybe that was because, though I felt sorry for her physical deformities, Eugenia seemed of all the characters to be most sensible to me, perhaps because her education most closely mirrored mine. I chuckled and shuddered in turn, and sometimes rolled my eyes, but I was grateful to wallow in these poor girls' emotional and mental dilemmas and the schemes of the attending adults and forget my own for an afternoon.

I nodded off, but not for long as my first thought when I woke was of Camilla, who had freed Edgar from their engagement and moved to Southampton. I caught the sliding book right before it fell out of my lap. It took a moment for the click of the closing door to alert me that my retreat had been breached.

"Beatrice has the maids cleaning in my study. We can talk in here," my father's voice broke the quiet.

There was a pause, and I heard my father and his guest

pull chairs away from the table. I began to unfold myself so I could stand and announce my presence but stopped when I heard his company's voice.

"You trust them?" My fickle heart still jumped as Robert spoke.

"I do, but I lock away any revealing documents before they enter."

"If the customs service is going to make a habit of surprise searches, we both should find more secure places for our sensitive papers," Robert thumped the table.

My father cleared his throat, "it is our good luck that you had already sent the last packet to Etienne LeFevre when the officials came to your house this morning."

I froze and closed my eyes in despair. There was nothing for it. I had to sit and listen, ensnared again in the trap I thought I had escaped.

"Yes, although I have taken more precautions in case they come again. They will not find anything that I don't want to be discovered," Robert's confidence angered me.

"And what have you heard of the search for LeFevre?" My father asked.

"They came close last week," Robert's chuckle surprised me. "He escaped moments before they knocked down the door of his place on the Quai des Celestins." Why would Robert find that amusing?

"And the information?"

"Yes, I received word that it arrived as expected," Robert's words pounded through me, "but someone gave notice at the last moment to His Majesty's 2nd Dragoons. They were alerted to the trap."

"Here is the next packet." I closed my eyes as my father's words proclaimed him guilty.

"I'll give it to Wilkins tomorrow night. They are planning to deliver their last shipment."

I stared blindly at the dying embers as their conversation moved from espionage and talk of another packet, to smuggling to every-day politics with an ease that still somehow surprised me. Even after they left, I sat for a long time thinking about what they had said.

My guilt for eavesdropping lasted barely a moment before I reminded myself of all the times over the last two days that I had hurt, and worried, and tried to find excuses for Robert's behavior. But no! He had deceived me. I had seen his—warmth as a serious interest in me. I had responded. Worse, I had lied for him, if not in so many words, at least in intent.

Maybe I could understand better if I thought that the horrors of war and the wound he had received were cause for some of his present actions. Maybe—at least I could tell myself that he wasn't himself—that it wasn't the Robert that I knew who was doing this. But I didn't really believe that.

Taking all that into account, Robert owed me the information I needed to save my father. He wouldn't give it freely, so I would take what I was owed.

It was a sign. I wasn't meant to ignore this situation. If Robert were discovered, it would endanger my father. It didn't matter how he came to be in this situation. I would have to continue, not for Robert—No! But for my father. And I was finished with watching, gathering information, and waiting for my chance to save my father. I would act more directly.

My decision brought me an unexpectedly profound and a demoralizing relief. I sat in stunned disbelief, then I chuckled despairingly as I finally faced the truth. Even now I loved Robert.

Oh, I knew I couldn't be with him. I would not live a life, as so many noblewomen in our country did, ignoring their husbands' philandering, expecting and receiving no more than discretion as they were repeatedly betrayed. I wouldn't. But I still could not sit back and let him die. Even if he was never to be mine, I needed to know that somewhere in the world, Robert lived, even if it was with a French seductress.

And yes, I realized my own bitterness. And realized at the same time, with some mortification, that there was some secret part of me that thought, even hoped, I might somehow still come between him and this woman. I laughed, again mirthlessly, but accepted my secret hopes.

I would just have to make sure that my feelings didn't weaken my resolve. Robert wasn't the man I'd thought he was, but I would remain his friend. I wouldn't stand by and watch him compromised by some foreign charlatan, no matter how enamored he was with her.

I looked down at my hands, still gripping Camilla, A Picture of Youth and felt very old. I knew I wouldn't be finishing the novel. I couldn't escape my life, no matter how I tried. I would just have to face the pain, the sorrow, the fear and move on.

The coals in the morning room fireplace were almost dead now, a mound of gray ash with only a few specks of lingering sparks. I was exhausted, but finally at peace.

Everything was different, but nothing had changed. I sorrowed, but I would still fight for him. I would still find a way to save them both.

Chapter 17

I detest the man who hides one thing in the depth of his heart and speaks forth another

French Proverb

If I hadn't already resolved to take action, my aunt's conversation at breakfast the next morning definitely would have moved me, at least to leave the house. My father had ridden off early for one of his trips to London, and after the servants had closed the door to the breakfast room, my aunt put down her napkin and cleared her throat.

"My dear," she squirmed a little then sat up straight, "I'd like to talk with you."

I lifted my brows but stayed silent as my heart sank. Those words never prefaced anything I wanted to hear.

"Yes, hmm," her eyes roamed the room as if looking for inspiration, "I've noticed," she grimaced, "and so has your father, of course," her hands played with her napkin, "that you've been feeling poorly."

"I'm feeling well enough today, thank you aunt."

She ignored me, "I can't help but notice that you have been often absent when Robert comes to call," her color rose.

Oh, please no, I thought.

"And equally apparent is your unease when you are in the same room with him."

I shook my head but realized that she was not looking at me and that nothing I could say would stop her when she thought she was doing her duty. I sunk down in my chair.

"I feel I must ask if," she came as close to cringing as I'd ever seen, "if he has done anything that has offended your sensibilities," her eyes flashed up briefly and lowered again and color rose in her cheeks, "I refer to anything improper."

"Of course not," I squeaked. Then memory of his mouth on mine, and his hands, oh those cunning hands, pulling me against his hard body, his lips, and his tongue following the line of my throat—ah, there was not any chance I would ever tell Aunt Beatrice about that.

I suppose, I redirected my thoughts desperately, that my sensibilities were offended by the smuggling and spying and definitely by that woman, but that wasn't what my aunt was asking, and I wouldn't be sharing that with her either.

"If there is an understanding between you," she squirmed, "you might tell us. It is my understanding that men have certain, hmm—desires that may, if you're not prepared, seem hmm—frightening."

"No, no, no," I stammered.

"And though," she continued doggedly, "before marriage, these," she cleared her throat, "passions should not be . . . given free reign, it is not all that uncommon that a man may, under certain circumstances, forget him—"

"Aunt Beatrice," I interrupted firmly, "Robert and I have no understanding. We haven't," I paused and felt the heat rise in my face.

Her shoulders dropped, "well," she sighed deeply, "well then."

Why did I get the feeling that under her relief there was some disappointment?

"Liza if that is the case, I must assume that you have argued with Robert."

"No, I——"

"I must tell you, Liza, that confrontational behavior is not the way to accomplish what you want. You must learn to find more subtle, resourceful ways of dealing with men—ways that don't encourage them to become irritable or defensive. You must know once a man has set his mind against something, there is no reasoning with him."

"Aunt, I haven't argued with Robert," which was true, sort of, but I felt ready to argue with my aunt. I was more than a little affronted at her assumption that I was at fault for any difficulties between Robert and me.

But when I looked up, I almost laughed at her look of consternation.

"I was sure, watching you this week that all was not well between you. You have been sullen and despondent."

I shook my head and decided distraction was what was needed, and definitely a change of topic. I smiled and said, "When we were walking on Sunday, Maris, Lady Helen, Miss Hatton and I, we talked about walking into town to-day for some shopping. If you don't need me?"

"Oh, I do like to see you spending time with girls your age," Aunt Beatrice picked up her napkin, and looked down at her plate. Then she grimaced and pushed her cooled food aside. "You'll want to ride over to the Squire's?" She asked as she went to the sideboard to fill a new plate.

"I thought I'd walk," I said as I rose to leave. There was no way I could have eaten another bite.

I neglected to mention to my aunt that the plans with my friends were for that afternoon, which allowed me time to pursue my own endeavors that morning. I took my spying clothes, as I had begun to think of them and hid them behind the stable, so I wouldn't have to go in the house and chance my aunt stopping me. Then I headed through the woods towards Robert's house.

Quin followed as I walked and thought. I discarded plan after plan as soon as they formed in my mind. It was obvious that I had to get those papers, and before tonight's meeting. With that in mind, but no particular plan, I made my way through the woods towards Amesley Hall.

I stopped short of the edge of the trees and watched the house. I was almost sure Robert and his father were away from home. They were still harvesting the field east of the grange. I knew they liked to spend some time every day in the height of the season with their tenants and workers. But the servants would be about. What were the chances I could get in and out without detection?

I looked down and noticed that Quin had left me to explore. When I looked up again, the side yard was empty. I ran before I knew I was going to, heading for the tradesman's entrance. I let myself in and leaned back against the door, breathless at my audacity.

Listening carefully, I made my way through the halls. From this direction, I avoided the grand entrance, the drawing room, dining and breakfast room. Only once did I hear footsteps, and I slipped into the billiard room and waited for them to pass. Luck was with me. The servants must have finished the ground floor cleaning and moved up to the first floor.

I took a deep breath to steady my nerves and moved quickly to the library and to the chess set. Not until I stood with my hands on the case did it occur to me that Robert may have any number of hiding places, but when I pushed the carved bird's beak and opened the compartment, there they were—documents that were tangible and clear proof of my father's and Robert's treason.

Even expecting to find it, my heart sank. I spent a few minutes reading, but a shadow outside caught my eye. I moved soundlessly, pressing myself into the draperies and carefully peeked out the window.

The library faced the park, which was empty, but when I pressed closer, I could see the stable. And there crouched down, resting on his heels, I saw my downfall—Robert talking to and petting Quin. Even as I watched, Robert stood and snapped his fingers as he walked towards the path that led to my home.

I had no choice. I rolled the papers and stuffed them down the bodice of my gown where they crinkled and scratched. I ignored the discomfort and made a cursory check outside the door for servants and ran through the house and out the door. The path he took was the easier way, but if I was quick, and careful, I could take a more direct route and head him off before he reached my house.

My path was rockier and steeper, but I kept up my pace. I was breathing hard by the time I came to the stream, which moved quite fast and had some tricky currents along that stretch. I checked that the papers were still secure and hidden and lifted my skirts in one hand and held the other away from my side for balance. My luck held until I was mid-stream and stepped on one particularly slippery rock.

I leaned. I rocked, and finally I stepped off the rock and down into the stream with one foot rather than fall. I thought I was safe, but the current pushed against me. I stepped off of the rock with my other foot to steady myself. Even then, I rocked dangerously for a minute before I finally regained my balance.

I sighed in relief and stood for a moment in swiftly bubbling water and took stock. My feet and my legs below my knees were wet and cold, but I was still standing. I'd kept hold of my dress, so it wasn't soaked through. I might be able to hide most of the effects of my mishap. The papers were still safe. I waded slowly to the bank and stumbled up the rocks there.

I ran until I came to the path between our lands. Here I stopped and put my hands on my knees and panted.

When I could breathe evenly, I stood and looked back toward Robert's house. The path was empty, but I heard a yip from the other direction. They had covered ground quickly. I smoothed my hair as well as I could without a mirror and brushed a hand over my skirts, then I clapped and called, "Quin. Quin, where are you? Here boy."

I stood where I was until my dog appeared with Robert not far behind.

As he walked toward me, I suddenly remembered the stolen documents. I looked down quickly to make sure they weren't visible then lifted my chin and smiled brightly.

"Oh, you found him," I dropped to take Quin's head between my hands and scratch behind his ears, "thank you."

I crooned to my dog for a few minutes as I searched for composure.

"If he continues to escape, you won't keep him a secret for long," I couldn't read his tone, but when I looked up I noticed the smile in his eyes. Though he looked tired to me, I steeled my heart.

"Yes," I didn't rise, "I'm working on it."

He cocked his head and studied me like I was a column of sums that didn't quite add up, "now that you have your dog, allow me to walk you home."

"That's not necessary."

He just smiled and waited for me to rise. There was no avoiding him, so I smoothed my features and tried for an expression of polite disinterest. I turned toward home, intending to walk ahead of him, but he reached down pulled my arm through his, and kept me by his side.

I babbled. I hated it, but when I was nervous—and I was nervous, and so very conscious of those documents stuffed in my dress—I babbled. I feared to even breath too deeply, but apparently breath isn't necessary to fill the air with inane chatter.

By the time we neared home, he wore a look of confused forbearance, and though I tried to resist, he slowed our pace.

"Liza, I'd like to talk with you."

It seemed the universe was conspiring against me. I wasn't sure I could endure another uncomfortable talk, but there was nothing for it. I nodded and watched uneasily.

"You look like you're going to be tortured," he paused, but I just scowled, which seemed to amuse him rather than deter him, "come Liza, we can deal better than this."

I kept my mouth shut and watched a hawfinch take wing.

He continued doggedly, "matters between us since I

came home have not been comfortable." He waited for a
response, but I didn't feel inclined to help him.

"Liza Lou."

Oh, not fair, I thought, not fair at all.

"What can I do? What can I say to bring us to ac-
cord?" He stopped our forward motion and turned his
searching gaze to my face, "I miss the easy discourse that
we have always shared."

I blinked to hold back tears. I missed that too.

"I think of it often, and with affection."

I was speechless, stuck between what his words made
me want and what I knew to be true.

"I understand that over the course of four years people change. We are, both of us, different. I wouldn't expect
that we could go back to those childhood interactions, nor
would I want that," his voice deepened, "we are adults
now."

I felt flushed. How did he do this to me?

He took my hand and pulled until there was only a
small step between us, "it has occurred to me I might not
have given enough attention to the effects of the war on
families and communities at home—to you. I have been
thinking only of my part of this war."

I had to be fair, "of the two of us, you are the most
changed, the most affected , I believe." I was proud of my
neutral tone.

"I suppose, but surely you, who know me best, can
recognize that which remains unchanged in me?"

I looked down and watched our feet, "sometimes I
think I do, but then . . ."

He leaned forward, "but then?" He repeated.

My breath huffed out, "then I don't." My bitterness

would not be contained, "Sometimes I don't think I know you at all."

He winced but took my chin in his fingers and lifted my head until I met his eyes, "Liza, through all the noise and confusion of the last four years, I tried to keep a place," he paused, and shrugged uncomfortably, "where I could keep unchanged the most important things—God, England, my Father," he paused, and then quietly, "—you."

I started.

"And then I came back and found that everything I thought was constant had changed." He paused in thought, "well probably not God, though I'm no longer as sure that I know Him as I once thought I did." His smile was pained.

"What I need, Liza, what I'm trying to do is to find, or perhaps rediscover the important things that yet remain. It is alright if those things are different than they were. I am just hoping they might still be recognizable."

He searched my face and seemed to be satisfied with what he saw, "I think—I hope that together we might recapture something or create something strong, something solid and lasting."

I searched his face in return. I wanted so badly to believe his earnest and sincere speech. I wished with all my heart that I could. I wanted that Robert of old that I had always trusted with a force that made me dizzy. I could only imagine what he'd experienced in war and in returning home to find so much changed. I clearly saw his pain and also his strength. But—I couldn't ignore what he was doing, and I wouldn't allow myself to be deceived any more.

I took a slow step in the direction of my home, and he fell in beside me. I asked myself, what was at my core when all the storms of life rocked and swayed? I looked inside and found those same things Robert had listed. God, country, family, Robert—yes, he was still there, marred and wounded, confused and erring though he was. It is that which hurt the most.

But all the insight in the world and all my care could not undo those moments on the beach when I saw him lift and carry, then wrap his arm around that woman. His unspoken questions, what I felt he wanted from me, those I could not answer, but perhaps I could help him again find his faith, his patriotism, and his place in his family."

We were in sight of my home, so I stopped and put my hand on his arm and looked up into those gray eyes and gave him what I could, "Robert, the truest thing I can say is that I am, always, your friend."

He winced.

"I will help if I can, though it may not be as you want."

He lifted my hand to his lips, watching me closely.

I tried to keep all expression from my face, but something he saw made him smile, "I think, if you will, we can build what we want."

Before I could think of a response, he bowed formally and took his leave. I heaved a huge sigh of—relief certainly, but also of confusion, and of sorrow.

Chapter 18

Falsehood flies, and the Truth comes limping after it

Jonathan Swift,
"The Examiner No. XIV"

I watched until Robert was out of sight while I tried to decide whether or not to sneak up to my room and change out of my wet shoes. I knew Maris would willingly loan me some of hers, so I locked Quin into the stable, tucked my spy clothes under my arm, and started out to meet my friends, my boots squelching as I walked.

There is a wooded copse not far from Sidley Green where Wrestwood Road crosses Hollier's Hill. I looked around to make sure no one was in sight before I slipped between the trees. I couldn't walk around all afternoon with stolen papers hidden in my bodice. I worried about leaving them, but I could think of no other option, so I tucked them in the pocket of my greatcoat, refolded all the clothes around the packet, and hid the whole bundle behind a tangle of bushes. With one last look to make sure it was truly hidden, I continued on my way to the manor.

I needed to find a way to leave my friends by late afternoon at the latest so I could return and change. It might be awkward, but I trusted that something would occur to me.

On the way to the Squire's, I strived to push Robert out of my mind—no easy task—so by the time I arrived, well before Amelia and Lady Helen, I was more than ready for a distraction.

While we waited for our other friends, Maris and I had time to visit as we played with the Squire's dogs. I threw myself somewhat desperately into the conversation. The recent neighborhood activities—Judith Bellerton's Al Fresca breakfast, a musical evening at the Hatton's, and the boating excursion got up by the Dinmores, provided plenty of fodder for our gossip, but mostly we talked about the upcoming grand ball.

However, even that couldn't dislodge the lump that stuck in my throat, the heaviness in my heart. I contemplated going home to rest before my evening's prowl. I knew I would be poor company for my friends.

I wasn't so preoccupied with my own concerns that I didn't notice how often Maris mentioned Mr. Phillip Martin's name in passing.

"Maris," I broke into her cheerful chatter, "Phillip? He's a great friend of your brother's, isn't he?"

She blushed hotly, but smiled merrily, "Well, and so he was. He is still I suppose, but," she giggled, "Frederick isn't so very in sight these days when Phillip comes."

"He's quite sporting mad, isn't he?" I suggested gently.

"Well yes," she shrugged, "but so is my father, and it has never bothered me . . . or my mother that I have noticed."

I sat back at her defensive tone and met her eyes that begged acceptance, even approval. I smiled at her. Of course, if Philip was her choice, I would be happy for her.

He had always been perfectly polite to me, but would he appreciate . . ., then I laughed as I thought about Maris' competitive nature. She was ever one to get up a game of real tennis or croquet. And she loved wholeheartedly an archery competition or a boating race. Nor could I remember ever to have seen her quibble about a little boisterous noise or dirt. Of course, Phillip would think her perfect. I reached forward, with only a little twinge of envy—okay, maybe more than a little twinge, and hugged her.

"I can see an active, vigorous future for you, without a need for anymore 'gathering of shells,'" I sighed.

What must it be like to find your match and be at peace with it? To love a man with confidence that he honestly returned your regard? I wondered if I would ever experience that. It seemed more than unlikely. Sorrow engulfed me, but this was my best friend. She deserved for me to forget my own problems and share her joy, so I pushed away my own concerns.

"And he has some other talents that I find quite . . . agreeable."

My eyes widened at her sly tone, "Maris!"

"Just sometimes" she assured, "when we have a few moments alone, and nothing too, too improper," her dimples made an appearance as she lowered her eyes modestly.

"Maris," I laughed with delight, "has he spoken with your father? Are things fixed between you?"

Her smile was blinding, and happy tears brightened her bluebell eyes. "The banns will be called starting this Sunday, but I wanted to tell you before anyone else."

Shopping took on a new delight as I looked with an eye to Maris' upcoming nuptials. I hadn't truly expected to enjoy our outing, but often during the afternoon, our eyes met gleefully. And though our happiness couldn't help but spread to our companions, I don't believe they guessed her news, which was its own pleasure.

Our plan had included tea at Amelia's and an offer of her carriage to take us all to our homes after. As tea-time approached, I sought for a way to separate myself from the group. Lady Helen, much to my surprise, generously provided the idea as we were walking past St. Peter's. She slowed her pace, looking up at the dark gray facade.

I remembered her praise of Mr. Jones and smiled in satisfaction, "it's such a beautiful church. I always feel such peace here," I said in an aside to Lady Helen.

As I had expected, she leapt at the hint, "if you don't mind going on without me, I'd like to stop in," she blushed, "I have a question of some doctrinal import if our curate has time."

Before Amelia or Maris could remonstrate, I took Lady Helen's arm and said, "I'll go with Lady Helen. We can make our way home after we have—communed."

Maris gave me a shrewd look, and then she sighed as she took Amelia's arm, "I'm not in need of church today. Let's go and have tea. And I, for one will accept your offer of a ride. I have walked enough for one day."

I flashed a smile of gratitude and waved them off.

Mr. Jones approached almost as soon as we entered the church, and Lady Helen whispered, "Liza, I wouldn't want to bore you—"

"Oh, I understand completely," and this fit perfectly with my wishes, "and your questions may take some time. I will spend a few moments in quiet contemplation and make my own way home."

She smiled in satisfaction, and I took a seat in the

last pew of the nave, nodding to Mr. Jones as he passed.
I clasped my hands, bowed my head and listened as Lady
Helen and Mr. Jones walked slowly up the aisle choosing
seats right in front of the chancel. Their voices were a
hushed murmur. When I looked up, they were both im-
mersed in their discussion and each other, so I slipped out
the side door and hastened up the hill out of town.

My clothes were untouched where I'd left them. I sat in
my little copse and listened. I checked the road three time,
and still I sat. I found it unaccountably difficult to disrobe in
the open air. I felt as if unseen eyes were watching my every
move, but as the afternoon shadows lengthened, I forced
myself to strip down to my shift. I looked around nervously
as I hurried myself into John's clothes, struggling as always
with the cravat, and jumping at every rustle in the brush. I
breathed a deep sigh of relief once I was able to slide into
my greatcoat.

By the time I came to Madame Fortunna's, the sun was
setting in a blaze of red, coral and orange. It painted the
ocean as far as I could see in matching hues. Sailors and
fisherman would be happy for the portent, but it looked
like an ocean of blood to me. I shivered as I moved into the
bushes at the side of Madam Fortunna's shop.

I had just settled in for a long wait when a strong arm
banded across my midsection and a hand covered my
mouth. I struggled against an unbreakable hold, bucking
and kicking. My screams were muffled by an iron grip.

"Liza," firmly, but quietly came the voice that I recognized immediately.

My relief turned my knees to jelly. He removed his
hand. Emotions flashed through me in quick succession—
overwhelming relief, sharp guilt, acute embarrassment,

angry resentment.

I did the only thing I could, "What do you think you're doing scaring me like that?" I attacked.

"What are you doing here?" His anger was palpable, but his voice was quiet.

"What am I doing?" I have always rejected any suggestion that I might resemble my aunt in any way, but though I too was quiet, I heard her shrill tone in my words, and my chin may have trembled with my emotion. "What am I doing?" I repeated, "I'm not the one who is . . . ." I narrowed my eyes, "wait, how did you know I was here?"

His laugh was harsh and not amused, "it was not difficult. I went home after talking with you, after I asked you for—" He bit off the rest of his sentence and glared at me.

I glared right back.

"Imagine my surprise when I found my documents gone."

"They are not yours," was my instinctive response.

His jaw tensed, and his eyes blazed with rage, "mine more than anyone's."

I shook my head hotly, but he just kept talking, "I talked with my father, with Perry, with the servants—everyone in my household, everyone that I have trusted with my life and could not find the culprit. Then it occurred to me how unusual it was that your dog was waiting so patiently outside of my house when I came in from the fields. How convenient it was that I met you on that path. I began to wonder if I'd found the reason for the reserve between us. I couldn't believe it of you, but I had to be sure.

Your aunt told me about your shopping expedition. It was easy enough to find four young women cutting a wide swath through town. I followed you."

"Followed me?" He followed me!

He nodded, "all afternoon. I almost lost you at the church, clever of you and brave to enter there, I'm surprised a bolt of lightning didn't bring down the building around you when you walked in."

I sputtered, and a red haze blinded me, "you have no right to speak about God's judgment. It's not me that's—"

He talked over me, "It took longer than it should have for me to remember the side door. Just as I rounded the church, I saw you turn the corner."

I backed away, but he took ahold of my arm. His grip, while not painful, was firm. I lifted my chin. His tone had been brutal, but his eyes were despairing.

As we stared at each other, the sharp sound of feet on shingles rang in the growing dark. Robert looked up, his eyes scanning deliberately.

He flattened us both against Madame Fortunna's shop. I leaned forward and looked around him and could see a few shadowed forms making their way up from the beach.

Robert turned back to me and made an irritated rumble deep in his throat. He put his hand on my shoulder and turned me away from the beach so abruptly, it took my breath. He pushed me down until I was bent over ruthlessly made me walk before him, "stay down," his voice was just a thread of sound.

With his hands guiding me, we made our way to the hedge behind Brook Lodge, three buildings away from Madame Fortunna's.

"I will ask again, what are you doing?" Though his voice was muted, I still heard his disillusionment.

Through my gritted teeth, I repeated, "What am I doing? How can you ask?"

Robert ignored my question as his eyes scanned the area. He took my arm and pulled me even farther up the hill toward a thicket of trees where I saw Saevio was tied.

"Now, Liza," This was the first time I had seen 'Captain Amesley.' And though I was intimidated, my fear didn't overpower my anger. "Answer my question."

"I don't need to answer to you," I followed his example and continued to speak quietly, but my voice was sharp.

He reached out and snagged the documents from the pocket of my coat. He held them up in front of my face, "I would have believed it of anyone, even my father, before I would have believed you capable of treason."

Shock held me frozen.

"Liza, you must stop," he took my shoulders and shook me, briefly, but not all that gently. "If you are caught, those who are searching, on both sides of this war, won't care that you are a woman. I won't be able to protect you from their wrath, at least not for long."

"Protect me—Robert you are not making any sense. It isn't me that is—" I shook my head, "Stupid man, I'm trying to protect you and my father.

He stilled and stared at me in silence.

"You are trying to—" A lingering sigh, and he was silent again, but his shoulders dropped, and his jaw eased.

He seemed to suddenly remember where we were, "now is not the time to talk. Just know that your part in this is finished. If I have to tie you up to get you to stop—"

"Me to stop?" I knew I needed to be quiet, but I couldn't control myself. I broke out of his grasp and took a step back, "I'm not the one," my voice rose," who is meeting smugglers and betraying soldiers," I drilled a finger into his chest.

He put his hand over my mouth, and breathed into my ear, "Liza, if you continue like this, you are going to get me killed."

My chin dropped with a sudden rush of indignation, but I lowered my voice to a mere breath, "I get you killed? It's not me that's fallen in with outlaws and murderers."

"Have you stopped to ask yourself why I would—What do you think is going on, Liza?" The sound of metal striking metal came out of the dark. He stopped and listened and took a deep breath, "Liza, this is not the time," he took a firm grip on my arm and pulled me toward his horse.

I squirmed in righteous indignation.

"Liza, be still."

I opened my mouth to argue. But he pulled me to him and kissed me mercilessly until I stopped struggling. Then he gentled the kiss, skimming his hand up and down my back until I wanted to respond, wanted so badly to sink into his warmth and the promise he held out, but I remembered that his promises were all lies. I steeled myself and stood firm.

Only then did he pulled back, and I looked up at his shadowed features. He kissed me once more, hard and brief, and swept me up into his arms and onto Saevio's back before I could utter a sound.

"You'll have to ride astride, but you're dressed for it," his smile was a white gleam in the dark.

"Robert," I pulled myself forward to dismount.

His hand on my thigh stayed me, "Liza," he shook his head, "Liza Lou, I see that I will need to tell you all, but not here, not now. Trust me for just a little while, my dear. Go home, and I will come tonight, and we will talk."

Comforted that at least he was finally going to talk to

me, I leaned back and searched his face, "Robert——"

He shook his head, handed me the reigns, saying, "ride fast, ride low."

He slapped Saevio's hind quarters, "Home, Saevio."

And Saevio took off so quickly that I was almost unseated. I pulled myself forward and leaned over Saevio's neck and held on as his strides chewed up the distance, but I looked over my shoulder and saw Robert's silhouette darker than the dark night. He raised his hand briefly before he pulled his cloak about him and walked back toward the shore.

All the way home, well not my home—the stubborn, but glorious horse would take no direction from me, but on the way to Robert's home, I had time to think. Unfortunately, I still had no answers by the time we rode into the stable yard a very short time later.

Magnus stepped out, holding a shuttered lantern, "Captain Amesley?" He whispered.

"No, Magnus, it's Liza. Liza Henshaw."

"Where is the Captain? Is he hurt?"

"He wasn't when I left." Even in the dark I could see Magnus relax.

He helped me to dismount and left me standing in the yard as he took Saevio into the stable.

He joined me a few minutes later, "I'll walk you home."

"I don't——"

"I'll walk you home," he repeated. He gestured, and I gave up and started walking.

Though I tried, Magnus was not a font of information. He followed me silently, and then silently waited on the edge of our grounds until I came to the servants' entrance of our house. I waved and saw him turn and lope off into the trees.

In my room, I changed quickly into a walking dress and slippers. I walked quietly through the house to make sure all the servants were abed. When I was sure all was secure, I unlocked the front door. After some thought, I unlocked the back as well and settled in the morning room to wait. I stirred up fire but didn't light any candles.

I felt confused but hopeful as I sat in front of the fire and waited. In time, the warmth, the series of late nights, and the relief from the terror and tension of this night caught up with me. I fell asleep.

My dream was a mix of angry men, clubs and guns, fire flickering, and Robert handing me a cask of brandy, too heavy for me to carry. Then, in the way of dreams, I was on the dock watching the pounding of the waves as the tide came in, the wind blew, and clouds scudded across the dark sky, but I could see something in the foam. I stepped closer, but a dark, deep voice said my name, "Liza." My hair flew across my cheek, hiding the view, "Liza."

Chapter 19

I will a round unvarnished tale deliver

Shakespeare. *Othello*

I opened my eyes and flinched to see Robert leaning over me. His hands were on the arms of my chair, caging me in, his face in shadow. He was so still that I waited and watched the reflected glint of the waning fire in his eyes and listened to his steady breathing for a long time.

"You thought I was a spy?" I said the first thing that came to mind.

"Not until you stole my communique."

"The communique that you stole and were giving to smugglers?"

"I didn't steal it," Robert stood upright and removed his gloves and cloak, watching me the whole time. Then with a sigh, he turned his back to me and walked over to drop them on the table in the center of the room. He returned and sat on the chair across from me, leaning his forearms on his thighs, his head lowered. He rubbed one hand down his face. I felt a moment's sympathy that I ruthlessly stifled.

"You thought I was a spy?" Lifting his head and pinning me with his glare, he repeated my accusation.

"I know about Etienne LeFevre," I scowled, "I know you're sending information about troop movement and arms deliveries to Etienne LeFevre."

He stood, took three quick steps, and towered over me again, "how do you know about Etienne LeFevre?"

"I heard you and my father talking about him."

He rocked back on his heels and folded his arms, "Who else knows?"

"No one," I was deeply offended, "well my maid Susan knows a very little. She is the only one I could trust to help me. And she won't tell anyone." I scowled, "why would you even consider that I would share such damaging information about you and my father?"

Relief flashed across his face and was gone in a moment, "Of course you wouldn't," He looked up as if searching for divine intervention. He chuckled and shook his head.

Sitting while he towered over me, I felt like a recalcitrant child waiting for a scolding. So, I stood, forcing him to step back, "I don't see anything funny about this!"

He rubbed his face again and the laughter disappeared, "no, it's not funny." I was paradoxically sad to see the weight of exhaustion and worry descend again. I shrugged uncomfortably.

"Etienne LeFevre?" I drilled my finger into his chest.

"It's a long story, the tale of Etienne LeFevre; are you sure that you want to hear it tonight?"

"Oh, stop being so evasive," I waved, "get on with it."

He smiled, took my hand and pulled me across the room to sit beside him on the sofa, "Etienne LeFevre is the code name for a man whose father, an Austrian royalist, died during the Terror. He and his French mother escaped—no one quite knows how—and settled in England. His understanding of the terrain, the politics, and the languages of the continent allows him to move in the highest circles in France. He is an invaluable resource for information and protection for our agents."

My sigh of relief shook my whole body, "So Etienne LeFevre is working for Britain?"

"Well, he would be, if he actually existed."

"What," I screeched.

Robert put his hand over my mouth, "Shush Liza, I don't want to explain to your aunt or your father why I'm alone with you in the middle of the night in a dark drawing room."

I looked up in trepidation. We both listened in silence for a minute, but no other sound broke the quiet of the house.

Then I narrowed my eyes at Robert. He smiled and tweaked my nose, "Yes, we created him. We leaked information about him over the last four months so that the French would know about him and his work in France."

"Robert," I growled in growing frustration, "you said you'd tell me all. Why did you invent a Frenchman who is a spy for England?"

He took my hand in both of his and started to play with my fingers. I felt it all the way up my arm, but I was determined I wouldn't be distracted now. I pulled my hand away and folded my arms. I inclined my head and raised my brows.

He smiled, but sighed and started talking, "If I'm to tell you all of it, I must start at the beginning. We've jumped way ahead with Etienne LeFevre."

"Very well," I nodded.

Robert spent a few moments pinching his lower lip. Finally, he stood and paced to the fire, picked up a seashell that rested on the mantle and put it back down. He looked back at me, shrugged and smiled before he walked to the window and leaned against the sill. I watched impatiently but remained silent.

He cleared his throat, "after the Dardanelles Blockade, I spent three months in a field hospital in Portugal. And another two months in hospital in London. I finally accepted that I would have to sell out," he paused looking out the window, but I don't think he was seeing the shadowed park, "I began to make arrangements to come home."

"You didn't want to come home?"

"I did want to come home," he turned to look at me and lifted his hands in frustration, "but I didn't want to leave my men or my ship."

I nodded. Robert would never desert his friends. Which was, among other things, what had made his actions so painful to me.

"Admiral Fielding came to me in London. He had spoken with Colonel Fitzpatrick from the Secretary at War office. They decided that, as I live in Bexhill, they had a job for me." He left the window and started prowling around the room, hands clasped behind his back.

He paused and flashed a glance at me, "they had traced the movement of some stolen documents this far and realized that the local smugglers were doing more than avoiding tariffs on spirits.

"So, you're trying to put an end to the smuggling along the coast?" I could hear the skepticism in my voice, "I don't think your plan is working."

He smiled, "You'd be right if that is what I was trying

to do. The smuggling is, of course a concern. The smugglers are determined, organized, and brutal. They are more dangerous because someone is controlling their runs, informing them of the schedules of the excisemen, the patrols of the militia and the legion forces, who are helping the customs service."

"He'd have to be pretty well-placed to have all of that information," I grimaced to think that one of my neighbors was involved in such deceit.

"Yes." He glanced in my direction, but I don't think he was seeing me, "but the bigger issue is that this same man—or as I believe a second man—is accessing and sending information to Napoleon's agents. It is limited information, now, but it is still more than we can allow our enemy to have. We've tracked the flow of information this far. We do know he, or they, are in league with this particular band of smugglers.

"The Wilkins gang," I supplied.

He glowered at me but continued prowling. His wanderings had brought him again to the fireplace. I watched mesmerized as he added another piece of wood, took the fire iron and stirred the coals. The fire quickened. His broad shoulders blocked the light from the fire. His actions were smooth and powerful. I felt a little light-headed and forced myself to take a breath. It would be so much easier for me if I didn't find it such a pleasure to watch him. I shook myself and asked, "This is why you have been working with the smugglers?"

He shrugged, "someone with means and opportunity is in league with the smugglers." Anger resonated through his voice "and he or someone working with him has helped French prisoners escape and arranged for transport back to

France. He has shipped French agents into our country. He has breached the lower levels of our security and is sending information to the enemy," his voice deepened. "His or their actions have, both directly and indirectly, caused injury and death to countless men," his hands fisted, "Do you know that Napoleon reads the Times, the Morning Chronicle, and The Morning Post every morning?"

I shook my head. "A smart man could garner a lot of information from reading the newspapers, even if just the attitude and morale of Britain."

"Yes, even if that's all that was getting through, it would be serious, but it is more," his jaws tensed as he ground his teeth. "Finding the man who is ultimately responsible, this spy or leader of spies is of the utmost importance. If he can get to one of our government officials, who's to say he won't be able to recruit another, one with more damaging information?" His fisted hands landed on his hips, "I am tasked with discovering him."

"And you think you will find him by joining in the smuggling here?"

"I might hear something helpful. I would be stupid not to try, but I think it more likely that if the spy thinks I am less than honest in my dealings but still have access to sensitive information, he might approach me and try to influence me to share what I know."

He fell silent then looked up. I watched him watching me and thought about what he'd told me, what I'd heard, what I'd seen when I'd followed him.

"I suppose it might work," I remembered the argument I'd heard in Madame Fortunna's cellar, "but I don't think most of the smugglers know who is controlling their movements."

He looked at me with suspicion, "what makes you say that?"

"Something I heard at Madame Fortunna's."

Robert stalked to the sofa and lifted me with a firm grasp on my arms. His sudden anger took me by surprise, and I hung for a few moments suspended before I started to struggle against his determined grip.

"Tell me you haven't been nosing around Fortunna's shop, at least no more than tonight when I found you."

I didn't' say anything.

"Liza don't think because she is female that she is any more safe than the rest of the smugglers. Women can be even more dangerous than their male counterparts."

"I know."

He groaned, "what have you done?"

"Put me down."

With a look of surprise, Robert did, but he kept a hold of my arms.

I pulled a little, but when he didn't let go, I huffed and said, "I went to buy some lace and thread."

"Liza," his growl was a warning.

"When she was busy with another customer, I—" his thunderous expression caused me to pause and edit my account a little, "I found a hiding place and listened."

He waited, and as the silence built, I had to continue, "I overheard her arguing with some men, some smugglers."

A lifted brow was his only response.

And so, I related that conversation that was engraved on my mind. I remembered the fear of the dark, closed in place, the smell of dirt, damp, spirits, the smell of my fear. I described the voices I'd heard, and I shivered with the memories.

When my gaze focused, I saw Robert staring into the space behind me with an arrested look.

"You know these men?" I asked.

"Hmmph, one of them, I believe. If I am right, he is employed at the Belle Inn. It might be interesting to speak with his employer, Mr. Conway." Robert didn't remove his hands from my arms, but I could tell he wasn't thinking of me. He wouldn't have revealed that last had he been.

I waited and watched him. When his attention returned to me, I flinched, "Liza, why would you risk going there?"

"I needed to know where their next smuggling run would land."

"Whatever you learned was not worth the risks you took," his voice, though quiet, echoed through the room. He glared at me sternly, "promise me you won't go back there."

"I won't," I paused as I considered, "not unless I absolutely have to."

He shook me, but gently, "my head-strong, fearless, foolhardy—" then he groaned and pulled me close. It finally settled into my mind that Robert and my father were not traitors. Relief made me boneless. I nestled into his warmth, my nose to his chest. He smelled of night, the sea, and the undefinable, familiar sandalwood and musk that was Robert.

I don't know how long I rested against him, long enough for him to tunnel his fingers into the knot at the back of my head, pulling pins at random. I felt my hair list, then fall. He ran his fingers through the disordered curls until he found the last two pins, tucking them in his pocket with the others.

"Liza," he whispered while he gathered my hair and bunched it in his hands, laying his lips at my neck. I felt a frisson of—it wasn't fear, but the danger was real, and it caused enough panic that I pulled away.

We watched each other, both of us breathing heavily.

I backed up another five steps and cleared my throat, "Etienne LeFevre?"

During the ensuing long pause, Robert watched me with a hooded, hot stare. When both of us were breathing a little more regularly, he leaned back, with arms folded, and once again looked at the ceiling. He took two deep breaths, brought his head back down and was once again in control, or close enough that he could continue, "Ah, and now we return to Etienne LeFevre.

"How was I to find our traitor? We don't know who he is; we don't know the details of his routes, the people he uses. I could watch and wait for him to make a mistake. Instead I—"

"Set a trap."

"A trap," he agreed, "and it begins to work. We know French spies intercept nearly half of the information we send to our Etienne LeFevre."

"And this is good?"

"Yes, it is good. Our traitor will want access to all I know."

"Won't they soon know that the information you're sending is false?"

"Well, that is the thing. It can't be false."

I gasped.

"Or it must close enough to the truth that it is believable, but we also do everything we can to make sure that, through seeming accidents of timing or providence, it does little damage to British concerns." The tension in his body reminded me again of that large, predatory cat, "And Etienne LeFevre, constantly moving from place to place, is a master of the convenient last-minute miracle."

"And once you catch the spy, Etienne LeFever can just disappear. Brilliant."

"Thank you, my dear." Robert bowed. "I would love to be worthy of your admiration, but there are no guarantees. We can only hope we will find the spy in time. The initial reason we created Etienne LeFevre was to follow the flow of information—who buys and retrieves the communiques? Who knows the information? Who tells whom? We watch and follow each lead, knowing it will lead us back to the spy here and ultimately to the leak at the war office."

"It's a good idea, I think."

"I'm so glad you approve."

I laughed at his exasperation.

He shook his head and continued, "but Etienne LeFevre will only work for a short time—a few months if we are lucky. The information is just slightly off, fifteen miles or two to three days off, only enough that the differences can be explained by a change in weather or geography or vagaries of troop movement, but each time we give information that is slightly off or that doesn't give them their anticipated advantage, we lose time. The longer we can maintain the charade and continue to control the flow of information, the greater safety and influence we keep."

I cocked my head, "safety?"

"Yes. Liza, because we have other men working in France, in Switzerland, Prussia, Austria, and Russia. And while Fouche and his agents, both in France and here in England are searching for Etienne LeFevre and the letters we send him—and we have heard that finding and eliminating Etienne LeFevre has become a matter of some urgency in French circles," Robert's smile was fierce, "one of my most trusted officers can safely carry information to our men."

I clapped my hands, "Mr. James!"

Robert narrowed his eyes at me and growled, "Liza, how do you know about James?"

I shrugged, "I saw you with him in the Belle Inn."

I lowered my head to hide my smile at his arrested look on his face.

"How long have you been following me and listening in on my conversations?"

"Well, I couldn't do anything when I was ill."

His breath hissed, "that long?"

I shrugged but remembered that first overheard conversation. I had a horrible thought. "Father knows all of this?" And before he could take breath to answer, "you think my father is the spy."

Chapter 20

Every man has his faults, and honesty is his

Shakespeare, *Timon of Athens*

A bark of laughter broke the quiet. We both stopped and listened, but the only sound was the crackling fire and the ticking of the clock, "No Liza, your father is not a spy for the French."

"Then why involve him?"

He laughed, quietly this time, "You've got that the wrong way. It was all your father's idea," he stated baldly.

My jaw dropped, and I blinked three times. "Father?"

"Liza, what do you think your father does on his regular trips to London?"

I blushed furiously because honestly, since his regular trips to London had started a year or so after my mother passed away, I had thought he had a, hmm—a ladybird in London that he visited. But I wasn't going to say that to Robert, "I don't suppose I have given it much thought." That much was true. I tried very hard not to think about it ever.

He shook his head.

"Tell me," I huffed in frustration.

"Liza, your father is—quite familiar to those who work at the office of the Secretary at War. He is a brilliant strategist. How do you think Colonel Fitzpatrick came to know about me?"

I felt stunned and a little breathless. I turned my head aside and stared into the dancing flames thinking of my, at least I had always thought, unprepossessing father, his love of the Greek philosophers and dramatists, his quiet voice, his steadfast love for my brother and me. A new place in my mind and heart unfurled and filled with knowledge of his unknown depths. I felt for a moment as if my father were a stranger, but an increasingly dear one. Tears pricked my eyes and I blinked them back.

I shrugged this new view of my father into place and felt a little larger, but also a little raw, for the new knowledge. When I turned back, Robert watched me with perceptive attention.

I bristled in discomfort and lifted my chin, "you could have, you should have told me all of this. It affects me as deeply as anyone," I couldn't stand still any longer and began pace around the room.

Robert pivoted in place and followed me with his eyes, "I could have, I know, but even now, Liza that wouldn't be my first choice. It is dangerous, and I don't want to endanger you."

"It's my—"

"Think Liza, only six men in all of Britain know of our plans—and now you."

That caused me to pause. I felt keenly the weight of his confidence in me, late though it was. I inclined my head in acceptance.

"Even now, I wish you didn't know. I need you to be safe."

I shook my head. Didn't he realize that I felt the same, and then unbidden came the memory of an inky night and Robert lifting that delicate girl from the boat, his protective arm around her shoulder. Maybe I didn't have the right to worry about his safety, but I thought rebelliously, if I didn't, neither did he.

I paced faster and my breath grew jagged. Robert watched perplexed. I turned in a burst of indignation, "did you tell that girl?"

The silence was palpable. I stopped pacing and faced him.

"That girl?" Robert repeated carefully.

"Yes," I began again to circle the room, "last week at Little Galley Hill, there was a girl who came in on a boat. You brought her ashore," I stopped at the window and turned my back to Robert and brushed away an escaping tear.

"You were there?" He sounded non-plussed.

"I was there." I pushed the words out, "I saw . . ."

I was surprised by his weary chuckle.

I turned, pushing myself back against the cold window and crossed my arms.

"Is this why you have—" he mumbled, as if to himself, "you thought I—" another muted chuckle, this directed at the floor as he raked his fingers through his hair.

He shook his head, "Lord save me. You have been sneaking around even more than I realized."

He crossed the room and firmly placed his palms on both sides of my face. "Liza, it is not what you think."

A sob escaped, and I shook his hands off and shouldered my way past him, putting the length of the room between us. "I know what I saw, Robert."

In vivid clarity the memory returned of Robert lifting this woman from the smuggler's boat and gently cradling her against his chest. Even though I was too far away to make out her features, I could tell she was beautiful, with a pale face and dark hair, small and delicate. Even from afar I had recognized his tenderness for her and her regard for him.

"You care for her. I could see that you care deeply for her."

He rocked back, looked up at the ceiling and cleared his throat, "I am fond of this girl, but not in the manner you believe."

"Robert." My cry was an anguished question.

He walked across the room in measured steps, never breaking eye contact. He once again took my face between his hands and lowered his head until his brow rested against mine, "no matter what you saw, there is no reason for you to fear." I shook my head but didn't break his hold this time.

"Liza, listen to me. There is no other woman for me," his lips pressed lightly against the corner of my eye, "there has been no other woman for me even before that day more than four years ago when we," he lifted my face and took my mouth with gentle, thorough fervor.

He lifted his head, "I know I'm asking for a lot, but can you trust me? Just a little longer, my love, until I can tell you all, will you trust me?"

"Tell me now."

"I can't. It is a long story and there is not enough time, Listen."

And when I turned my attention away from Robert

and my own traitorous body, I heard the difference. I felt
the difference that is always present in a house that is waking. As yet I didn't hear the servants in the halls and on the
stairwells, but it wouldn't be long.

"You will tell me?"

"Yes. Soon. I promise."

After all he'd told me that night, I could finally believe
that he was still the loyal man I had always known. But I'd
also seen him on the beach that night with my own eyes. Of
course, I now knew he wasn't a traitor. Did that also mean
that he wasn't a liar? Could I trust what he was saying?

It was hard for me. I wanted an explanation of that
woman who he had brought to England, and I wanted it
immediately. But I looked into his eyes, at the clear confidence and strength, and yes, the honesty that blazed as
distinct and real as any of his physical features. I lowered
my head and weighed and measured, and finally listened to
my heart—and I made a choice, a choice to trust his word,
believe in his feelings for me and mine for him.

"Please Liza Lou. I am telling the truth when I say that
you have nothing to fear from that woman on the beach."

I nodded.

And, I thought, if he didn't tell me very soon about
this French girl, I would find out myself.

In the next moment my thoughts flew as Robert lifted
and explored my face with searching fingers while his
searing eyes held mine. "Liza," I felt his whisper on my lips,
and a pulse of heat slid and tingled over my skin, "my Liza
Lou," he dipped and kissed me again, "there is only you."

I wanted him to keep kissing me forever, but I gasped
as his mouth roamed, nipped at my ear, pressed a kiss to the
tender curve of my neck. His hand gently brushed down

my arm, his hand linking with mine, his other sliding down my back, pressing me closer.

I may have moaned. With a satisfied chuckle, Robert scooped me into his arms, smiling warmly when I squeaked in surprise. He carried me to the sofa and sat with me across his lap. His lips grazed my temple as he gathered my hair in his hands and buried his face in the wild mass and breathed in deeply.

"Mm," the tremor in his voice woke an answering pulse through my body, "On my ship, surrounded by too many unwashed men, I dreamed of the smell of lilies." His lips returned to mine and plundered. I closed my eyes and the world faded. I was carried, dipping and rising on a sea of dazzling sensation. His touch swept the curve of my hip, his broad hand burning through my muslin dress. I arched into him, wanting, waiting.

"I thought of that kiss when I lay in my bunk," he murmured, "and later in my cabin."

"You could have written that," my voice was a breathless whisper.

He laughed against my throat and shivers raced down my spine, "what would I have written? That I ached for you, that in my carnal dreams we loved by the side of that river,"

"Ah," I swallowed, "Robert,"

"Hmm?"

"Robert," Only his name escaped.

"You were not yet sixteen," more kisses and his teeth grazed my jaw, "even seventeen was too young for the kind of thoughts that occupied my quiet moments, the hopes that grew stronger rather than faded over time."

His lips returned to mine. Dizzy and panting, my head

fell back.

The clock chimed four times. He paused. The quiet was broken by our labored breathing then by his pained groan. "We need to stop now, Liza," he put his hands on my waist and pushed gently.

"Hmm," I kissed his chin, the corner of his mouth. I slid my fingers into his hair, "Robert," I slipped my tongue out and tasted the hollow between his jaw and ear.

He moaned, "Ah, Liza," his laugh was strained, "I really think," he captured my hands and kissed them, "I must leave now. They may start in the drawing room, but it won't be long before your servants come to clean this room and light this fire." He rose from the sofa, lifting me with him. We stood looking at each other in silence as my heart pounded and the fire crackled and burned.

"Am I acquitted in your mind, Liza, of treason and of betrayal?"

My eyes went to the sofa where we had been kissing. I lifted my brows and met his again. He didn't look away.

I supposed that after the reassurance of his ardor, I could give voice to the depth of my earlier distress and my overwhelming relief. "The thought that you and my father were treasonous shocked and frightened me, but I could make a plan and do—something. I could help. But when I thought you had chosen someone else," I shook my head in remembered pain, "what could I do about that?" I felt a prickling pressure behind my eyelids and blinked away the sudden moisture.

"Even seeing what you did, I can't believe you thought that of me."

"You will admit the evidence is overwhelming. And I knew you were keeping secrets and telling lies." I scowled, "you're still keeping secrets."

"Not for long, promise you. And about the other, you know why."

"Yes," I was still reeling from the revelations of the night—and from his kisses. I lowered my eyes.

His response was wry, "well I can't have you following me, showing up at meetings with smugglers or," he stopped with an arrested look.

"Liza please, now that you do know, I beg you, will you stop your involvement, stop your dangerous questions, stop following me and inviting the interest of these ruthless men?"

I looked into his pleading eyes. Part of me wanted so much to say yes, just to make him happy, but I would not leave him alone and defenseless in danger.

"No," I said gently.

He pulled back and shook his head, "Liza . . ."

I lifted my hands and bracketed his cheeks and felt the bristled growth of his beard, "you feel it's your right to protect me. Is it not my right to do the same?"

He closed his eyes as if in pain.

"Isn't it, Robert?"

He pulled one of my hands down and kissed my palm, "but Liza—"

I spoke over him, "but I won't follow you without your knowledge. I won't lie to you. And I will be more careful. Now that I know what's at stake, I know better what not to ask and of whom. I won't be careless, but I won't leave you alone, surrounded by enemies. I won't. I can't."

"Liza, you aren't trained for this, not prepared. You—"

"Then help me, Robert. And let me help you. You're smart. Think of ways I can help, places you might not be able to go where I might hear something."

"Liza."

"Before you say more, perhaps you might take some time to think and who I am. Remember all that you know of me, you who know me best." I pulled away from him and walked toward the doorway.

He caught my hand and pulled me the other way toward the window. He turned to face me, his face filled with frustration and anger—he looked a little lost for a moment. He opened his mouth, and I could tell I wouldn't like what came out. But his deeply ingrained manners came to the fore. He turned and leaned his head against the window, then took a deep breath and lifted the sill. He took my hand one more time and bowed over it, holding my fingers to his lips.

"Good evening. Good morning, now" he looked deeply into my eyes, "but we will talk more of this later."

"If you like," I said gently. "And you will tell me about this girl."

His grin, as he lowered himself out the window, was a brilliant slash of white in the dark. He backed up two steps, "Thank you, Liza. Your trust means more to me than you can know."

He turned then, and I watched as his shadowed form walk briskly away until it merged with the shadows of trees. I pulled down the sash, and the window closed with a click. As I turned the door opened and the maid squeaked.

I was hard pressed to come up with a believable reason for being there. The servants obviously saw through my attempts at subterfuge but nodded and kept their mouths closed. Unfortunately, I knew that wouldn't last for long. I sighed to realize that I might indeed be trying to explain my night's activities to my father and aunt before the day was out.

It was only as I was finally preparing for bed, as I picked up John's trousers off of the floor where I had dropped them earlier, that I remembered the unavoidable feeling of being watched as I changed into my brother's clothes in that wooded copse. I blushed hotly. I had sensed—no, I had known someone was watching. I felt the heat of my blush all the way through my body.

And I tried to be scandalized. My wicked, wicked love. We certainly would talk later.

Chapter 21

For truth has such a face and such a mien, as to be lov'd needs only to be seen.

John Dryden,
"The Hind and the Panther"

I floated down to breakfast the next morning awash with goodwill toward the world and everyone in it. I should have felt tired, but vast relief and memory of Robert's kisses filled me with an invigorating vitality. Everything was beautiful, even the cloud filled sky couldn't dampen my mood.

Though I was later than usual, my father and aunt were still at table, their conversation desultory.

"Elizabeth." Aunt's brief greeting didn't disturb me.

"Liza, my love, good morning," the warmth of my father's love settled over me. I gazed a little misty eyed at this man, whom I finally recognized again as the smart, loyal, upstanding gentleman I had always known. I now knew that others, in high places, respected him, even looked to him for guidance and leadership. How proud I was—proud and so very grateful. I blinked away the moisture that rose to my eyes.

I smiled tremulously and walked to the sideboard to fill a plate and compose myself.

The pound cake was especially light today, and the chocolate richer and more flavorful. The gray light filtered through the clouds was soothing in our beautifully appointed breakfast room.

I looked up and noticed that both my father and aunt were watching me in concern. I realized suddenly what a mindless, sentimental twit I must look, staring into space with a mawkish smile. The breakfast parlor seemed to lurch, and everything in me settled into place. My brain started working again. What was I thinking, gazing into space with a silly smile pasted on my face? I had work to do.

I had to figure out a way to convince my aunt to visit the Amesleys so that I could discover who the French girl was. I trusted Robert, but the sooner I knew who she was, the happier I would be. I also needed a figure out how to help Robert discover the murderers of the two riding officers, the man who was running the smugglers, and the spy. This was no time to be simpering and dreaming.

I began eating with more attention, and my family stopped watching me so closely. After a few minutes I stole a peek at my father and my aunt.

My plans were interrupted when Phillps opened the door to announce with unusual solemnity, "The Amesley family has come to call. I put them in the front drawing room."

"Very good, Phillips," my father folded the newspaper and placed it by his plate. He rose and offered his arm to his sister, who had also risen and stood with her mouth gaping open.

"The family?" My aunt whispered.

My father shrugged, "I know no more than you, but I'm sure it will become clear when we get to the drawing room."

Well, I thought, Robert had promised. I should have known he wouldn't leave me to wonder for long.

We walked into the drawing room and my eyes were drawn to the young woman who stood between Mr. Amesley and Robert. I studied her and felt her appraisal in return.

She was five inches shorter than I with a tidy sylphlike figure, her dark hair curled in shiny, and enviably well-behaved waves. Her heavily lashed eyes, quickly lowered, were a familiar perceptive gray, and I sighed. Those eyes were unmistakable. She was obviously very closely related to Robert, though her expression was livelier and more curious than Robert's quiet reserve.

My eyes flew to Robert's and his subtle smile was amused. All of us stood for a few moments staring at each other.

Mr. Amesley broke the silence and came forward to bow to Aunt Beatrice, "Miss Henshaw, may I introduce my daughter, Miss Sidonie Amesley?" He took Miss Amesley's hand and brought her forward, "Until recently I had believed that she died with my first wife, but Robert was able to find her, and to our delight he was able to slip her out of France and bring her home to us."

There was only one small gasp from Aunt Beatrice exposing her surprise at not only a daughter, but a first wife. But in a moment, she eased into the refuge of polite usage. I couldn't help but think how pleased she would be later to have received this information before any of her friends,

"Oh my dear girl, I am delighted to make your acquaintance. What a charming surprise to have another young neighbor. I think it's a wonderful thing that you here and safe, with your father and brother."

"I am hoping that you will be able to advise us on how best to introduce Sidonie into the neighborhood," Mr. Amesley said.

My aunt nodded, managing to look both gratified and magnanimous, "Of course, Charles. I would be delighted." She smiled at Sidonie, "and aren't you lovely. I think you'll be breaking hearts all over the parish."

Miss Sidonie blushed, but very properly answered, "how do you do? I am pleased to meet you." Her English was quite good, with a lilting and very pleasing accent.

Mr. Amesley saved her further embarrassment, "my dear, may I introduce my good friend, Mr. Henshaw?" They said all that was proper.

And finally, since we'd been exchanging fleeting looks at each other since I had walked in, Mr. Amesley brought his daughter to me, "and dear Liza, will you allow me to introduce my daughter. I know she will be comforted to know someone closer to her age."

"Miss Amesley,"

"Miss Henshaw," we both curtsied

"I am very happy to make your acquaintance," I answered her smile.

"Miss Liza, I feel I already know you, a little bit. Robert," she pronounced it Ro-bear, without the final t, "does mention you, often." She had dimples that showed themselves in a mischievous smile. And I relaxed a little. If she could tease Robert, I thought we might be able to be friends.

I led Sidonie over the window so we could talk, "You

can't know what a relief it is to me to finally meet you. You are not so very frightening."

"Frightening?" She was surprised.

"You see, until yesterday, I believed you and Robert were——" I waved my hands hoping she would fill in the rest.

Sidonie lifted perfectly arched brows in incomprehension.

"I thought you were his paramour," I said baldly.

Sidonie gasped, then coughed, then laughed—a light, musical gurgle, but she caught herself quickly, "I'm so sorry, I'm sure it was very distressing. But no—oh no."

My lips quirked. I smiled, "now I can see it is funny, but I was hiding on the beach when you came ashore, and he was so attentive and gentle with you."

"Yes. He is," now she waved her hands, "but this is something very interesting that I want to know, why were you hiding on the beach?"

"I was following Robert of course. He had been acting so secretive, and I knew he was involved in something," I paused and replaced 'disgraceful' with, "dangerous. I thought if I knew more, I could save him."

She nodded, "and there was some danger—those men on the boat, they are not good men, and then you saw him bring me?" She clapped, "This is a story I would like to hear more. How angry you must have been with Robert."

I looked over at Robert and was just in time to see him leave the room with my father.

"What is he doing now?" I scowled and met Sidonie's secretive smile. My heart gave a little bump.

Aunt Beatrice called us over, so I had no opportunity to question Sidonie further. The discussion of the best way to present Miss Amesley was paramount. The words were familiar—tea, musical evening, grand ball, but none of it made much of an impression on me. My mind was in my father's study, until the suggestion that we get up a group of young people to ride over to view Herstmonceux caught my flagging attention.

The outing would take a full day, so Aunt Beatrice wasn't encouraging, but Herstmonceux Castle, built in the fifteenth century, one of the first brick buildings in Britain, is glorious, and even better, it is surrounded by three hundred acres of the most amazing woodland and beautiful gardens. I thought I might be able to persuade Robert to come, so I thought the idea brilliant and was eloquent in my support.

Mr. Amesley nodded at my aunt, "I know how busy you are with preparations for the ball. A full day away would be too great an imposition," in one stroke he crushed my hopes, "and that's not even considering the time to plan and prepare." My heart sunk lower, and then with a guileless smile, he said, "perhaps Lady Ramsgate or Mrs. Crossley could be persuaded to take care of the planning and act as chaperon."

Which just proves that insight and intelligence is a familial trait. After Mr. Amesley's considerate suggestion, nothing could have kept Aunt Beatrice from leading our expedition.

Planning was well advanced when my father and Robert returned. My father, once he understood the project, gladly entered into the discussion, but my whole attention was caught by the heat in Robert's eyes.

"If I might have a word with Liza?" He asked the room at large.

I blinked and my heart stuttered. But Robert didn't

wait for a response. He took my hand and tucked it into his arm and led me across the hall to my father's study. The door closed with a click, and he turned and pulled me into his arms and brought his mouth down on mine.

I slid my arms around his neck and clung to him, trying to move closer to him, and closer still. He held the back of my head in one firm hand and his other hand moved achingly down my back, gently pressing. With a lurching half dance, Robert backing up and pulling me after, we stepped and swayed, kissing and moving together until Robert's legs met the desk.

His thumb moved around to caress my jaw, "Liza, lovely Liza Lou," he sighed against the corner of my mouth and with what sounded like a satisfied chuckle, he said, "your father has given me permission to pay my addresses."

My heart leapt, but before I could answer, he took my lips again. One brief kiss turned into two, then more. Our lips clung, but he finally lifted his head a whisper away and asked, "are you going to let me——," another kiss, "pay my addresses?" I opened my mouth to answer, but he angled his head and brought his lips back to mine.

"Robert," I turned my head to the side with a gasp.

"Hmm?" He nuzzled my jaw and worked his way to my ear.

I laughed and slipped my fingers into his hair and let them furrow through the thick waves, "I do so love the way you address me."

He laughed and we kissed some more.

Finally, and frustratingly, he pushed me back a few inches and took a deep breath, "Is this a yes, Liza? This had better be a yes."

I looked up into his clear gray eyes, darkened in passion, "Yes, please Robert," I pushed against his hold on my hips but he held firm and I could only lean forward, "I need you to address me some more right now," I kissed his chin, which was all I could reach until he moaned and pulled me to him again.

I don't know how long we kissed—a minute or fifteen, with Robert propped against my father's desk and with me leaning boneless against him. His fingers moved in sweet rhythm against the fluttering beat at my throat and his other hand slid to my hip, pulling me closer when I was brought back to the present by the clearing of a throat.

"Now children," like a douse of cold water, my aunt's voice put out the hottest of the flames, "perhaps it would be a good time to rejoin the others and share your, I assume, good news?"

The word Robert said under his breath made me laugh, but I stepped back and straightened my dress. Robert patted his cravat into place and ran his hand over his hair, and we followed my aunt into the drawing room.

Sidonie squealed. Mr. Amesley hugged me and whispered in my ear, "my fondest hope has always been that you would join our family. I'm glad to see that Robert has finally found some sense."

My father, too, held me to his chest, and whispered, "I have always liked Robert, but if you're not happy," he pulled back and studied my face and smiled resolutely, "well then," he said and patted my shoulder.

Aunt Beatrice said nothing, but it was all in her face— her pride, her relief, her self-congratulation.

We had been busy before with the planning for the grand ball, but adding my nuptials to her list, my aunt's organization now became militant. She seemed to take great pleasure in making sure that every moment of my day was planned and accounted for.

Not for nothing was my love acquainted with spying and sneaking. Almost daily, Robert, with as much skill as any smuggler, found a way to slip away from watchful eyes. Only ever for a little time, but it was enough to leave me yearning for more. As our kisses became more ardent, I walked around obvious of so much that was around me, but aware of my own body in a way I'd never been before, and ever more aware of Robert's.

And always just when I was ready to melt into a molten puddle, Aunt Beatrice would appear, and with a long-suffering sigh send Robert away.

The third time she caught us kissing, this time in the stables, Aunt Beatrice said, "Captain Amesley, surely you have more important things to do than bring your," she looked down and sniffed, "little—dog over here and distract Elizabeth from her duties."

Robert bowed to her with an irascible smile, kissed me, and whispered, "I wonder if you're marrying me so your aunt never finds out about your dog," he winked and whistled his way out of the stable.

"Elizabeth," Aunt Beatrice's voice was severe, "your father and I have agreed it is best you have a short engagement, but even then, if you're not careful, in eight months-time, the neighbors will be counting on their fingers." She ignored my blushing protests, took my arm and pulled me toward the house, "I expect you to act with a little bit of decorum."

From that day she hardly allowed me to leave the house unattended, and her eyes followed me everywhere. My salvation was that, to keep me busy, she assigned to me the running of all required errands.

Daily, sometimes twice a day, I was sent around the parish to arrange some detail that would make the grand ball 'The Event of the Year.' Susan was required to accompany me when I didn't have a friend along, but she didn't seem to mind now that I wore a dress—one of my own—and my activities were not stealthy.

I almost always took Quin up on the cart with me, I sometimes invited Maris or Amelia along with me. If my errand took me near to St. Peters, Lady Helen was always willing to come. She seemed to have many doctrinal and ethical questions, but I was beginning to question whether her frequent visits were due to religious fervor or due to Mr. Jones. I didn't even try to imagine what Lord and Lady Ramsgate would think of that.

But my most frequent companion on my errands was Sidonie. She was a pleasant companion, which boded well for our continued amity when we became sisters. She was gifted with a cheerful, unshakable poise and a sneaky humor that delighted. She took dramatic pleasure in everything around her and often seemed very young and carefree. And I felt young and carefree when I was with her.

And then in a sudden about face, her continental broad-mindedness would shock me, and her discerning, if slightly cynical insights and occasional and embarrassing risqué asides reminded me of the six years between us and her difficult life before she came to England.

And sometimes, when she thought no one was watching, her eyes would fill with a world-weary sorrow that made her seem ancient and ageless. But she never talked about her experience, and I didn't like to pry. And after a short time, she would always shake her head, lift her chin, and smile again at the world.

It really wasn't my fault that, on one such outing, my period of self-interested and happy diversion came to an end.

The sun had just past its zenith, and Sidonie and I were driving down Church Street on our way to the Manor to deliver linens.

As we neared the Belle Inn, over the rumbling of the carriage I heard a voice that sent a shiver down my spine. That rough deep voice was unforgettable. I looked around in a panic, wishing for a place to hide. People thronged the street, going about their business, and I took a deep breath telling myself that the smuggler didn't know I'd heard him in Madame Fortunna's cellar. It was not dark. I was not alone. If I didn't announce my fear, no one would notice me. I took one more deep breath before looking around discreetly, hoping to put a face to the voice.

Though the argument had lowered in volume, the red face and looming threat of violence revealed the smuggler. His mien match his heavy voice. He was a giant of a man, both in height and girth, but without any fat. What was most remarkable was that this man, that I knew to be so very dangerous, would boast such a young, open freckled face and bright red hair.

The man with whom he argued had his back to me, but it was easy to recognize the burnished blond hair and impeccable elegance of Mr. Hugh Hatton.

Chapter 22

Rather fail with honor than succeed by fraud

Sophocles

It couldn't be. I hadn't even been thinking about smugglers, yet there he was, arguing with Mr. Hugh for all the world to see. I slowed the carriage, and with sudden decision, pulled the horses into the drive leading to the inn's stables.

Sidonie didn't demure. She just sat in watchful silence. My admiration for her grew.

"We are stopping for refreshment?" She suggested lightly when I pulled up the horses.

That might work, I thought, but then realized that I wouldn't be able to listen to the smuggler and Hugh from inside.

"Did you notice those two men arguing in front of the inn?"

"No." She folded her hands in her lap, "They are important?"

"Yes." I lowered my voice to a whisper. "One of them is a smuggler who knows—ah, some information that Robert needs,"

I looked behind me and addressed the ostler who was approaching, "We won't stay long. If you'll just tie the horses here.

"I see," Sidonie ignored the ostler, but waited until he walked away before saying, "and Robert is not here."

"Robert is not here," I agreed, "but I can't let this opportunity pass by."

"Well," with a gallic shrug she said, "we shall have to see what we can find out for him."

I reached over and hugged her. She returned the hug and sat back and smiled gamely.

"Let's see, what is it possible for us to do?" She tapped her lip with one delicate finger, "it seems to me very much that we need a diversion."

"Yes, but what?"

"See me," with lifted brows and a grand gesture, she pointed to herself, "I will go into this inn and ask to speak to the proprietor. I will make much disorder. Yes?"

"Are you sure?" I had a moment of concern.

"Oh pah, being on the stage, this is a life I would not like, but in this inn—it is such a small role in front of an audience of only a few. You will see. I have been trained to be an actress. Well," she lifted one delicate finger, "a singer, but singers are actresses as well," she nodded as if to herself, "while I provide this performance very diverting, you hide and listen." Without waiting for a response, Sidonie climbed down and, with a lift of her chin, walked into the inn.

I wasted no time slipping as close as I could to the side of the inn where the two men talked. And taking a steadying breath, I crouched at the corner of the building.

"I tell you again, keep your voice down," Hugh hissed,

"Better yet, let's take this inside."

"Don't need to go inside. Just pay me," the smuggler weaved a little, and I thought his belligerence might be born of some liquid courage.

My theory was born out as Hugh stepped back and wrinkled his nose, "I paid the agreed upon price. I didn't ask you to do more. In fact, your actions were unnecessary. The weak rumblings of Perry Gerow's conscience didn't require such extreme warning. I was well able to ensure his continued loyalty."

"Well you didn't need to. I took care of it, didn't I? And I expect to be paid for it."

Hugh sneered, "You take too much upon yourself."

The smuggler poked his sausage-like finger into Hugh's waistcoat and said in a peevish voice, "You just wish you thought of it first."

Hugh looked down his nose and brushed the finger away, "initiative in this organization, you will learn, is not always a good thing. Nor is being bringing attention to those who prefer to remain anonymous. If I were you, I would get back to work, and avoid letting Mr. Conway see that you're drunk on the job." I recognized the threat. So did the smuggler as he scowled at Hugh, "you'll regret that, you will," he spat, but he turned and walked, mumbling, to the inn.

While Hugh watched him, I scurried back to my horses. I stood at their heads and tried to decide what to do. How was I to let Sidonie know we could leave, and I really wanted to leave now.

"Miss Henshaw," I jumped and turned to face Mr. Hugh Hatton's narrowed eyes, "What a surprise to see you here. What brings you to the Belle Inn this afternoon?"

I thought fast and smiled in what I hoped looked like innocence, "I am waiting for Miss Amesley. She had an errand here. Have you met Miss Amesley?" He opened his mouth, but I smiled brightly and continued, "Well she is Captain Amesley's long lost sister, can you believe it? Who is recently come from France."

I peeked at him from under my eyelashes, looking for that glazed look men sometimes get when women chatter, "Anyway," I waved my hand in front of my face, "I told her I'd wait here, but now I wonder if perhaps the proprietor has refused to deal with a person from France, although of course, it's not her fault that that terrible Napoleon wants to take over the world. But people will be people. I need to go in and help her. It was a pleasure to see you. I will see you next week at the ball. You are attending?"

"Of course," Mr. Hugh took my hand and bowed over it, "I hope you will save me a dance?"

I tittered and may have fluttered my eyelashes a little as I curtsied, "Of course, Mr. Hugh. Well, good day."

As I walked away, a drop of sweat slid down my back where I could feel Hugh Hatton's eyes follow me all the way into the inn.

Apparently, the proprietor of the Belle did not have anything against lovely, young women from France. He had three bottles of brandy on the counter and was prosing on about the comparable benefits of each. His chest swelled under her admiring gaze.

When Sidonie saw me, her smile brightened, "Oh, la. I can't decide. I'm sure they are all of them very good. Why don't you send all three? It is his birthday, and he may have friends over, don't you think?" She leaned forward and patted his arm. I didn't trust his smile, but Sidonie returned it fully, and he looked stunned. Then she turned, took my arm, and grandly swept both us out the door.

I was relieved that Hugh was gone when we got back to the carriage. After Sidonie's masterful performance, I felt I could tell her everything I had heard, both that afternoon and in Madame Fortunna's cellar. The telling, interrupted briefly when we dropped off the linens at the Manor, lasted until we were almost back to the Amesley's.

I didn't expect Robert to be happy, but I didn't expect the scolding he gave both of us.

"We've talked about this, Liza."

"You talked, Robert."

"Liza," how I hated that long-suffering tone.

"Robert," I mimicked, "Of course, I had to—"

"Smugglers, Liza, you know the danger. You have seen what they are capable of. And to bring my sister into such a situation is unconscionable."

I winced and then when he didn't speak, I took a deep breath, "Robert, he was right in front of me. I didn't go looking for him. I didn't draw his attention. And now we know he works at the Belle Inn. We can—"

"We can't." I didn't miss the strong accent on the 'we.'

"So just because you didn't find this information on your own, you will ignore it?" I sniffed, "I never thought you'd be too proud to—"

"I am not proud. I'm trying to protect you," he sighed deeply and ran his fingers through his hair, "and no, I'm not so foolish as to ignore intelligence just because I don't like the way it was gathered."

"Well, okay then." I sat with relief and ignored his glower.

"And Sidonie," he turned to his sister who sat quietly

in a chair in front of his desk, "don't think I have forgotten your part in this," but the worst of his ire had been spent on me. He began a gentler scolding, talking of vague dangers, reminding her of her unfamiliarity with the people and area and enjoining her not to join in "Liza's folly."

Watching Sidonie's response was instructive. I knew I couldn't duplicate her patience, but I had to admire it. Through Robert's tirade, she sat with folded hands and lowered eyes. Every once-in-a-while she would look up at him, from under her lashes, with a measuring glance. Then she would lower her eyes again. She inclined her head when his voice rose, but the only other movement I saw was the regular tap of her thumbs against each other. Against the promontory of her poise, he butted his head until finally he just wore down and stopped.

Then she rose, smiled, and kissed Robert's cheek and glided out, unbent, undefeated and unfazed. As she passed, I looked up at her face. She winked at me and closed the door after her.

I waited a moment before I suggested, "maybe Hugh is like Perry, involved against his will?"

Robert looked doubtful, and when I considered what I heard, I was inclined to agree, "Well, I hope for Amelia's sake that he isn't too deeply involved. I've decided," in my new confidence in Robert's esteem, but I didn't tell him that, "that I quite like Amelia. I wouldn't like for her to be hurt by something that Hugh has involved himself in."

Robert just grunted, but he did drive me home, and during the ride unbent enough to discuss the overheard conversation. "Liza, if they were talking about the riding officers who were killed, it means Hugh Hatton is neck deep, even perhaps in some position of power in this ring."

I thought about that, but it was hard to be gloomy riding next to Robert through the early dusk.

He drove our carriage into the stable yard and handed me down. I invited him in, but he declined. He did kiss me thoroughly before turning away to begin his walk home. Before he had gone too far, he stopped and called back, "watch that nose of yours, Liza. I like it right where it is, and if you keep sticking it where it doesn't belong—"

I rolled my eyes, "I wasn't sticking my nose anywhere. Can I help it if as I'm driving along, Mr. dangerous smuggler pops up right in front of my nose?" I wrinkled said nose.

He laughed and shook his head.

"Besides, what are the chances that I will see anything like that happen again? I'm sure I'll be as safe as can be from now on."

"That is my fervent hope."

And it happened just as I predicted. For the next few days, the most exciting thing that happened to me was an afternoon spent helping Sidonie with the final fitting for her ball gown.

And then after our long wait, the day of the ball came. Aunt Beatrice and I left early with her list of last-minute appointments in hand. She had arranged to have the use of one of the upstairs rooms at the manor so that we could change into our ball gowns without the inconvenience of a trip home. Accordingly, we were followed by a second carriage packed with gowns, slippers, stockings, feathers, combs and brushes and pins, jewels, fans, gloves, wraps, ribbons, handkerchiefs, perfumes, creams, powders and somewhere under all our finery, my aunt's dresser and Susan.

It seemed to me as the day progressed, that my aunt

and her friends became more of a hindrance than a help to the servants as they scurried to and from the Manor kitchen, the ballroom, the greenhouse, the gardens and back to the ballroom. Tempers grew short, and every setback took on the characteristics of a major crisis.

Through the windows of the ballroom, the peace of a golden sunset called to me. I decided to step out onto the Manor grounds and take a little stroll. Surely no one would notice my absence. My plan took on added pleasure when, while walking around the perimeter of the ballroom, I looked out the window and recognized Magnus leading Saevio to the stables. I picked up my pace.

On my way to the ballroom's double doors, I heard Lady Ramsgate's querulous voice, "she does it just to vex me. She knows I don't have time to worry about her. And why, of all times, does she feel the need to go to church today?" I didn't hear my aunt's words but recognized her attempt to mollify.

I made it to the doors a moment too late as Aunt Beatrice turned and caught sight of me, "Elizabeth dear," she called, "Lady Ramsgate is concerned that Lady Helen is delayed at the church." Her eyes commanded my assistance.

"I'd be happy to go and find Lady Helen," I complied, only slightly put out. A stroll to the church, I thought, was as well as a stroll around the grounds. Either would get me out of the frantic last-minute emotion, and if I saw Robert and he joined me, it was all the better.

As I walked out, I heard Lady Ramsgate continue her complaint, "she is spending an inordinate amount of time at the church these days. Of course, I have no complaint with the church in general, and I did donate the new alter cloth, but it is unseemly to be so zealous in religious observance."

"Now, don't you worry, Lady Ramsgate," I heard Aunt Beatrice say, "Elizabeth will find Lady Helen and bring her back. We still have time before we need to change into our gowns."

"Elizabeth, take—" I heard my aunt say before I closed the door. I definitely didn't want to take Susan. She would be, as the French say, de trop in the situation that I was hoping I could create.

My plans were frustrated as I didn't see Robert even though I ambled slowly around the grounds. I comforted myself that I would see him, talk with him, dance with him tonight. And maybe he would arrange a few private moments. I shivered in anticipation. But first I needed to find Helen, so I set out at a leisurely pace toward St. Peter's. I paused where Church Street met Hastings Road and waited for a carriage to pass. I thought how if Lady Helen's parents were mine, I might find solace at the church as well.

My thoughts made me inattentive. I didn't see Hugh Hatton until he was upon me. I had an unfortunate moment of undiluted fear, and when he saw it, his features hardened, and he took a firm grip on my elbow.

"Miss Henshaw, it looks like you and I should have a talk."

"Oh, no," I answered, "I couldn't possibly visit now. I've been sent to walk to the church and bring Lady Helen back—to the manor." I tried to communicate to Hugh by the power of the litany in my mind—I am no trouble, ignore me. I've seen nothing; I've heard nothing.

He obviously didn't hear my thoughts. "You're going to St. Peter's, are you? And all alone. We can't have that," he pulled me across the road, "that's as good a place as any for our talk." His grip tightened painfully, "I'll accompany you."

"That's really not necessary," I said firmly and tried to remove my arm, but he dragged me along beside him.

"It is necessary to me," he said grimly.

I pulled harder against his grip and looked around, hoping for some familiar face.

I looked back and thought I caught a glimpse of dark hair and a dark cape that gave me some small hope.

I looked again, hoping to make sure, but Hugh pulled harder, glowering and mumbling, and I had to look forward or pitch forward onto my knees. We reached the wide wooded field between the shops on Hastings Road and St. Peter's grounds, and Hugh pulled me into the clearing behind the trees.

I snuck one more desperate look behind me and then turned back to Hugh and lifted my chin.

And stopped breathing when he pulled a pistol out of the pocket of his cloak and pointed it at me.

Chapter 23

Great talker, great liar

Homer

I froze, my eyes fixed on that black hole. It swelled
to fill my whole prospect. The world began to spin until I
realized I wasn't breathing. I dragged a breath in, and then
I started to think.

"What are you doing, Mr. Hugh?"

"Don't play innocent with me. I know you've been
following me." He reached out and grabbed my hair and
pulled me across the clearing. Sharp pain brought tears to
my eyes, and I stumbled into the shadow of the trees and
fell to my knees.

"I have not been following you," I squeaked. In spite
of the risks of my situation, I was insulted.

"And it's you that has been talking out of turn and
causing me problems."

"I don't talk out of turn." If he hadn't had the gun, I
might have lost my temper and hit him. But with that gun
pointed at me, I stayed where I was on my knees.

"You were there at the Belle last week, and ever since

that day, I can't step out my door without someone following me, watching me. And now my loyalty is being questioned—I'm being threatened." He leaned down and grabbed my arm in a bruising grip and pulled me to my feet. The fevered light in his eyes frightened me almost as much as the pistol.

Was Robert having him watched? It seemed likely, but I wished whole-heartedly that he would find more experienced men to do the following. "I don't know what you're talking about. All of that has nothing to do with me. Even if I wanted to follow you, do you think my aunt would let me do something so improper?"

That seemed to give him pause, but then he snorted, "I think your aunt doesn't know the half of what you get up to. Now, move."

"Well, perhaps that's true," my breath was labored, but I was afraid of what would happen when Mr. Hugh decided to stop talking, so I pressed on, "but you have it all wrong. I haven't been following you. I have been following Robert. Robert Amesley, you know." Surely he could hear the truth in my words.

His laugh grated against my nerves. His grip on my arm tightened, and he pulled me forward. I instinctively jerked back, and my sleeve ripped, leaving my shoulder bare.

The look he turned on me scared me as much as the pistol, which he lowered and rubbed against my bare skin, "if I didn't know better, I would think you were trying to distract me."

I shook my head, but he pulled me against his chest.

My breath hitched and I struggled in earnest.

He purred, and my dread grew, "it certainly is tempting."

I shook my head, "Mr. Hugh, please don't."

His laugh shocked me, "Keep fighting, my dear. I like a woman with a little spirit."

I froze and looked up at him. Yes, he meant what I had thought he meant.

He threw back his head, and his laughter rolled through the trees.

And then suddenly, unnaturally, he stopped laughing. Only his heavy breathing broke the silence. "It would serve you right. I'd like to show you what you get when you follow a man."

The moment slowed and lengthened with me breathing hard and fast and Hugh holding me tight against him, his eyes lit with frightening sparks.

I turned my head, and he leaned down and whispered, "and I would, if I didn't have somewhere else I need to be. Although—"

"Release her, now." Robert stepped out of the trees behind me.

Hugh's grip loosened slightly, and I twisted and pulled free, almost falling again in my desperation to get away from him. I found my balance and didn't stop moving until I was standing next to Robert. Panting and shaking, I bent over to catch my breath. My pistol hit my knee. I had forgotten about it in my fear. I closed my eyes for a moment. Together and armed we had a much better chance.

Robert put his hand on my back, but his attention, I could feel, was largely focused on Hugh.

And I knew Hugh's pistol was now pointed squarely at Robert. Somehow, that was worse.

"What are you doing here?" Hugh growled.

"I saw Liza leave the manor and walk this way. I came to find her and escort her back." I felt an inappropriate laugh bubble up at Robert's matter-of-fact response.

"I'm afraid you'll be disappointed. She won't be leaving with you. She's been following me. But now that I've caught her, she will pay the consequences," Hugh sneered.

"I haven't been following you, I tell you." I gasped, still bent over and panting, "I was following Robert."

"Surely you can come up with a better story than that."

"I'm afraid she is telling the truth this time." Robert's voice was wry. "She was following me, which has caused me some few problems, but not as many as you will have. You see, I am the one who has been following you, or at least having you followed."

I forced myself to stand up. I turned, pressing myself into Robert's side. Lowering my head, I whispered, "I have my pistol."

Robert slid his hand down my back, kissed my forehead. "Good," he said and pushed me behind him, turning to face Hugh more fully.

"Very affecting," Hugh said, but his face gave lie to his words. He pointed his pistol at Robert and said grimly, "Give me your weapons."

Robert shook his head. "unlike you, I don't go armed to supper and a ball."

"Show me."

Robert spread his cloak, and I pulled my pistol from the pocket of my cloak.

"You should have stayed for supper."

"I didn't want Liza to be alone."

"That's regrettable—for you, Captain," Hugh stepped

forward. "You both are going to come with me."

In Robert's shadow, I stiffened. My hands shook. I had practiced shooting both stationary and moving targets and seldom missed. I suppose I could have hit a rabbit or bird on the wing if I were starving, but the thought of shooting a man, even one as morally flawed as Hugh Hatton? I didn't think I could do it.

I thought if only Robert could lower his hands, I could give him my pistol, but Hugh's site was trained on Robert and didn't move as they talked. It was up to me.

Robert shook his head, "I don't think we should." I knew he was trying to give me time, and perhaps get some information from Hugh. "You will only have one shot. What are you going to do?" Robert's composure worked to slow the racing of my heart a little.

"You are right," Hugh's eyes narrowed, "but I can adapt. I will just kill you now and take the ever-delectable Miss Liza with me. I can kill her later."

"Like the two riding officers you killed?" Robert shook his head, "that wasn't very smart Hugh."

Hugh's eyes narrowed, "is that why you're having me followed? I didn't kill those men."

"Oh, I think you did," there was no question in Robert's voice. "I think you've involved yourself with the local smugglers and have got yourself in a serious fix."

Hugh dipped his head like a bull ready to charge, "It wasn't me I tell you. I didn't kill them, but I will kill you. You've ruined everything," His voice raised. And then he seemed to hear himself, and he stopped abruptly, breathing in and out for a few moments.

"But I can still fix it," he said in a quieter voice, but his breath was still labored.

"By killing me here; by taking Liza? That will just cause you more problems." Robert's reasonable tone brought a flush to Hugh's face.

"Look around, Captain Amesley. There is no one to tell the tale. By the time anyone arrives, you will be dead, and Miss Liza and I will be gone." He looked at me and smirked, "maybe I won't kill her for a while. We were just talking about that when you interrupted."

"You're speaking of my future wife."

A bark of a laugh made me jump, "No! Truly? Well people are always saying that you are a brave man."

I growled. It was bad enough that he was a blackguard, it was a bit too much that he was also an insulting and pompous boor.

His eyes focused on me, "she is a beauty, and with that touch of red in her hair, I'd lay odds she would have given you a good ride—if you were going to survive. But instead you'll die tonight, knowing that I'll be the one riding her, and then I'll kill her."

"And then you'll have two more bodies," How could Robert sound so calm? But then I felt the rigid muscles of his shoulders and understood his suppressed anger and his determined control. "And what will the man who is running your organization do? I can't imagine he'd like even more attention focused on his activities. He must already be angry about the two riding officers you killed."

"Just shut-up." Hugh's voice roughened in fury.

"But why did you bring them to my doorstep, so to speak?"

"It wasn't me, I tell you," his voice raised again, and spittle flew out of his mouth. "I didn't kill those men.

"And it was their own fault anyway. We couldn't have

them show up during the smuggler's run. They should have just kept their doubts to themselves and obeyed their orders. But no, they had to ride East. It was their own fault."

"So, you killed them and carried them all the way to my property." Robert shook his head.

"No, how many times do I have to tell you, it wasn't me." Hugh waved his arms, "It was Mr. Goodlee. Mr. Goodlee was more than willing to take care of them—for a fee. But the fool just had to take it one step further." Hugh began pacing, "his greed and ambition led him to go too far, but it wasn't my fault. I told him it was all Mr. Goodlee."

I could feel Robert's intense concentration as we watched Hugh unravel before our eyes. "Him?"

Hugh laughed "You'd like that, for me to tell you, but I'm not a flat. I'm fly to the time of day."

"Why did he bring the bodies to me?" Robert asked quietly.

"It didn't have anything to do with you, you fool." Hugh scowled. "Anyway, I told him, it was a stupid thing to do," his movements were fitful and jerky, "but he thought it would be a good to deliver a totally unnecessary warning,"

"To Perry?"

"I see you know. Did the fool confess?" he snarled.

Robert's hands fisted, "The information you were getting from Perry was not worth the trouble those two deaths have brought down on you."

"You're right, the estimable Mr. Gerow hasn't been very useful to me—but he had potential to be." He waved his gun, but brought it right back, "killing the two officers was necessary for the smuggling run, but Perry would have heard about it in the natural course. And I could have taken care of his . . . wavering in a more subtle way."

"Any hope of subtlety is gone, Mr. Hatton."

"It's not my fault!" he bellowed, then he stopped and stared unseeingly at us, "I'll have to take care of Gerow too."

"Liza," Robert said.

"I can't," I whispered into his back.

Hugh's attention quickened. His smile gleamed in the growing darkness, "Yes, say your goodbyes."

On the thread of a breath, Robert said, "Liza, you must."

I grimaced, "Oh, alright," I whispered back.

I took a deep breath and tried to think about the scent of the beech hedge and the sweet chestnut trees, the sound of the breeze, the sight of the low clouds illumined by the moon. I inhaled deeply once more and stepped to the side, lifted my pistol, sighted down the barrel, exhaled and pulled the trigger.

Mr. Hatton dropped his pistol and clapped his hand to his arm, above his elbow. He swore violently at me. Even in the dark, I could see a deeper shadow of blood seeping down his arm. My knees turned to jelly, and I sat abruptly. And in a fog, I saw Hugh drop to his knees and reach for his pistol, but Robert was there first. He scooped it up and booted Hugh to his back, keeping Hugh's weapon aimed at the writhing, swearing man.

I felt queasy and a little dizzy, but Robert's sudden laughter was like the slap of fresh wind, shocking and bracing.

I looked up into his grinning face. "I never thought I'd see the day when I was grateful for your unerring aim. It used to make me livid that you never missed."

I didn't tell him that I wasn't aiming for Hugh's arm. The pistol was still gripped in my fist, and my hands were still shaking ever so slightly.

I looked up again and saw Robert's perceptive compassion. When he spoke, his voice was brisk, "Liza, you saved my life," His gaze cooled as he looked at Hugh again, "and though he may not have the use of is right arm, he will live, and he will tell me everything he knows."

My body felt boneless, but I pulled myself up and stumbled over to Robert, who slipped me under his left arm.

"What made you bring a pistol, Liza?" he murmured against my temple.

"I started carrying one with me everywhere some time ago. I've been practicing, but—" I moved closer to him, seeking warmth.

The sudden sound of another gunshot broke the quiet of the wood, and both Robert and I jumped. Hugh rolled slightly and came to rest in unnatural stillness. In the light of the full moon, the shooter's form was clear for two seconds before he turned and ran.

Robert swore and ran in pursuit, leaving me looking at Hugh's prostrate form on the grass. I felt sick, but I refused to succumb. I closed my eyes for a moment and swallowed. There was nothing I could do for him, so I turned and followed Robert's path through the rustling bushes.

I broke out of the wooded area and entered the churchyard next to the cemetery of St. Peter's quite a distance behind Robert. He yelled, but the shooter ran, weaving through the headstones. Some movement to the side drew my attention. Mr. Jones and Lady Helen walked out of the church.

After a moment, Mr. Jones leaned down and picked up something from the ground. He pulled back his arm and threw at the fleeing man. With a bellow, the shooter fell forward. Robert was on him in a trice, pulling his arms behind him and sitting on his back. I ran to catch up, and when I saw how he continued to buck and struggle, I sat on his legs. Though still writhing, he was powerless.

Robert leaned down and whispered, "Mr. Goodlee, I presume." The man kicked hard, almost heaving me off of his legs.

"This is the man that Hugh was arguing with at the Belle," I told Robert breathlessly.

I didn't hear their footsteps over the struggle, but Mr. Jones and Lady Helen appeared at our side, "I hope I did right to stop this man," Mr. Jones voice was a surprisingly calm after the last few minutes. My heart was still racing, my breath coming in gasps.

"Yes. What did you throw?" Robert was also unflustered.

"A rock. There are many of them in the cemetery."

"You're aim is uncommonly good."

Mr. Jones grinned. "My given name is David. I spent my youth practicing with a sling but found I was better throwing."

"Well, Mr. Jones," Robert's voice was wry, "I'm glad you haven't lost your ability or your aim."

Lady Helen stood slightly behind Mr. Jones, serenely surveying the field of battle, "perhaps we could use a few of the choir stoles to tie this man?" She asked Mr. Jones.

At his nod, she turned and entered the door of the church.

"I was worried for Lady Helen's sensibilities," Mr.

Jones huffed, "but she is quite composed, isn't she?" He looked after her with admiration.

It wasn't long before Mr. Goodlee was trussed up as tightly as a Christmas goose. Robert stood and ushered the three of us a little distance away and cleared his throat.

Before he said a word, Mr. Jones spoke, "we heard two shots and came out to investigate. I'm relieved to see that you and Miss Liza are unharmed, but I can't help but notice that this man has not been shot either. Are there other wounded who need my care?" He studied Robert's face with interest and relaxed when he shook his head, "something to do with the two unfortunate riders that Miss Liza found some time ago, I surmise?"

Robert nodded again and smiled at the curate's perception, "Yes, Hugh Hatton identified this man you brought down as the smuggler who killed those two riding officers. Liza and I witnessed as he shot and killed Mr. Hugh."

Lady Helen gasped, "Oh, poor Mr. Hatton and poor Amelia."

Questions chased across Mr. Jones face, "That accounts for one shot," he cocked one eyebrow, "I feel that there is more to this unfortunate story."

"Yes," Robert said slowly, "and much I still don't know." We waited in silence while Robert studied the ground. After a deep breath, he lifted his head and continued, "most importantly you must know that these two men were just a small part of a darker plot, and I'm more likely to get to the bottom of it if the details of tonight's events are not generally known." Robert and I looked at the curate and Lady Helen.

"I won't lie," Mr. Jones said slowly, "but neither do I feel honor bound to satisfy the curiosity of those not directly involved. You tell me that this man is the killer of the two riding officers. He is the one who shot Mr. Hugh Hatton. If this is the truth," Robert nodded, "then this much, and no more, I can ethically say."

Robert looked at Helen.

"I can't imagine being called upon to say anything. I so seldom am," her half-smile was self-effacing, "and all I witnessed was a man running across the churchyard and brought down by Mr. Jones."

Robert nodded and before my eyes transformed into 'Captain Amesley.' After a quick look at his pocket watch, he sent Mr. Jones to the Manor with a short list of assignments—the squire must be informed and brought back. A servant must be sent to find the riders' commanding officer. Mr. Hatton and Miss Amelia must be carefully told the sad news. And above all, discretionmust be maintained.

Helen insisted that she accompany the curate. I watched her walk at his side, his hand at her waist guiding her, and I couldn't help but think that her great capacity for quiet would comfort Amelia.

After that I had nothing to do but repeatedly recount a vastly edited version of my part of the evening for each party as they arrived. It went something like this: Mr. Hugh Hatton had seen me on the street on my way to the church to get Lady Helen. He decided to accompany me. Robert joined us as we were entered the wooded field, south of the church. The trussed-up man, whom, by the way, I happened to have seen arguing with Mr. Hugh at the Belle Inn some days before—I had the impression he felt he wasn't adequately remunerated for some trifling service—shot Mr. Hugh and ran here. We were chasing the killer when Mr. Jones, who with quick thinking and resourcefulness, stopped him. Every word the truth.

I wondered how Robert would explain the gunshot
wound in Mr. Hugh's arm, but I said nothing about it and
neither did he.

The churchyard filled with a surprising number of
milling men. Unfortunately, Lord Ramsgate arrived with
the Squire. His, "what is the meaning of this?" and, "disgraceful, disgraceful," rang out at regular intervals. He hint-
ed that there was something more than coincidence that
Robert was again present at a disturbing death. Everyone
ignored him.

Colonel Abernathy, commander of the local militia
barked orders to a handful of his officers, which accomplished nothing.

The Squire gave Robert a shrewd look that promised
that a later accounting would be required, and it was he
that quietly managed to get the work done.

Robert and I stepped back, then back again. We settled
on a bench that was in sight of the commotion and kept
our own counsel.

With Robert's arm firmly around me, his chin on my
head, I finally began to feel like myself again. If we didn't
have a killer trussed and struggling within sight and a dead
man in the woods to our right, it might have been romantic.
As we sat, Robert's hand slid up my back and his fingers
brushed into my hair, kneading until I felt my tension dis-
solve.

The full moon, encircled by a misty ring, rose higher
above the line of the trees, vast and round, and glowing
white in the cloudless black sky. The silvery light edged the
black and gray trees and bushes with sharp white lines. The
hedge along the churchyard bent in a late breeze as though

from the passage of unseen beings. I shivered and Robert's arm tightened. I laid my head against his shoulder and sighed.

Then I had a horrifying thought. I sat up straight and tried to pat my hair into order, "I don't know what Aunt Beatrice will say. We're sure to miss supper. And there is another dead man. I'm sure she'll find a way to lay the fault at my feet."

Robert smiled, "I don't think she'll care as much if we tell her we'd like to announce our upcoming marriage tonight, yes?"

I sighed deeply. "Yes."

Chapter 24

An honest man's the noblest work of God

Alexander Pope,
"An Essay on Man"

I thought my dress, ordered in Brighton soon after my aunt's committee started planning the ball, was particularly beautiful with an elegant white satin slip under an overdress of silk netting with gold embroidery, beads, and fringed sleeves. I also wore my mother's pearls and tiara. Susan grumbled the whole time she buttoned and combed and twisted and pinned, but she worked fast.

She was also thoughtful enough, as I had missed the light repast my aunt had planned before the ball, to bring me some bread and cheese so I wouldn't faint from want of food before supper was served at midnight.

I don't know when Robert managed to speak with my aunt, as he'd told me he would have to question Mr. Goodlee and would be late. But somehow he must have found the time.

So it was that when I was almost ready to go down, Aunt Beatrice burst into my room, "Elizabeth, my dear," she advanced in a cloud of perfume and powder, and gave me a loose hug, patting my back gently, "how awful for you. Are you certain you are able to attend tonight?

"Of course, I will be disappointed if you can't, but we really must do what is best for you," she looked like it took all her resolution to offer. But she couldn't stop there, "your father and I are thrilled that you want to announce your engagement tonight. I think it will be most romantic," she waved her hand as if pushing that thought aside, "but I will put my foot down and absolutely refuse if it is too much for you." She finally stopped and looked at me with expectation.

"I will strive to bear up under the pressure," I said, hiding my smile. "I would like to go down with you now. I would hate to miss the ball after all your work. I'm sure it will be an enormous success."

"How brave you are," she clasped her hands to her bosom, "I must say you look divine. This color brings out the green in your eyes," she bit her lip, "you look so very like your dear mother."

"Truly?" I blinked quickly, "it is exceedingly kind of you to say."

And thus it was that we descended the stairs in complete amity and swept into the wide entry.

The ladies knew the power of a first impression, so they kept the guests milling outside the ballroom until a crowd had gathered. Then, in well-planned drama, they opened the ballroom doors.

I felt like I was entering a dream. The contrast between the terror and dread of not even an hour before and this dazzling sight caused a momentary dizziness.

In addition to the gas lanterns, three hundred candles and their reflection in the multitude of mirrors filled the room with sparkling light. Already the musicians were warming up on the balcony above, a lilting melody drifting lightly through the air.

The ladies of the committee, determined to follow the latest style, had hired an artist to chalk the dance floor in an intricate sweep of carnations, lilies, and roses that matched the flowers that filled every corner and table and hung in draped garlands through the room.

And I tried to let the light, the music, the talk and movement replace the frightful recollection of that small, but vast black hole pointed at me, then at Robert. I tried to forget the grim satisfaction in Hugh's voice as he calmly announced he would kill Robert and take me, the feel of the gun in my hand, the smell of the powder, the sight of Hugh's body crumbled on the ground.

And sometimes it worked. I was temporarily transported to a magical place where everything was beauty and cheer. Then memory and horror would return. Back and forth, my mind jumped in a wavering succession of odd, fragmented impressions.

After the first set, which I danced with my father, I noticed Lady Helen near the door and made my way to her.

"Lady Helen, this is a lovely gown," I linked my arm with hers and we sauntered along the edge of the ballroom where, if we talked quietly, we might have some privacy. "Tell me, how is Amelia?"

She nodded at Mrs. Crossley and Mrs. Bellerton and, in a lowered voice she said, "when I first told her, Amelia gave me such a piercing look, I thought she was about to ask for particulars. I had a moment of disquietude wondering what would be best to say, but then her father commanded all her attention. Mr. Hatton was quite overcome and had to be put to bed. His servants know how best to help him of course, but Amelia was all concern, and I was saved from prevarication."

We both smiled as Lieutenant Walter bowed. "Poor Amelia." My heart ached for my friend, "I will visit her tomorrow and try to find what I can do to help. She might feel—"

Our private conversation was interrupted by Lady Ramsgate, "Miss Henshaw," she nodded, "Helen dear, come along. Lord Holloway is here tonight, and I especially want you to speak with him."

"I'm sorry mother," Helen's voice was surprisingly firm, "but here comes Mr. Jones to claim the dance I promised him.

I turned and found that indeed, Mr. Jones was coming our way, smiling warmly at Helen.

When he reached us, he bowed to all of us, "Lady Ramsgate, I must thank you for allowing your daughter to help me as I informed the poor Hattons of the passing of their son. Lady Helen was a special comfort to Miss Amelia."

And Lady Ramsgate was distracted, "Oh Mr. Jones, it's a shockingly terrible thing, isn't it?" He nodded gravely, "why, Mr. Hugh! and in the middle of town, how did this come to be?"

Without a flicker of a glance to Helen or me, Mr. Jones leaned forward, "Lady Ramsgate, I know I can trust your discretion," I felt my eyes widen, but Lady Ramsgate nodded regally. He lowered his voice, "I believe only a desperate man would do such a thing. He must have felt quite threatened in life or livelihood," Lady Ramsgate looked thoughtful. "I can tell you" he assured, "that the shooter was apprehended, and the authorities are talking to him as we speak," he stood straight again, "now, of course, as good Christians, helping Mr. Hatton and Miss Amelia must be our first concern."

"Of course," she agreed, "quite right."

"Lady Helen, shall we take our place for the Scotch Reel?"

Helen put her hand on Mr. Jones' arm and glided away with head high and a contented smile. I couldn't remember a time I hadn't known Lady Helen, standing quietly in her parents' shadow. But only in the last two months did I feel I had really seen her poise, her tranquil strength, and understated beauty.

I wondered with consternation what else might be right in front of my face, that I might missing. It was a disturbing thought that troubled me until Frederick came to take me out on the floor. I found comfort in his familiarity. Surely, at least Frederick—even all the Davies family—were an open book to me.

Sidonie, on the other hand, was a small, dark, mystery. Beautiful in white satin with pink trim, with a teasing half-smile and that tantalizing accent, her appeal was universally noted and appreciated, at least if the crowd of men around her was any indication.

Between dances, she saw me on the fringes of her train and, with dancing eyes and charming dexterity, she gently scattered her gentlemen admirers, "Oh, Mr. Fox, I would so like one of those ices. It is very warm, yes?"

Once he scurried away, she turned to Lord Holloway, "but I wouldn't want to get chilled. I think perhaps I might have left my shawl over by that potted plant," she smiled up at him. He bowed and disappeared into the crowd.

With a finger to her chin, she looked up, "Oh, dear, have you seen my brother?" When Frederick and Lieutenant Lentz shook their heads, she tapped her chin, "he might be in the card room, do you think?" Frederick dashed away, "or perhaps——" Lieutenant Lentz smiled, bowed, and sauntered away before she finished her sentence.

Only Mr. Routledge remained, looking hopeful. "Now I think again, perhaps to see my father would be better, don't you think?"

Her last swain left her side, looking dazed and hopeful. Sidonie said, "they are all like sheep a little, yes? They can be tiring."

"You're not enjoying yourself?"

"Oh yes. I am. It is all very beautiful. This music is very nice, and I like, very much, the dancing. And everyone is so kind," she let out a sigh, "it still doesn't seem to me very real that I am here."

She leaned back and waved her hand from her neck down, "see me in this dress; for the cost of this one dress, my aunt and I could have feasted for months," she shook her head astounded, "and, note these stockings," she lifted her skirts a very little, "——silk!" She raised her brows. "And tonight, when we return home, a servant will warm the bed, and I will wake in the morning and drink chocolate."

She paused as if to fully appreciate the magnitude of her present prosperity.

With a laugh and a shake of her head, she waved it away, "Liza, I do have a question for you, does Mr. Routledge ever speak of anything but his Millfield Mansion?" Her smile was wry.

"Well, not that I've ever heard. It is a little ridiculous I suppose, but harmless, I think."

She nodded, "so I thought, too. And Mr. Frederick, if he's going to ask pardon every time he swears, why does he take such pains to swear so regularly?"

I laughed. "Frederick lived a few months in London last spring, and he likes to remind us that he is accustomed to spending time in more sophisticated company."

She laughed with me, "Oh here is Lieutenant Lang to talk to me about Hanover while we dance." He presented himself hopefully, and Sidonie smiled and lowered her thick lashes. Lieutenants Lang's jaw dropped, and he almost stumbled. She placed her hand on his, and as they walked onto the floor, she looked back at me and her dimples flashed.

After dancing the Roger de Coverley with Captain Richter, I joined Maris and her mother, sitting in chairs set up along the side of the ballroom.

Like everyone else, they were full of speculation.

"There will be difficult months ahead for Miss Amelia and for Mr. Hatton. Will they stay in Bexhill, or do you think the painful memories will drive them away?"

I hadn't thought to wonder. It would be a shame, I thought, for them to leave the support of the friends they had made here. Amelia, at least, had become a good friend. Of course, she would be in mourning for three months, but I would like to be able to condole with her.

Mrs. Davies shook her head, "Very sad, I know how Amelia was looking forward to this ball. It is certainly a reminder that we never know what tomorrow will bring."

In the middle of this melancholy thought, I noticed Maris was watching Philip across the room. Their eyes met and clung. I was so pleased that my best friend was preparing for her happy event but thought it a little ridiculous the way she—

Ah, in the middle of a commotion by the door, my eyes caught a flash of dark hair and that familiar tall, lithe form. Robert's eyes scanned the room, and when they met mine, I shivered and sighed.

He smiled and walked toward me, lifting a glass of raspberry shrub from the tray of a passing servant and presenting it to me with a smile.

We stayed to visit the Davies long enough for propriety, but soon were strolling through the crowd. After a few moments Robert looked around and pulled me by the hand and out the door onto the balcony.

"What did he say? Mr. Goodlee?" I asked before we'd taken a dozen steps.

Robert gave my hand a squeeze and walked down the steps onto one of the well-lit garden paths.

I had a sinking feeling. Did he plan not to tell me? If he thought he could— I stopped and turned to him, ready for battle.

Robert lifted a finger and outlined my lips. He stepped closer and in a voice that was a mere thread of breath against my cheek, he said, "Not here, Liza. I will tell you, but not here surrounded by so many people."

I felt the tension leave my body and nodded.

He led me deeper into the garden, putting his arm around my waist, and under his breath, he said, "not that he said much that was to the point. I believe Hugh would have been a better source of information. Mr. Goodlee is just one of many smugglers, smart enough to know that there is more going on than movement of run goods, ambitious enough to want a bigger role, and willing to do anything to accomplish that, but not in the leader's confidence and not overly bright. The only good outcome is that we now have the names of a few men for Lieutenant James to watch more closely.

"That is something," I matched his quiet tone.

He stopped in the shadow of a large beech and pulled me to him, "You needn't worry, Liza, that I will keep things from you any longer. I never want to experience anything like I did tonight walking into those trees and seeing that gun pointed at you." He shuddered and squeezed me, a little too tightly. "I won't have you dashing about in ignorance when there are men willing to go to such lengths to protect themselves and their endeavors."

I gasped, "I don't dash about—"

He chuckled unhappily, "you do have an uncanny ability to be where things are happening. I hope knowing more will help you recognize and avoid danger."

"And I'll be more able to help you, because Robert, those men who were following Hugh weren't very good. Maybe I could give them some hints."

Robert shook his head, "Hugh only saw the men I wanted him to see."

"Robert!"

"I thought he would wait until he was sure he had shaken his shadow and then lead us to the leader of the smugglers or perhaps to the spy. That plan misfired. I had no idea he would assume it was you who had exposed him."

"Well, your plan seems very smart to me. If he hadn't been so foolish as to accost me, it might have worked."

"His accosting you leads me to fear that you will be in more danger as my wife, and that I should wait to claim you.

I shook my head and laid it on his chest.

"No," his hand stole up my back, spreading a languorous warmth, "No, I've waited long enough," he dipped his head and kissed my temple, "but I do want you to continue to carry your pistol," he said as he followed the line of my jaw with more light kisses.

"I will," my head fell back against his hand, "though it's John's pistol," I said breathlessly.

"I will get you one of your own," his lips slid across the hollow beneath my ear, "we will practice."

"Yes," I sighed and clung to his shoulders, "practice."

He slid a finger over my throat and collar bone and smiled, "I won't lose you now when you've finally agreed to be mine," his finger paused to feel the fluttering in the hollow of my neck, and his eyes darkened, "I will protect you."

"And I, you."

He sighed, "Very well. We will keep each other safe."

And we spoke no more for a time as he brought his mouth back to mine and we kissed. I kneaded his shoulders, seeking to learn the strength and texture of bone and sinew.

His hand cupped my elbow, drifted up my arm, and slid over my short sleeve, exploring my sensitive skin with slow circles. I shrugged, lifting into his seeking touch, his clever fingers.

He murmured something I didn't understand before his lips again met mine in another exploring kiss. The breeze hummed through the leaves of the beech and filled the air with the scent of lavender. Against my lips, Robert breathed, "Liza, I love you."

"I love—"

"I declare—"

At the sound of my aunt's voice I jumped then hast-

ily pulled and rearranged my shawl. Robert took a deep
breath and straightened his waistcoat and placed his hand
on my waist, keeping me close when I turned to face Aunt
Beatrice.

"One would think you both would show a little more
discretion at a ball."

Robert whispered in my ear, "perhaps I should hire
your aunt. She has the uncanny ability to discover us no
matter how cunningly we hide." I giggled.

"Elizabeth Louisa, your hair," she looked horrified,
"you cannot go back to the ballroom looking like that.

I raised my hand to tidy the disorder caused by Robert's hands. He tried to help. But finally, Aunt Beatrice, with
a deep sigh, stepped in to smooth and re-pin Susan's artistic
arrangement. Then Robert and I linked arms and followed
her back to the ballroom and onto the dance floor.

He kissed and squeezed my hand and then swept me
into place in line. I looked up into my beloved's face, and
the music began. We met and parted but watched each
other through all the forms of the dance.

He held me close for a moment after the music ended,
smiling into my eyes.

"Liza," my father asked, "Are you ready?" I looked and
saw that my aunt was there as well.

"Yes. I am ready," I placed my hand in my father's.

"Friends," my father's voice rang out. It took a minute
for the room to quiet, but when it did, Papa lifted my hand
to his lips. "Please join me in my happiness as I announce
the upcoming marriage of my daughter Elizabeth Louisa
Henshaw, to our neighbor and good friend, Mr. Robert
Peter Amesley."

My neighbors and friends clapped, and few shouted.

I knew most of these people well, and felt such a fondness for them, in spite of their foibles. But, even though we had found the man who killed the riding officers, there were still villains in our midst, endangering our coast, our families, our country. They were liars and traitors.

I also was a liar, but I had good reason for every lie I told and every truth I withheld. So much had changed, but not that. The difference was that my deceptions and secrets were founded in love. Did that justify my actions? Perhaps not, but I comforted myself that my father knew. Robert knew; I would keep no more secrets from him. For the rest, I felt that protecting those I love and protecting our coast and country, might require an invisible web of secrets and lies.

Epilogue

'Tis not the many oaths that make the truth, But the plain single vow that is vow'd true

Shakespeare,
All's Well That Ends Well

A month later, in the middle of Robert's mammoth mahogany four-poster bed, I lay with my head on Robert's chest, chewing on my knuckle and thinking again about secrets.

"Liza," his lazy voice stirred me, "If you're worrying now, we didn't do this right," he slid my head to the pillow and rolled to his side, his head on his hand, "maybe we need to practice."

I laughed. "You know it was wonderful," and I shivered as his hand came to rest on my stomach. I breathed in deeply, "but we can practice," my voice squeaked a little.

"Well, it sounded like you were pleased, but—"

I hit him on the chest, then let my hand linger. I felt his heartbeat quicken and wondered that my touch could do this.

He took my hand and lifted it to his lips and nibbled,

"if not that, what are you worrying about?" He rolled back and pulled me with him until I rested on top of him. "Surely you're not thinking of the spy—I will find him and stop him."

"We will find him." I asserted.

I ignored his grimace. "But it's not that." Now I leaned my elbow on his chest, put my head on my hand, and looked down at my love-rumpled husband.

"Okay my love?" His voice rumbled through my body.

I laughed again, but this time my laugh came out deeper, more breathless. It was hard to talk, so aware as I was of muscle, and bone, and sultry warmth. His fingers slid along my spine and caressed the dip of my waist but stopped there. He waited, watching me with smiling, curious eyes.

"I know I promised never to tell you another lie . . ." He quirked his eyebrow, "and I won't, though, of course, I know I must keep secrets and lie to everyone else."

"But not to me."

I looked him in the eye, "no. I won't lie to you. It's just that . . ." I lowered my eyes, "being like this, so ah—so unguarded—well so open. I'm not saying it well—"

"You are," he leaned up and kissed me long and deep, "when we are like this, just the two of us with nothing between us, it feels—profoundly sensitive, and exposed?"

"Yes," I blinked in surprise, "for you too?"

"For me too."

I huffed in relief, "no lies—at least with you—well that's not so hard, but I feel that now I won't have any more secrets either, and nowhere to hide."

He lifted my hand, kissed my palm, and placed it back over his heart. I felt the strong, regular beat, and I basked in the warm glow of my love's eyes and the gently amused quirk of his beautiful mouth.

"Liza, my love, my life. I will treasure all your secrets. I will give you all of mine. We'll make them ours," he murmured as he pulled me even closer to his warmth, "and I will keep them always in my heart."

Thank You!

I hope you enjoyed *The Secrets We Keep*.

The Secrets We Keep is the first novel in my Illusions series. Other books in the series include:

- *Smoke and Shadows*, an Illusions Novella
- *The Lies We Tell*, Illusions Book 2
- *The Masks We Wear*, Illusions Book 3

While they are a series, every story can be read on its own, but I do hope you get the chance to enjoy them all.

Connect with me at:
- gigi-lynn.com
- gigilynn.forromance@gmail.com

If you'd like to read an excerpt from *The Lies We Tell* just turn the page . . .

Chapter 1

So I stood up, pretending I had more Breath than I had been feeling that I had, And said: "Lead on! I'm strong. I have no fear."

Dante Alighieri,
Divine Comedy

I thought I would be able to practice courage in a few small things first, just to get in the way of it. Fate and my stepbrother Hugh had different ideas.

We had only lived in Bexhill a few months when Hugh was shot dead by a smuggler, ironically in a peaceful wooded field situated between the shops on Hastings Road and St. Peter's church, right in the center of town.

Then everything changed, and there was no time to dabble in courage. I must spring right in, or perhaps I should say, be plunged in, whether I would or not.

Long sideways looks and awkward pauses in the days after his death made me question the circumstances surrounding the shooting, but Hugh's father, and mine for fifteen years, was devastated at the death of his only son. Brought down to his sick bed, his need for my support took precedence over my need to find answers. So, I worried and wondered while I sat by Papa's bed and took notes of the funeral details that he deemed necessary.

With tears coursing down his face, he said, "only the best for my Hugh—every honor must be his," his head rocked back and forth on the pillow. "Everyone who knew him recognized his worth, but so many here didn't have the time to really know him."

My mother had married Hugh's father when I was five years old. Since then I had shared a home with Hugh, but I still didn't feel I knew him. I tried to remember Hugh as he had been on that day I met him, a tall, blond, good-looking boy of twelve. You would think the entrance of a new, unknown mother with her small, meek daughter would have discomposed Hugh. Far from it! He looked me over with one lifted brow and said, "Amelia Anne, is it?" He shrugged and proceeded to ignore me with supercilious indifference until I was eighteen years old and ready to enter society. His heavy-handed attention then was not an improvement over his previous neglect.

Papa brought me back to the present when he reached out and grasped my hand convulsively, "Amelia, I depend on you to see that everything is the very finest."

I patted his hand, "Don't distress yourself, Papa. I will do everything that is needful."

I began, tentatively, with Mrs. Hattie May, the garrulous midwife who, I was told, could prepare Hugh's body. She was the first to push me into uncomfortable daring, as she required me to help her, in spite of my single state.

If I was uncomfortable at first, with the weight—the reality of Hugh's lifeless body, the midwife's brisk manner soon eased my awkwardness. She set me to washing Hugh's hair. And as she washed his body, she chattered, "well, isn't he a fine-looking young man. Though, I don't always trust the handsome ones. My first husband turned my head, he was so handsome, and charming—he could charm the birds out of the trees. But let me tell you, I didn't much mourn his passing. Now my Patrick, he's not much to look at, but he is as gentle as a lamb, except," her eyebrows wiggled, and she smiled in delight, "when I don't want him to be. Now when you decide on a man, you want . . ."

Well, I won't even repeat the stories she shared. I felt my eyes stretched wide and looked away quickly. I might not otherwise have noted the second bullet wound—not a death wound—on Hugh's right arm if I hadn't needed the distraction from her robust, earthy description of her husbands and her unlikely, even unbelievable account of men and marriage.

No one had said anything about that second wound in the furor following Hugh's death, so I asked the midwife to keep quiet as well. But that gunshot wound convinced me that my doubts were valid and gave me serious reservations about the honors we were heaping upon Hugh.

But to please Papa, I ordered the coffin from the local cabinet maker, made of wide planked knot-free elm, not pine, with coffin furniture made of brass attached to the lid. His breastplate, engraved with his name and the date of his death with an angel above the plate and flowers below, gleamed in flawless splendor. The decorative handles on each side must needs also to be in brass.

I worked with the local upholderer to furnish all the textiles for the coffin covering, a deep purple silk velvet, attached with a double round of decorative brass headed nails, the interior of the coffin, padded and lined with a

white fine weave crepe. Hugh, of course, must have a mat-
tress and pillow, Papa had tearfully insisted, so it must be.
And the pall—the large cloth that would cover the coffin
from the time it left our home until it reached the grave-
side—must be of black velvet.

From his seventeenth century bed on the second floor
of our home looking over the sea, Papa fretted. No detail
was too small for his attention.

For three days I worked without rest from dawn until
late. Finally, two days before the funeral, he rose from his
bed to take charge of the hiring of the vehicles, all painted
black, one to carry the coffin and one for him. He sent to
London for tall black ostrich plume head-dresses to be worn
by each of the Belgian black horses.

Hugh must have six bearers, each wearing black
cloaks, hatbands and gloves and six pages as well, each with
a black hatband and gloves, and I ordered many more pairs
of black gloves as gifts for the funeral guests.

We had the servants drape the drawing room with
black baize and bring in a table for Hugh's body, encased in
a silk shroud of the highest quality, so the neighbors could
pay their respects. But Papa and I kept the overnight vigil
alone as he didn't want visitors in the depths of his sorrow.

Papa paid to have the church draped in black, and of
course we paid the small fee to have the bells rung. Vicar
Tolison came out of retirement to walk in the procession
and officiate. If the vicar's face was any indication, he had
been more than generously compensated for these services
in addition to the burial fee.

It seemed to me, after all the preparations, the height
of irony that women are considered too delicate to attend a
funeral. Though it caused an unpleasant argument, I stood

firm. I was determined to be at the church and the cemetery. Perhaps that was the first brave act that I chose myself. And I found that after the initial storm, Papa seemed
comforted by my presence. And so, I was rewarded for my
courage.

After Hugh's coffin was lowered into the grave, the
men gathered in groups like dark clad twite, nodding and
pecking. As the only woman present, I stood a little apart
under a lowering sky. I listened to the muted sound of the
sea and the mournful cry of a great Northern diver as the
grave workers shoveled dirt onto the wood of the casket in a
regular thrumming beat.

I wondered, now that the funeral was over, what our
life would become. As Hugh's sister, in practice if not in
affection, my mourning would only be three months, but I
knew I couldn't leave my father too much in his own company for the six months of his mourning.

What should I do to interest the only father I remembered in life once more? Could I convince him to stay in
Bexhill where we now had friends?

Colonel Abernathy, commander of the militia in Bexhill approached me, "Miss Hatton, let me accompany you
to your carriage."

I flashed a look at my father. He was still taking his
leave from the Vicar. So, I placed my hand on Colonel
Abernathy's arm as we walked toward the road and our
carriage waiting there.

The Colonel cleared his throat, "you may not know
that your brother and I were friendly."

He was right. I hadn't known. I looked up at him as he
strolled confidently next to me.

Colonel Abernathy was a regular fixture at all the

neighborhood events, but I didn't really know him. He was generally well liked as he was well-born, attractive and amusing. A clever conversationalist and a willing and accomplished dancer was always welcome in society.

He smiled at me with that ever-present twinkle in his deep blue eyes, "he spent quite a bit of time with my officers. I feel like I knew him well," his smile widened, "if I weren't a gentleman, I could tell you some of the scrapes they got into—but of course, no worse than young men everywhere—just high spirits." He patted my hand.

I wondered nervously under what circumstances Hugh spent time with the officers of the militia.

"May I have permission to call on you, and your poor father, later this week," he smiled gently, "he might enjoy hearing some of the more innocent stories I could tell."

I nodded and thought he was correct. Papa would enjoy stories of Hugh.

"And perhaps," his pause caught my attention, "perhaps, I could help lift some of the burden you face by going through Hugh's papers."

Without thought, I shook my head, "You're very kind, but—"

"Hugh often talked about his interests and activities. We even discussed some of his business ventures and shared in one or two."

He couldn't know that his claim of a close connection to Hugh didn't necessarily fill me with confidence.

"I feel sure that Hugh would have liked for me to save you and your father any pain and extra work during this difficult time."

I decided right then that before anyone entered Hugh's study, especially my father, I would find a way to go through his papers. But that was something I wouldn't share with Colonel Abernathy, so I lowered my eyes demurely, "I will certainly tell my father of your generous offer, but—"

Then I saw Mr. Perry Gerow approach, hat in hand, blond hair stirring in the breeze. My heart picked up a little and I suddenly felt quite flushed.

"Miss Amelia,"

Oh, and with that deep voiced greeting, I felt a sigh escape. I smiled and let my eyes wander over his handsome face.

He looked at me in concern, "You can imagine how surprised I am to see you here. Even in his sorrow, I can't believe your father willingly exposed you to such a difficult ordeal. Most irregular. I'm sure you are distressed."

The sun went behind a cloud. I felt a chill and my stomach knotted.

"Perhaps this week," he moved to my other side, away from Colonel Abernathy, "I could call and condole with you." He leaned closer to me, "I had an idea of how I might be of service to you. I could go through Hugh's things so that you won't be bothered by unimportant details. Of course, I am used to doing this kind of work for my cousin."

Confusion distracted me from my disappointment. Hugh and Perry had not been friends. In fact, Hugh had said some fairly unflattering things about Perry and had even ordered me to suppress Mr. Gerow's pretensions.

I wondered fleetingly if Hugh's dislike had been part of the attraction I felt for Perry. I pushed the thought away as unworthy. And if I increasingly felt constrained—even upon occasion a little vexed with Perry Gerow, maybe it was only a part of growing up to realize that no man was perfect. After all, how many men could be expected to see beyond the decorum and pretty manners that my mother and, after she died, Mrs. Riding and Miss Singer at the Mansion House Private Seminary for Young Ladies had nurtured in me.

While I had been thinking, a polite, but intense argument had sprung up between Colonel Abernathy and Mr. Gerow.

". . . time together. I think my claim of friendship is the greater, I'm sure the Hattons—" Colonel Abernathy stopped and flashed a quick look at me.

"In your cups, both of you, I would wager," Perry said under his breath, but I think he meant me to hear.

The Colonel bristled, "Look here—"

They were like a pair of scrapping sparrows. This kind of brangling made me uncomfortable and anxious. I looked around for some way to distract them, and I met the curate's eyes. He looked at both men with understanding and lost no time coming to join us.

If it had been my choice, I would have asked Mr. Jones to conduct Hugh's service, but he is only the curate, and papa wanted Hugh to have the best. I have always preferred Mr. Jones Sunday services, though I admit I may be somewhat swayed because my friend, Lady Helen Ramsgate, held him in such high regard. Mr. Jones' gentle manners and calm good sense had comforted us in the storm after Hugh's death.

"Miss Hatton," at his deep voice the churning waters of the disagreement subsided, "your father has been telling me what help you've been to him this last week." I removed my hand from the colonel's arm and the curate bowed over it. "I know he finds consolation in your devotion, but we don't want you to exhaust yourself. Perhaps now, you will be able to find a little time for yourself."

"I am well," I felt flustered at the attention, "but thank you."

"Well, I will come this week and check on both you and your father."

Papa approached, and the curate turned to the Colonel and Mr. Gerow, "Maybe you two men could give me your opinion about this—" his voice faded as he adroitly led them away.

The clouds darkened as we drove toward home, but Papa tried to lighten my mood with a forced jocularity that broke my heart, "I couldn't help but notice the two young men paying special attention to you."

I smiled and patted his arm, "it is the oddest thing. They both asked to come and visit."

His chuckle was sincere. "I don't find that so odd, my dear. You are lovely, and now you are my only family. You will be a very wealthy woman."

I gasped, "don't talk like that," then tentatively I said, "you are not so very old, not yet fifty, and still quite handsome." He smiled and shook his head, but I continued, "you may yet remarry."

He patted my hand and shook his head mournfully, "I don't have the life in me to start again."

"That is just how you feel now. In time we will both heal. We will have many, many more years together."

He gave me a searching look, "well, no matter how long we have, I realize that I need to get my affairs in order."

"There is plenty of time for that. You shouldn't overtax yourself."

"It needs to be done. I'll have to drive up to London and meet with to my solicitor, Mr. Call."

"Oh, no you mustn't. Not now."

"No," his resolute look faded, "you're right. Of course, I can't leave now." He was silent for a few moments. "Perhaps Mr. Call would drive down, or maybe he will know a good man closer to us."

"That sounds like the best way," I said. Hopefully it would give me enough time to go through Hugh's study and see what everyone was so anxious to get a look at. If Hugh had been into something that would hurt Papa, I would have time to take care of it before he found a new advisor.

He flicked his finger down my nose, "Don't worry, my dear, it will bring me peace to know that no matter what happens, everything will be in order and you will be taken care of properly.

You wouldn't think that this talk would lift Papa's spirits, but so it was. He seemed more himself as we drove home, but then he visibly drooped when we turned into the drive leading to Edgecombe and he saw the hatchment over the front door.

"Drive on Coombs," he waved his hand weakly, "we'll use the side entrance."

I walked papa, who now leaned heavily upon my arm, to his room and left him in the care of his man. Before I could talk myself out if it, I made my way down the stairs and to the door to Hugh's study. Maybe Papa was right, and Colonel Abernathy and Perry were simply looking to fix the interest of an heiress, but the fact that both men asked to get a sight of Hugh's papers made me think they were after more than that.

No one was in the hall. So, I stepped forward telling

myself that I was not doing anything improper. I was not, after all, infringing on anyone's privacy. Hugh was dead. Still I took a deep breath before I turned the knob, and quietly eased the door open. I stuck my head through the small opening and stopped in surprise.

Mr. Canless, Hugh's personal secretary opened and shut one desk drawer after another, barely taking the time to look at the contents. He was visibly flustered and muttered to himself as he threw quick looks out of the window, "where is it? Where did he put it? Ah—" He thrust some papers deep into a canvas bag on the desk.

Chapter 2

Fools rush in where angels fear to tread

Alexander Pope,
"An Essay on Criticism"

I ignored the roiling in my stomach and stepped through the door. Mr. Canless straightened, gasped and went pale. He looked behind me and then seemed to gather himself. "What are you doing here?"

I lifted my brows in surprise.

"I mean," he coughed, "how may I help you, Miss Hatton?"

I shook my head, "what are you doing?

He cleared his throat, "before he—earlier—Mr. Hugh asked me to gather some—documents that he wanted delivered. Even though he's not here, I think it's important to finish my work according to his direction before I move to my next situation." Once again he cleared his throat, "it is nothing for you to concern yourself with."

I was a woman and new to asserting myself, but this man's attitude toward me was beyond insolent. He was a servant, and upon his employer's death, had been given notice. All of this ran through my mind while we stared silently at each other.

He seemed to come to himself and looked down at the canvas bag that rested between us, "is there some way I may serve you Miss Hatton?" He reached out and grabbed the strap of the bag.

I stepped forward and put my hand on the corner of the bag closest to me. I needed him to leave, but I was sure he shouldn't leave with anything from Hugh's study. I picked at a loose thread on the bag while I thought quickly. "I believe that Barrows has some questions before you leave." Barrows was our steward. And surely, he had some questions, even if not for Mr. Canless.

I stood grasping the corner of that canvas. Without taking my eyes off Mr. Canless, I waited. His eyes darted to my hand on the bag then back up. He cleared his throat and once again glanced quickly at the bag. I could tell he didn't want to leave, but I was the daughter of the house, and though my heart was beating so hard I was surprised he couldn't hear, I stood firm.

After a few moments he bowed to me and walked out. I rushed over and listened at the door until I heard his footfalls fade down the hall. I pulled my handkerchief out of my sleeve, where I'd tucked it that morning before the funeral and blotted my brow. Back at the desk I opened the canvas bag. I sunk into Hugh's chair and stared at the bundle of bank notes. I know Hugh didn't pay his secretary that much money, and under the money, there was a sheaf of papers.

I didn't dare take the time to go through them, but I was determined that Mr. Canless wouldn't leave with them.

And then the difficulties presented themselves to my mind. I looked around Hugh's study. Where could I hide the bag to keep Mr. Canless from taking it when he returned and until I had more time to read those documents? I knew he would come back. He'd been too frantic and determined to simply walk away.

I listened for a moment at the door. Footsteps in the busy front hall, though muted, were frequent. There was no way for me to slip away unseen with a canvas bag hanging over my shoulder. I turned back into the room and searched the drawers of Hugh's desk until I found the key for the study door. I locked the door and slipped the key into my bodice. Our housekeeper, Mrs. Poole had keys to all the rooms in the house, but I couldn't imagine what reason Mr. Canless would give her for needing one, and in the busy main hall, I didn't think he would have time to break the lock.

I sat at Hugh's desk and once more opened the top drawer, but the longer I sat, the more my stomach rebelled at the thought of Mr. Canless' knock on the door. I would search Hugh's study for anything else that might raise eyebrows when I was sure his secretary had left the house for good. I again listened at the door then paced around the room, feeling trapped. I really needed to get out.

On the second circuit around the room, I paused at the window that faced the folly to the North. Low dark clouds, but no rain as yet, and there was no one working within my sight.

A possibility occurred to me. I shook my head. No lady would do such a thing.

I circled the room again and stopped for longer at the window. On the ground floor, the drop from window to the ground was no more than five feet. If I slid around backwards and supported myself with my arms, it would—no, I couldn't. I turned and faced the room and turned back again, my breath fast and unsteady.

Before I could talk myself out of it, I dropped the canvas bag out the window, tied up my skirt with my sash, opened the window and climbed out, dropping down behind the line of camellia bushes our gardener had recently planted. And stopped. Now what?

Made in the USA
Las Vegas, NV
16 May 2021

23153380R00173